BEGGAR'S CHOICE

Other Nick Polo Mysteries by Jerry Kennealy

Vintage Polo
Special Delivery
Green with Envy
Polo's Wild Card
Polo in the Rough
Polo's Ponies
Polo, Anyone?
Polo, Solo

For my agent,
Dominick Abel

BEGGAR'S CHOICE

A Nick Polo Mystery

Jerry Kennealy

ST. MARTIN'S PRESS

NEW YORK

Design by Ellen R. Sasahara

Library of Congress Cataloging-in-Publication Data

Kennealy, Jerry.
      Beggar's choice / Jerry Kennealy.
          p.   cm.
      "A Thomas Dunne book."
      ISBN 0-312-11478-8
      1. Polo, Nick (Fictitious character)—Fiction. I. Title.
PS3561.E4246B4   1994
813'.54—dc20   94-32376
                                                          CIP

First edition: December 1994

10   9   8   7   6   5   4   3   2   1

CHAPTER 1

◄►

The long gray line stretched up Leavenworth Street, doglegged to the left, and continued along the adjoining block. I could see the bleary eyes of the early birds waiting for the door to open at eleven-thirty. They'd been there since eight o'clock, with nothing else to do, nothing else to hope for.

Father Tomasello walked by in his dark brown robe, looking as if he'd just stepped off the label of a Frangelico liqueur bottle, complete with a silver-dollar-size bald spot at the back of his head. His deep-socketed blue eyes twinkled behind thick tortoiseshell-framed glasses.

"Are we all ready, ladies and gentleman?" he asked in a cheerful voice.

"All ready," we chorused back, holding knives, spoons, forks, spatulas at the ready.

The good father opened the door and they streamed in. The mix was always about the same, a ten-to-one ratio of males to females. Their ages ranged from early teens to a few old-timers pushing ninety, their faces creased with pain, grief, or embarrassment.

I was at my usual post, which I manned on Tuesdays, serving mashed potatoes and turkey dressing. The first time Jane Tobin and I had volunteered to help out at St. Matthew's Kitchen, I had been put in charge of desserts. But I had been a bit too generous with the peach pie slices, and we had run out well before the last of the lunch crowd passed me by. After that they put me in the "spud well." We never ran out of mashed potatoes.

The men, women, boys, and girls came by slowly, metal trays

at the ready, and I began scooping out the potatoes and turkey dressing. Turkey was a regular entree at St. Matthew's. Father Tomasello had a friend who owned a turkey farm in Stockton, ensuring us a steady supply of that once-noble beast.

Most of the diners kept their eyes down, examining the food, paying no attention to the servers. It had been a real culture shock to me at first. I had expected to see a bunch of wine-soaked street-sleepers and some rough-and-tumble addicts down on their luck. And those ladies and gentlemen did show up. But it was the others that really got to me. Pimply-faced kids, a goodly portion of the females pregnant. Kids having kids. The ones with the shakes, badly in need of a fix, be it booze, heroin, methadone, speedballs, crack, or the latest designer drug on the scene. They stood patiently in line, shivering no matter what the weather.

Then there were the straight-backed old-timers, gently, or not so gently, pushed away by their children, their pensions barely enough to cover the cost of a one-room apartment. And the former well-to-do, wearing once-expensive clothing now in need of a cleaning, with buttons missing and elbows that were worn thin.

I had seen men I'd gone to high school with. Had been in the service with. Once I recognized a former client, an attorney who ran an office of more than twenty lawyers. He had been infected with that rich man's disease, a cocaine habit, and inhaled himself out of business, his home, and his marriage. I sought him out in the dining hall that day. He wanted no part of me, and he never came back. At least not on my Tuesday tours of duty.

"Hey, Two Scoops. I want to talk to you after lunch," called a raspy voice.

I looked down the line and saw the grinning puss of Scratchy. Full name Charles Nelson O'Hara. But everyone called him Scratchy, for reasons I'll go into later. After lunch.

He worked his way up to me, and I ladled a hefty portion of taters and dressing on his tray.

"What's up, Scratchy?"

"Hey, Polo. I'm not kiddin'. I gotta talk to you."

"Sure. Soon as I'm through here."

The line kept moving. The large, industrial-size trays of potatoes and dressing were refilled several times before the last customer scuttled by at two o'clock.

Father Tomasello had a firm rule. No servings after two o'clock. He had a limited budget, and the donations of money and food stretched only so far.

I headed straight for my next assignment, the sink. Most of the volunteers have two or three tasks. The regular volunteers, that is. The celebrity types who show up for Christmas, Thanksgiving, and Easter have their pictures taken with a carving knife in hand, then tiptoe out the back entrance as soon as the reporters and photographer leave.

There are usually ten to twelve of us on Tuesdays, an eclectic mixture. A couple of retired firemen. A former deputy chief of police. A banker who is a charter member of AA. A woman who somehow manages to volunteer two days a week and still find time to raise her five children. A nurse who goes right from the dining room to her shift at San Francisco General Hospital.

And there is Vernon, a very good jazz drummer, who kept up a steady tempo while drying the pots as I washed them. And Jane Tobin, a reporter/columnist at the *San Francisco Bulletin,* and for want of a better description, my significant other.

I was trying to make it more significant than it was, but Jane had suffered through a rough marriage and was in no hurry to "make a dumb mistake again."

So there I was, up to my elbows in soapsuds, humming to the beat of Vernon's "Green Dolphin Street" encore on the soup pots, wondering what Scratchy wanted to talk to me about.

Scratchy described himself as a "sidewalk architect" when questioned about his profession. I had paid no particular attention to him during my first few months at St. Matthew's, and didn't recognize him when I approached him at his "office," the freeway off-ramp at Eighth and Harrison streets in San Francisco.

Scratchy had a regular beat. Eighth and Harrison on Monday,

Wednesday, and Friday, then on Tuesdays and Thursdays he wandered over to Fourth Street by the Moscone Convention Center and hit on the visiting business types. Saturdays and Sundays he played the field. Depending on the action, he might be found at a Giants game, a 49ers game, a play at the Geary Theatre, or the Opera House. Wherever crowds gathered, Scratchy would be there, with his VET WILL WORK FOR FOOD cardboard sign at the ready.

A friendly tip. Never, ever offer these poor souls the opportunity to actually work. I'd heard Scratchy blister the ears of a couple of naive do-gooders who suggested that they had some gardening or window-washing chores for him. His response was a string of curses and something along the line that holding up that stupid sign all day was work enough, and if they didn't want to fork over a few coins they could perform various acrobatic sexual practices upon themselves.

Scratchy was at his freeway off-ramp office one day when a three-car collision took place. I was working for the insurance carrier for the car in the middle. Scratchy had witnessed said accident, and his brief statement on the police report was favorable to our client, so the insurance company wanted me to locate Scratchy and get a formal statement.

Scratchy wasn't all that cooperative when I first approached him, then he recognized me. "Hey, you're Two Scoops from the kitchen, right?"

I hadn't realized I had a nickname, but apparently my heavy-handedness with the chow put me in the good graces of several St. Matthew's regulars.

Scratchy was in his mid-forties, but looked much older: five foot eight, rail-thin, toast-rack chest. His sunburned face was etched with a network of lines. His hair was smoky gray, thick and long. Have you noticed that about the so-called street people? So few of the men are bald.

The reason he went by the name Scratchy had nothing to do with his raspy voice. The reason was, well, it's because he scratched a lot. All over. Scratchy claimed it was the result of Agent Orange and other defoliants he was subjected to in

Vietnam. He also blamed the army for his drug and alcohol dependencies. The government apparently agreed, a little, because Scratchy received a monthly disability check, though not as much as he wanted or considered his due.

Scratchy turned out to be an excellent witness. He remembered where the cars were before the collision, as well as their positions after impact. He even recalled some of the rather hot statements made by the drivers once they'd gotten out of their mangled vehicles.

It took some time for me to get a full statement from him, because of his penchant for running into the street with his sign when cars coming off the freeway were forced to stop for the red traffic light. At first I thought he was stringing me along and would ask for a sizable "donation" before signing the statement I'd prepared. But no, he signed on the dotted line without asking for a penny.

I reported my findings to the insurance carrier, and, even though they were aware that Scratchy might not make the most reliable witness, they decided to subpoena him for a deposition.

Have you ever been involved in a deposition? Lawyers from all sides in a civil case gather to take the statement of a witness under oath. Questions are asked by all. Sort of a mini-courtroom scene.

Scratchy's deposition was a classic. He had no permanent residence address, his sleeping arrangements sometimes changing each day, so I arranged to meet him at the corner of Market and Powell streets and escort him to the deposition, which was set up in a conference room in a sleek, modern office building in the financial district.

The room was as sleek and modern as the building itself. We arrived on time. The stenographer, a thin, hard-faced woman in her forties, watched in general disbelief as I escorted Scratchy into the room. There was a tray with coffee and doughnuts in the middle of the long, polished walnut table that filled most of the room. Scratchy was never one to pass up a free meal, so he dove in, slurping the coffee and dunking away with the doughnuts.

The stenographer almost panicked when I left the room to check on why the attorneys hadn't shown up yet.

She followed on my heels. "Don't you dare leave me alone with that—that man."

Scratchy had not bothered to overdress for the occasion. He wore a pair of crusty jeans, the legs so short that they flapped in the wind like flags, a pile-collar nylon jacket that had once been a dark blue but was now faded in the spots that weren't covered by stains, and a bird-bombed baseball cap with the emblem of the New York Yankees unraveling at the front. A sporty plaid scarf with several small holes and tears in it was draped around his neck. The stubble on his chin looked several days old, and, from my downwind walk with him, I could tell his last bath had been taken some time before his last shave. "Dumpster grunge" is probably how a couturier would describe the ensemble.

Two of the attorneys arrived and wrinkled their noses in unison. Their idea of grunge was switching from a Brooks Brothers suit to a Giorgio Armani sport coat.

Scratchy could take a hint and started regaling everyone with a joke about an attorney, a judge, and a donkey. You wouldn't want to hear it.

The lawyer I was working for, the lovely and competent Kathy Kirby, came in five minutes later and bestowed a winning smile on Scratchy. He was smitten. He stopped scratching and cleaned up his language, at least refraining from using the dreaded "f" word, which came along about once every sentence in his normal narrative.

"Are you finished?" Jane Tobin asked, bringing me out of my reverie.

I submerged the last of the turkey roasters into the pool of murky soapsuds. "Just about. I've got to meet someone out front. It'll just take a couple of minutes."

Jane, who stands a little over five feet and weighs not much more than a hundred pounds, frowned as she pushed back a strand of auburn hair that had dropped over one of her malachite-green eyes. Being a reporter/columnist (the / gets her about a hundred bucks more a week), she's always in a hurry.

"I've got to get back to the paper," she said anxiously.

We'd traveled to the kitchen in my car. Jane had a VW convertible, and convertible tops were susceptible to knife-blade attacks if they're parked in the vicinity of St. Matthew's. "Just a couple of minutes," I repeated. Poor old Scratchy probably just wanted a loan, I thought.

If only it had been that simple.

CHAPTER 2

◀▶

Scratchy was sitting alone at one of the well-worn green Formica-topped tables in the dining hall. There were a full dozen tables, with benches bolted to them, each of a size that could handle thirty people. If they squeezed in real tight.

"Got a cigarette?" he asked, his mouth bent in a crooked grin. "Mine are still in the machine."

"I gave them up, Scratchy."

"Sure, sure. I remember now. Listen, Polo. You still in the shamus game?"

I put a foot up on the bench and rested my elbow on my knee. "Yes, still at it."

He took a sip of his coffee, then dropped the cup to the table with a minor clatter. His hands were shaking badly.

"I need your services." Though the room was empty, he swiveled his head around slowly, like a quarterback studying a defensive formation.

I waited him out. He took off his baseball cap, a Detroit Tigers model today. There was a red mark across his forehead from the headband.

"Can you run some plates for me?"

"Plates? You mean license plates?"

"Sure, sure. What else, Polo? Dessert plates?"

I hesitated. "Scratchy, what do you need license-plate information for? Someone pass you by at the office?"

He rubbed a long finger behind his ear, as if checking for an injury. "No. Nothing like that. It's these regulars. They stop all the time, slip me some pretty big dough. I'd like to be able to call them by name, butter them up a bit, you know." He dug a hand in his coat pocket and pulled out a jagged piece of paper. "Here. Check these out for me—I'll pay you for your time."

There were two license plate numbers printed in pencil, in large block letters and numbers. "These are California plates?"

"Sure, sure, Polo. Whaddya think? Switzerland or something?" He started to stand up.

I waved him back down. "I'm not checking these out unless I know what they're really for, Scratchy."

His hands started shaking again, and the veins on his neck looked as if they were sending out a Morse code signal. "Listen, Polo. These people are nice as hell to me. I just want to let them know I appreciate it. You call people by their name, they think you're something special." He stood up and jammed his hands in his pockets. They moved as if he were counting coins. "Just do it. Please?"

I dropped Jane off at the *Bulletin,* then drove back to my flat in North Beach. Mrs. Damonte, my one and only tenant, fluttered her Venetian blinds at me as I trudged up the front steps. Mrs. D, a lovable, cantankerous octogenarian, leaves the flats unattended only for such important occasions as parlor visits: funeral or bingo. She starts each morning with a short Manhattan and a thorough reading of the morning paper's scratch sheet, the death notices. I'm firmly convinced that she zooms in on those names starting with the letter P, wondering if Nick Polo has finally gotten his due, thus leaving the flats to her.

Mrs. D has lived in the flats longer than I have, and I was born in the room that I now use as an office. When my parents were killed in an airplane crash a few years ago, they left the property to me. The one stipulation was that in the event I should precede her to that interview with Saint Peter at the Pearly Gates, and if I have no heirs, the property goes to Mrs. Damonte, who had come over from the old country with my grandmother. Though she's got forty-plus years on me, she's determined to outlive me.

The odds grow stronger in her favor every day. The fact that she still pays almost the same amount of rent as she did twenty-five years ago helps her to tolerate me. Meanwhile, she manages the flats as if they were already hers and on par with the jewel of Donald Trump's real estate portfolio. She constantly upgrades the electrical and plumbing services, finds dry rot where no termites dare to tread, and contracts out all the minor construction chores to compatriots who, no doubt, kick back a goodly portion of their fees to Mrs. D.

As a peace offering, she allows me full run of "her" vegetable and herb garden, and gives me nibbles of the fantastic dishes she creates in her kitchen. How good a cook is Mrs. D? Nero Wolfe would have willingly dumped Fritz Brenner if he could somehow have managed to lure her to that old brownstone on West Thirty-fifth Street in New York.

I thumbed through the mail, finding three checks for work done on insurance cases some weeks ago. There were no messages on the answering machine. I took out the paper Scratchy had given me with the license plate numbers. What did he really want them for? That story about wanting to know the names of some generous "regulars" was thinner than the chicken consommé St. Matthew's had given out at lunch.

There are several ways to find the registered owner of a license plate, most of them perfectly legitimate. Address information is harder to get since that well-publicized case wherein a mentally deranged guy paid a Texas private investigator to get him a motor vehicle owner's address in California, then promptly went to Hollywood and slashed the identified person to death. Present rules at the Department of Motor Vehicles call for the release of a person's address to a licensed private investigator only if the stated purpose for receiving the information is "service of process." In other words, laying a subpoena on them.

The government is much less worried about releasing the name only. As long as you're licensed, bonded, and have an account with the state, all it takes is a phone call.

I thumbed through the Rolodex for the DMV number and made the call, jotting down the information as the clerk read it from her all-powerful computer.

Vehicle number one was a new Toyota 4×4 Land Cruiser registered to the International Auto Leasing Company in South San Francisco.

Number two was a little more interesting: a Mercedes 190E coupe, belonging to Lester Maurence. Maurence was a name known to everyone who spent any time at all in the Bay Area. A bit of a mystery man, he made his millions in Hong Kong in the shipping business and commercial real estate. He settled in San Francisco about six years ago and immediately began making a splash. His name hit the financial and social columns on an almost equal basis. Like so many people with seemingly too much money, he'd been bitten by the political bug, and he'd managed to get elected to the San Francisco board of supervisors.

I don't know how politics work in your town (do they actually work in any town?), but here in the City by the Bay, we have a mayor, then next in line of power comes the board of supervisors: eleven citizens elected at large, who serve four-year terms before ponying up the necessary monies to run for office again. The job pays less than two thousand a month, and they've been running up campaign costs of several hundred thousand dollars every time they throw their hats into the ring, so you figure it out. Dedicated public servants? Or somewhere in those once-smoke-filled rooms, perhaps mucho real money is made.

Several prominent people have used the board of supervisors as a stepping-stone to bigger, though not necessarily better, things. Dianne Feinstein became mayor, then United States senator after serving several terms as a supervisor. Then there was Dan White, a former policeman and fireman, who was unable to get his job back after he tragically changed his mind about retiring from the board, snuck into City Hall with a gun, and killed Mayor George Moscone and fellow supervisor Harvey Milk.

The board's penchant for sticking its collective nose into the problem of apartheid in South Africa or inviting Fidel Castro over to explain the glories of socialism rather than concentrating on mundane regional issues such as potholes in the streets, overcrowding in city jails, and vacant downtown office buildings had earned it several nicknames, "board of stupidvisors" being one of the less graphic.

Lester Maurence seemed to favor Feinstein as a role model. He made no secret about his desire to be the city's next mayor, and the governor's office in Sacramento or a Senate seat were strongly rumored to be in the cross hairs of his political sights. "A poor man's Ross Perot" was the way one local reporter described Maurence. We should all be that poor.

So, the possibility existed that Maurence was the type of guy who would roll down his window and toss a few coins at a homeless type like Scratchy O'Hara.

Scratchy telephoned bright and early the next morning, asking if I'd had made any progress chasing down the license plates.

"You should have recognized the man in the Mercedes," I told him. "Lester Maurence. He's a city supervisor. Shipping tycoon. He was at St. Matthew's Kitchen last Christmas doling out the turkey."

"Lester Maurence, huh? What about the other car?"

"It's leased. A Toyota Land Cruiser. No name other than the leasing company."

"Shit," Scratchy cursed, then went into a coughing fit. "Can you run it down, Polo? Find out who it's leased to?"

The alarms started going off in my head. I was sorry now I'd passed on the information about Maurence. "What the hell are you up to, Scratchy? Why the interest?"

Conversation was held up several moments because of the sound of a large vehicle with a perforated muffler rumbling by whatever pay phone Scratchy was using. He coughed some more—the raw, sandpaper cough of a heavy smoker. "Listen, Polo. This could be big. Real big. Worth a lot of dough. It could be my ship comin' in, pal. Can you run it down for me?"

"No. Not unless you tell me just what you're up to. Why are you interested in Lester Maurence? Why the hell do you need this information? You told me—"

"Gotta go," Scratchy said, then hung up abruptly.

I dropped the phone on its cradle and bundled up the notes with the DMV information. I was about to toss them into the wastebasket when I hesitated, smoothed out the paper, and impaled it on the brass message spindle next to the phone, promising myself I'd get to the bottom of it when I saw Scratchy next Tuesday.

CHAPTER 3

◄►

Scratchy left a message on my answering machine on Saturday, while Jane and I were out picnicking in the wine country around Calistoga. Another license-plate request. Another plea. "Get it for me, Nick. I'm not kidding. This could be big for both of us. I got a couple of other things I want you to look into. I'll pay you Tuesday at the kitchen."

I jotted the plate number down, but didn't bother to run it, just tucked the information in my wallet. I was going to have a long talk with Scratchy and find out just what the hell he was up to.

Scratchy was a no-show the following Tuesday. After lunch, Father Tomasello tapped me on the shoulder and motioned me away from the sink.

"Can I speak to you for a minute, Nick?" he asked in a hushed-confessional tone.

"Sure, Father." I dried my hands on my apron and followed the good padre out of the kitchen, across a small cobblestone courtyard, and into his private office.

His office was a dusty, cluttered affair, one wall taken up with floor-to-ceiling bookshelves groaning under their heavy load. A spindle-legged walnut desk sat in the center of the room, the top littered with folders and accounting spreadsheets. An adding machine perched in a corner of the desk, the paper spilling from its mouth and curling onto the floor.

"Sad news, I'm afraid, Nick," he said, heading straight for a shoulder-high steel safe, the type that Butch Cassidy and the Sundance Kid would have needed several sticks of dynamite to blow open. Father Tomasello twirled the safe's dial with blunt-tipped fingers. "Have you heard about Scratchy?"

"No."

He swiveled to face me. No twinkle in those periwinkle-blue eyes today. "Gone, I'm afraid. Car accident. Poor man had a difficult life, didn't he?"

"When did this happen, Father?"

"Last night. I just found out about it this morning." The safe's door swung open on well-oiled hinges. I could see dozens of brick-red business-size envelopes, secured by rubber bands. Father Tomasello thumbed his way through them until he found the one he wanted. "Some of my parishioners use me as a sort of bank, Nick. They have no place else to keep their papers, their documents. I don't do this for everyone," he said with another heavy sigh. "I just don't have the time or the storage space. But I've kept Scratchy's papers for a couple of years." He dropped the envelope on his desk. "Usually they leave their birth certificates, service discharge papers, Social Security cards, that type of thing. Maybe some pictures of their loved ones. A watch, or a ring that holds some special meaning to them, but they know that if they carry it on the street, it will be stolen. And their wills. Not that any of them have much to leave, but there are things like Social Security benefits, veterans' benefits." He paused and managed a pale smile. "And burial arrangements. You'd be surprised how many of them salt away enough money for a decent burial."

Father Tomasello settled himself gently into an elaborately carved heraldic chair, gesturing for me to use its twin on the opposite side of the desk. He bent forward, pulling a bottle of Glenfiddich single-malt Scotch whisky and two glasses from a desk drawer.

"You know, Nick," he said, "many of these fallen angels we feed every day have lost the battle with demon rum, but to tell the truth, there are times when I need a good stiff drink."

He poured a shot into each of the glasses and handed me one. I raised the glass in a toast. "A libation on the altar of friendship."

"Mud in your eye," he responded with a grin, then took a sip of Scotch. "Scratchy came to see me on Saturday. He had something he wanted to put in his bank." Father Tomasello handed me the envelope. "Take a look."

I slipped off the rubber bands. The first thing that caught my eye was the money. I upturned the envelope and dumped the contents on the desk.

"Six hundred and fifty dollars," Father Tomasello said. "I counted it when I heard about the accident. The police called me. He had a St. Matthew's holy card in his wallet. And not much else, I gather."

The money was all in nice crisp fifty-dollar bills. I riffled the edges. In addition to the money there were several pieces of paper, a photograph, and a zip-lock plastic bag. The bag contained three military medals: a Purple Heart; a Vietnam Service Medal, showing a dragon behind a grove of bamboo trees; and an Army Distinguished Service Medal, displaying a bald eagle, wings spread across a royal-blue enamel circle. The photograph was an old black-and-white of a young man holding an infant in his hands, smiling at the camera. The years had been hard on Scratchy. He was quite handsome when the picture was taken. One of the papers was a folded piece of inexpensive white note paper with two notations written in pencil: DUKE? SHARK? The final item was a reddish piece of pasteboard. A pawn ticket from Sam's Jewelry and Loan Company. The date stamped on the back of the ticket was for Saturday, three days ago.

I handed Tomasello the pawn ticket and the scratch paper. "Any idea who this Duke might be, Father?"

"No. I've no idea."

"And Shark. Maybe Duke's a loan shark. But what self-respecting loan shark would lend money to Scratchy?"

"I don't know. I do know that he put all that money in his envelope on Saturday."

"You're sure about that?"

"Positive."

"Did he put the pawn ticket and the paper with those names in the envelope at the same time?"

"I'm not sure, Nick. All I noticed was the money. He was very excited about it. He told me that he had some money to deposit. I had no idea how much. He said something about more money. A lot more money. And giving some money to

Susan. Then he asked me if you were going to be working on Tuesday. He said he wanted you to find this Susan, whoever she may be." Father Tomasello put a hand under his glasses and rubbed his eyes. "His will is there. He made it out two years ago. Left everything to St. Matthew's, Nick. I feel a little odd about it. He didn't really have anything then. Now there's this money. And that pawn ticket. If he does have someone, a mother, a wife, or children, I think they should get the money. Susan. I wonder who she is?"

I examined the will. Written in pencil on plain paper; "I, Charles Nelson O'Hara, being of sound mind," etc. The other papers were related to his discharge. The one interesting piece of information they contained that could be helpful was Scratchy's Social Security number.

I picked up the zip-lock bag and stared at the medals. "He probably has some veterans' benefits coming, Father. Enough to cover his funeral expenses."

Father Tomasello drained the remains of his drink and let out a polite burp. "I've dealt with the Veterans' Administration before. They've been helpful. There'll most likely be a life insurance policy of some type, too. I'll give them a call."

He handed me back the pawn ticket.

"I'll check this out if you want me to, Father."

"Please do. Would it be a problem for you, Nick? Checking into this for me? Finding out what Scratchy was up to? Running down this Susan? I've asked some of the regulars, but none of them ever heard Scratchy mention her name."

I slipped the pawn ticket and piece of note paper into my pocket. "No problem at all, Father," I said, hoping I sounded more confident than I felt.

San Francisco has its share of beautiful buildings, my own preferences running from the French High Baroque City Hall, to the Ferry Building, to a couple of the graceful downtown buildings erected prior to the "Manhattanization" of the area. I even go against local sentiment and like the TransAmerica Pyramid Building.

We also have more than our share of downright unsightly edifices, the cream of that particular crop being the jukebox of a hotel Marriott put up on Fourth and Market streets, and the Hall of Justice, an ominous gray square block of a monstrosity that, if properly described, would necessitate adding three extra u's to the word "ugly."

The Hall houses a jail, the district attorney's office, the city's probation department, the criminal courts, a district police station, and the detective bureaus.

On the main floor, just prior to the grime-smudged glass doors leading into the Hall itself, is the coroner's office. Coroner. Nice, harsh, sturdy word. You know what you're getting when you hear it. Maybe "coroner" is a little too descriptive, because the powers that be are changing it to "medical examiner," which brings to my mind a newspaper for doctors or a proctologist with long fingers. Next they'll be changing "morgue" to "deceaseds' dormitory."

The medical examiner on duty was Dominique Hutches, a lithe, olive-skinned woman with sultry coffee-brown eyes. She was cooperative, especially after I told her I was working with Father Tomasello in hopes of finding Mr. O'Hara's next of kin.

Scratchy didn't have much on him at the time of death. A moldy leather wallet, the foggy plastic insert showing his California DMV ID card. With Scratchy's booze and drug problems, he had no chance of getting an actual driver's license. The address shown was that of the Veterans' Administration Medical Center on Clement Street. A card from a local blood bank, showing Scratchy to be a regular contributor. A holy card showing St. Matthew holding up a cross. On the back was Scratchy's handwritten note, asking the authorities to notify Father Tomasello in an emergency. I guess death falls into that category. A ten-dollar bill and three ones. A black plastic comb with several teeth missing. His clothes and shoes were in a separate bag, but I didn't bother with them.

The ME's report showed Mr. O'Hara had been picked up at three-twenty in the morning from Second and Brannan streets. The cause of death was multiple injuries from an unknown vehicle. Hit-and-run.

"You want to see the body?" Hutches asked.

I said yes, but regretted it as soon as we walked back to the refrigerated storage room. If you've never had to go to the morgue to identify a body, consider yourself lucky. It's just as grim and clinical as it is in the movies. All-tile floors, walls of stainless-steel drawers, the drawers on heavy casters so the body rolls out easily. Hutches pulled back the grayish sheet covering Scratchy, and I winced. I took a long look, squeezed my eyes shut, and turned around. "Jesus. What the hell hit him?"

"Whatever it was, it was heavy. Looks like he was hit, then backed over. You can see by the way the skull is crushed here, and the . . ."

She went on like that for a couple of minutes, while I pinched my nostrils shut and tried to look as if I wasn't going to litter the tile floor with some of Father Tomasello's turkey.

"Do you know who's handling the case for Hit-and-Run?"

Hutches slid the drawer shut. It closed with a solid metallic click. "New fella. Davall."

CHAPTER 4

◄►

At one time I thought I knew just about every one of the inspectors assigned to the various detective bureaus: Aggravated Assault, Burglary, Fencing, Fraud, Homicide, Missing Persons, Narcotics, Homicide, Robbery, Sexual Assault, Vice Crimes, Hit-and-Run. I'd spent a good ten years of my career bumping from detail to detail. But once you're gone a few years, you're really gone.

I took out my old badge and showed it to the receptionist in the Hit-and-Run detail, a doleful-faced woman who looked as if she hadn't laughed since Johnny Carson left *The Tonight Show*.

"I retired a couple of years back," I informed her. "Is Inspector Davall in?"

It seemed like a simple enough question, but her eyes squinted shut and her forehead furrowed as if she were in sudden pain.

"What's it about?" she asked in a no-nonsense tone.

"Charles Nelson O'Hara."

She punched the name into her computer. "Yes, that's Inspector Davall's case. What is your interest?"

I passed her one of my cards. "I'm working for his family." It really wasn't much of a fib. Father Tomasello was probably the only family poor old Scratchy had.

"I'll see if Inspector Davall is available," was her unenthusiastic response. I watched her shuffle away from her desk and disappear through an open doorway. She came back moments later and grudgingly waved me through to the inner sanctum of the Hit-and-Run detail.

Personnel may change, but civil service decor doesn't. The

room was full of gray desks and gray filing cabinets, the walls dotted with city-issued calendars and cartoons cut from magazines.

A tall, well-proportioned man in a snowy-white shirt and dusty-red paisley tie waved a hand toward me, then plopped back into his chair. He kept his eyes on me as I approached. He looked to be in his late twenties, with a long, angular chin and fine-spun blond hair. He snapped my card under a manicured nail. "You're Mr. Polo?"

"Yes." I showed him my badge and got much the same response as I had from the receptionist. I dropped a few names of people I knew who used to work Hit-and-Run. They were all strangers to Davall.

"What's your interest in Mr. O'Hara?" Davall asked.

"Father Tomasello over at St. Matthew's Kitchen asked me to look into Scratchy's death."

I could see from the dull look in Davall's cloudy gray eyes that he didn't know who Father Tomasello was. Bad news. Anyone who read a local newspaper on a regular basis should know of Father Tomasello. "He runs a kitchen for the homeless in the Tenderloin. Scratchy, Mr. O'Hara, was a regular there."

"Oh," Davall responded. He was either the strong, silent type or stupid. I was beginning to fear it was the latter.

"Father Tomasello keeps a sort of bank for some of the regulars." I told Davall of the money Scratchy had left in Father Tomasello's safe. "Six hundred and fifty dollars. All fifty-dollar bills. Scratchy just had a ten and a few one-dollar bills on him at the time of his death."

The clouds in Davall's eyes thinned. "How do you know that?" he said, looking at me suspiciously.

"I saw the ME's report."

The heat stayed in his voice. "Who gave you permission to do that?"

Oh God, I thought. I hoped he wasn't going to be one of those. "O'Hara left a will. The money will go to St. Matthew's Kitchen if no relatives are found." I paused. "Father Tomasello is a good friend of Chief Leahy's. Leahy comes to the kitchen every Thanksgiving and Christmas, with the mayor, the board of supervisors. They all help dish out the holiday food."

Davall pursed his lips and looked at the row of neatly stacked manila folders in the gray metal desktop file organizer on the corner of his desk. All he had to do was reach for the one with the name O'Hara on the tab and hand it to me.

"I'll have to check with my lieutenant before I allow you to see my report."

Oh, God. He was one of those. I thought about swapping him the pawn ticket for the file, but once he got hold of the ticket, I'd never find out what Scratchy hocked. "I understand. Let me ask you a couple of questions, okay?"

I got a minimal nod, which I took as an okay. "Any suspects?"

Another brief nod, this one a negative side-to-side.

"Any leads on the vehicle that hit Mr. O'Hara?"

Davall's head swung back and forth a good two inches. I hoped he hadn't hurt himself.

"Have you come across anything to indicate that O'Hara had a family?"

Another nonaerobic shake of the head.

"Did the crime lab come up with anything at the scene?"

The question must have aroused Davall. He actually spoke. "No."

I leaned my face in his direction so he had to look at me. "Davall, I'd like to help on this. Anything I get, naturally I'd give to you. But if I'm to help you, you've got to help me."

He shrugged his shoulders, leaned forward, and plucked O'Hara's file folder. The folder was thin; it couldn't have held more than ten or twelve pages and a few photographs. He swiveled his chair so that there was no possibility of my getting a peek at his precious reports. "There's really nothing here, Mr. Polo. A waste of your time. Mr. O'Hara appeared to be a . . ."

I saved him from searching for the appropriate word. "Bum. Yes, Scratchy was a bum. He also was a war hero, with a disability. A human being. Just a guy trying to make it through to the next day. Now he's dead. Hit-and-run. The ME told me it looked as if he'd been hit, then backed over. And he just came into a large sum of money. A very large sum of money for a bum. Doesn't that make you a little curious?"

Davall snapped the file shut. "You can be sure that I'll look into that aspect of the investigation, sir."

Sir? I'd been called a lot of things by policemen, friend and foe, over the years. But never sir. "I'm going to work on this, Inspector. With or without your help."

Davall looked at me with an air of studied superiority. "Thanks for coming in and talking to me about this, sir."

There were slight drifts of steam spilling from my ears as I headed directly for the record room. It took almost half an hour, but, after filling out a request form and indicating that I was working for the life insurance carrier for one Charles Nelson O'Hara and plunking down seven bucks, I was given a copy of the traffic accident report.

Three pages, made out by the first officer on the scene, a solo motorcycle cop. There wasn't much of interest, just a description of the weather and Scratchy's remains, and a diagram. It was what was missing in the diagram that drew my attention. No skid marks.

I prowled the halls looking for a friendly face, finding my old partner, Paul Paulsen, at his desk in the General Works detail.

"You know a guy named Davall in Hit-and-Run?"

Paul, a robust ginger-haired man who never met a lunch he didn't like, gave me a cautious smile. "Bill Davall. Nice-looking kid. Part of the new breed."

"The new, uncooperative breed." I gave Paul a rundown on Scratchy, including the money and pawn ticket left with Father Tomasello.

"It'll be interesting to see what's in that pawnshop. That has to be where he got the money."

I agreed, then told Paul about the two license-plate requests I'd run for Scratchy.

Paulsen pulled at a finger joint until it popped. "Lester Maurence. The big leagues."

"Yes. But he could be just what Scratchy said he was. Someone who stopped and handed him a dollar bill every now and then."

"Maurence might slip him a buck or two. What about the leasing agency?" Paul asked.

"I haven't checked that out yet. There was another license plate. Scratchy called, left it on my answering machine on Saturday. I haven't run that one yet." I handed Paul the paper with the "Duke?" and "Shark?" notations.

Paulsen's handsome face formed a scowl. "Who the hell or what the hell are Duke and Shark?"

"I don't know. This was in Scratchy's stash at St. Matthew's. Maybe something will turn up on the license plate number."

"Let me take a wild guess. You want me to run the plate."

"That would be nice. And if you could pull anything available on Scratchy, it would be appreciated."

"I'll bet," Paulsen said, struggling to his feet. "I'm going to need a little more ID than just Scratchy."

I gave Paul Scratchy's full name and the date and time of the hit-and-run.

For a big man, Paul is very graceful. He wove his way through the barricades of desks and cabinets to the detail's computer. Oh, the wonders of police department computers. They have direct access to so many things that would make a private investigator's life so much easier: local criminal records, incident reports, national criminal records, and DMV records, with those all-important addresses.

Paulsen came back minutes later, ripping the perforated edges off the computer paper. He handed me the documents, then pointed a thumb skyward. "Mr. O'Hara was not unfamiliar with our overnight facilities on the seventh floor."

Scratchy's rap sheet showed he had indeed been a guest at the Hall of Justice's jail: a dozen or more arrests, all for drunk-and-disorderly.

The hit-and-run incident report that Inspector Davall had protected so diligently was barely worth the paper it was printed on—most of it was just a reworded version of the motorcycle officer's traffic accident report. There was a notation that the driver of a newspaper delivery van spotted Scratchy's body at 0240 and called his dispatcher, who relayed it to the police. No witnesses. No skid marks. No debris left at the scene, other than poor old Scratchy.

"Hit-and-run. No skid marks," I told Paulsen. "A little unusual, don't you think?"

"Could be," Paul agreed halfheartedly. "What was his alcohol blood count?"

"Point two oh," I said, remembering the details from the ME report.

Paulsen said, "You can get busted for drunk driving with a point oh eight reading. That's about four shots of straight hundred-proof alcohol in the bloodstream. Your boy was smashed."

"Scratchy probably woke up every morning with a point oh eight count. He was putting away a half gallon of cheap wine a day, at least. But not all in one sitting. Just a day-long intake of swigs from the bottle. What are you smiling about?"

"Maybe the late Mr. O'Hara was psychic." He handed me the DMV printout.

The plate number Scratchy had left on my answering machine was listed to a Rolls-Royce. Name of the registered owner: the Stockton Street Mortuary.

CHAPTER 5

◄►

It was an almost perfect day. The baby-blue sky was dappled with sun-rimmed clouds. A slight southerly wind rustled the leaves and food wrappers in the street.

The spot where Scratchy's life ended had a lot more food wrappers and old newspapers than leaves. The closest tree was a hundred feet away, a lone, gaunt ficus, its knucklelike roots buckling the concrete sidewalk.

Second and Brannan streets. An old industrial area, cornered by old brick warehouses built in the 1920s. Most of the buildings were chopped up into multiunit affairs housing everything from small contractors to accountants' offices to off-brand clothing manufacturers.

According to the police department's accident report diagram, Scratchy's body had been found sixteen feet east of the southeast corner of the intersection.

The commuter traffic was in full force, so I had to wait for a couple of signal changes before I could go out and give it a good look. The "no skid marks" notation puzzled me. Put yourself in the place of the driver. You're going along, suddenly you see something in your path, feel the impact. You'd slam on your brakes, right? Skid marks. Unless you were driving very slowly. But if you were driving slowly, how did you hit that someone in the first place? Why didn't that someone see you, or hear you coming? According to the medical examiner, it looked like whoever had hit Scratchy finished off the job by backing over him.

We had a case in town recently where a member of the medical examiner's staff went out to the scene to investigate a body that had been hit by a truck. The man parked, examined the deceased, got into his meat wagon, and, in taking off, actually drove over the body lying in the street. He hit the brakes, then, I kid you not, obviously not knowing what had happened, stopped and backed over the poor devil. The crowd of observers was said to have run away from the scene in shock, their curbside places taken immediately by attorneys looking to console the unknown dead man's soon-to-be wealthy relatives.

I studied the accident report on Scratchy, then paced off sixteen feet, keeping a wary eye on the traffic light. The grimy gray asphalt was ribboned with stains from oil, rubber, and God knows what. But no visible skid marks. Just the fading traces of the chalk marks that had outlined Scratchy's body.

Somehow, an old joke came to mind. Do you know what you find at the end of a rainbow in New York City? An empty pot of gold and a chalk outline of a leprechaun.

I raced back to the relative safety of the sidewalk just before the light changed again and the homeward-bound commuters sped away to wait at the signal on the next block down.

What was Scratchy doing in this neighborhood at two-forty in the morning? Though, Lord knows how long he lay on the ground before the newspaper delivery driver called in the report. The bars close at two o'clock sharp, so he could have been wandering home. But where was home? There are a dozen or more homeless shelters scattered around the city, but Scratchy wasn't a shelter type. He was a true, old-time street person who'd find a hideout and stay there until he was kicked out, then find another hideout: a vacant building, or one that wasn't vacant but where the occupant foolishly left a window open at night.

At one time the undersides of freeways were popular spots, but they'd been taken over by the hard cases, the druggies, the just plain wackos who ran their hovels like warlords and demanded payment, in money or services, for a cold strip of cement partially sheltered from the wind and the rain. They were a tough, vicious bunch. Sex often reared its ugly head. A streetwise beat cop working out of Southern Station told me that there were more cases of male rape then female rape on the streets now. The reason was purely mathematical. There were a lot more males than females living on those streets. The rapes were seldom reported, the victims being either young strangers lured to the Paris of the West, only to find themselves broke, strung out and unprotected, or poor defenseless cripples, physically or mentally, who didn't have the strength, savvy, or inclination to do anything about it.

Not Scratchy's lifestyle. He was an independent cuss. He wanted no part of the gang scene and scorned the cramped, barracks-style shelters the city provided. He'd have a haven somewhere. But where? I looked around the area. The possibilities were endless. A back alleyway stacked with empty cardboard cartons. An abandoned car that could be used for a week, maybe a month, before the city got around to towing it away. And who knows? Maybe Scratchy had a friend. With a real room. Electricity. A stove. Television. All the comforts of home. Almost.

Pawnbrokers. Have you noticed that they've gone upscale lately? They used to be housed in small storefronts in the seedy sections of town. Now you find them in suburban shopping malls, their display windows looking like plush jewelry stores.

I've worked the Robbery detail and have spent quite a bit of time in pawnshops, tracing stolen goods. A wise broker tipped me off to the business. "Nobody comes to me to buy or sell anything for themselves. It's always for their brother, their mother, their boyfriend or girlfriend, but never for themselves."

He was right. Nervous-faced customers would enter the store, and whether they were looking for a watch, a ring, a guitar, a camera, or a television set, it was always for someone else.

The man behind the counter at Sam's Jewelry and Loan Company on Sixth Street looked at me with shrewd battle-aged eyes. He was in his sixties, with thick hair that shone like polished silver.

"Can I help you, sir?" he asked politely.

"Is Duke in?"

"Duke? I'm afraid we don't have anyone by that name here."
It was worth a try. "Susan?"

He eyed me with suspicion. "There is no Susan here either, sir. Are you sure you've come to the right place?"

I dug the pawn ticket out of my wallet and handed it to him. "Redemption time."

He studied the ticket, then me, then disappeared behind some curtains at the rear of the store. The uniformed rent-a-cop leaning against the showcase near the entrance eyed me suspiciously. If I looked suspicious I wondered what he had thought of Scratchy.

The pawnbroker came back carrying a small white plastic tray. The bottom of the tray was lined with pool-table-green felt. Sitting majestically on the felt was a gold watch, separated from its thick gold bracelet.

"You're not the gentleman who pawned this merchandise, sir."

"No. But I've got the ticket. Is there a problem?"

He coughed into his hand. "There could be."

He set the tray down on the case in front of me. I picked up the watch. The dial said Rolex.

"Is this a real Rolex?" I asked, hefting the timepiece in my hand.

"Unfortunately, no."

I went for the bracelet. It felt heavy as hell. "Looks like real gold."

Another cough into his hand. "Yes. That's because it is real gold. Eighteen-karat."

I took another look at the watch. I'd heard of dozens of phony Rolex stories. This one certainly looked legit. "It would have fooled me," I admitted to the pawnbroker.

He tugged at an earlobe. "It would fool a lot of people. I've seen my share of them, and I assure you, this is the best." He held out his hand for the watch, and I dropped it in his palm.

"See here," he said, holding the watch between a thumb and forefinger, "the model number is stamped on this area at the top of the watch, twelve o'clock"—he twisted the watch around—"the model number on the opposite side at six o'clock. Usually on a phony, they don't bother with that, but someone did a magnificent job on this one."

"But you were suspicious when Mr. O'Hara brought it in to you."

"He did not appear the type of gentleman to be wearing a Rolex, but one never knows."

No, one doesn't. "What makes you so sure it is a phony?"

"Well, for one thing, the second-hand sweep. Rolex has a rather distinctive second-to-second sweep. This one rather flows along. I opened it up. A cheap quartz movement. The kind you can find on any ten-to-one-hundred-dollar watch made in the Far East."

"How much did you lend Scratchy on it?"

"Scratchy?"

"Mr. O'Hara. The man who pawned the watch."

"He didn't tell you?"

"No."

He clasped his hands in front of him like a professional mourner. "How unusual. The amount was six hundred and fifty dollars."

"How'd you arrive at that figure?" I inquired.

"The gold. Purely on the gold. Six ounces of eighteen-karat gold. The spot price on twenty-four-karat at the time of the transaction was three hundred and eighty dollars an ounce. Figure four ounces of pure gold, that came out to fifteen hundred and twenty dollars. I usually only go up to forty percent on deals like this, which would have made the amount six hundred and eight dollars. However, your gentleman friend looked like he was in need, so I rounded it off to the six-fifty figure."

My, my. All that without an adding machine. And how nice of him to think of Scratchy's needs. "What's the watch actually worth?"

He touched his chest with a finger. "To me? Well, that's hard to say. It's hard to put a figure on just what someone would pay over and above the metal value."

I reached for my wallet. "You take credit cards, don't you?"

He cocked his head and looked at me. "I'm not really sure I can release the item. There is the problem of its being a forgery. The Rolex people would be quite interested in getting a look at it."

I dug into my pants again, this time coming out with my old badge. "They'll look at it and take it away, and you'll be six hundred and fifty bucks to the shorts."

He pondered that while I dug my Visa card from my wallet. Of course, he already knew about the Rolex company's interest. He also must have figured that a gentleman of Scratchy's breeding might blow the six hundred and fifty bucks in a couple of days and have no way of ever redeeming the watch. "Put the bracelet back on it, please. I think I'll wear it home."

A movie reviewer once wrote an article about a film noir festival. His favorites were the movies based on Raymond Chandler's books: Bogart's *The Big Sleep;* Dick Powell's *Murder My Sweet* version of *Farewell My Lovely;* George Montgomery's *The Brasher Doubloon,* based on Chandler's novel *High Window.* He even mentioned the Robert Mitchum remakes of *The Big Sleep* and *Farewell My Lovely* and the attempts of James Garner, Robert Montgomery, and Elliott Gould to portray Philip Marlowe on the big screen. The reviewer's point was that the reason for the continued popularity of these movies, and other private-eye flicks, was that everyone, at some time in his life, for the briefest of moments, maybe just when he's alone in a theater watching one of these movies, wants to be a private investigator. Well, that may be stretching it, but it is interesting how many people tell me, "Gee, you're a private eye. I've always wanted to be one."

Well, nowadays if you want to become a PI, forget about Bogie's trench coat or Marlowe's revolver. The first things you have to learn about are computers and fax machines.

I drove back to my flat and went through some useless exercises on the computer, running Charles Nelson O'Hara through the on-line templates of a variety of database searches, coming up with nothing.

The first three digits of his Social Security number, 050, indicated the card had originated in the state of New York, but that's about as far as I got.

I wasted almost a hundred dollars running the complete numbers through six data searches, coming up with nothing but a San Francisco address, Forty-second and Clement streets, the address for the veterans' hospital. It was the same address Scratchy had listed on his Department of Motor Vehicles ID card.

Marriage records in California were negative. I checked Charles Nelson O'Hara through civil filings in San Francisco, looking to find an old divorce action. Again, as we investigators like to pronounce in our written reports: negative results.

I hoped Father Tomasello was having better luck getting information from the Veterans Administration.

I then ran the Stockton Street Mortuary through the computer. It was a corporation. The name listed for responsible managing partner sent a small shiver down my back. Henry Lee. A common name, especially in a town with a large Asian population like San Francisco. The Henry Lee that came to my mind was the one who ran most things in Chinatown. Things like gambling dens, prostitution, loan-sharking, and smuggling rings.

Lee operated out of a small alleyway, Pagoda, in the heart of Chinatown, which happened to be just around the corner from the Stockton Street Mortuary. I dug through the phone book for the mortuary's number.

A cool, professional voice answered the phone.

"Henry Lee, please."

"Who is calling?"

"Inspector Dreyfus from the Immigration Department."

There was a long pause on the other end of the line. "You had best contact Mr. Lee at his headquarters."

"I don't have that number. Is it on Pagoda?"

"That is correct." He hung up without saying goodbye.

It was the same Henry Lee, all right, and Mr. Lee was not known for his charitable contributions. To sidewalk architects or anyone else.

I went back to the phone book, known in the private-eye trade as a list of confidential sources. You'd be surprised at the number of cases where an investigator is hired to locate someone and, after going through all kinds of elaborate searches, finds the wanted person's name was sitting right there in the phone book all the time. You automatically assumed the client had checked this first. But you know what they say about the word "assume." No San Francisco listing for Lester Maurence.

I tried to find his shipping company in the yellow pages. Nothing. It's a sad story. The San Francisco waterfront's docks were once filled with passenger and freight lines, unloading their well-dressed voyagers and exotic cargoes on a daily basis. The Longshoremen's Union workers, with their broad shoulders, denim shirts, and white caps, were an everyday sight along the Embarcadero, strolling the sidewalks as if they owned them, stopping in for a 3:00 A.M. coffee and brandy at a battenboard saloon that wasn't supposed to open until 6:00 A.M. A couple of quick ones before climbing down those holds, then hours of backbreaking work while, just like in the Harry Belafonte song, the tallyman tallied their bananas, or pineapples from Hawaii, copper from South America, spices from China. There had been some bloody battles between the longshoremen, the police, and the teamsters back then. The city had a good, rough blue-collar tinge to it in those days. But those days were gone. Now most of the piers along the bay were just vacant, rotting lumber waiting for the demolition ball to smash them away, to be replaced by a restaurant or amusement pier.

Most of the ships had moved across the bay to Oakland. Oakland, once famous, thanks to Gertrude Stein, as the town with "no there, there," now had almost all of the Bay Area's ships, shipping lines, and related jobs.

I tried the Oakland directory. Sure enough, Maurence Shipping was listed, at Pier 17.

Back to the computer. As a member of the San Francisco board of supervisors, Maurence would have to have a San Francisco residential address. The assessor records came up snake eyes again.

Since Maurence was a supervisor, he'd have to vote. At least for himself. I found him in the voter registration files: 310 Buena Vista Terrace, San Francisco. Some people are foolish enough to include their home telephone number on their registrar of voters forms. Maurence was not among that group.

A quick switch back to the assessor base showed that 310 Buena Vista Terrace was listed to K. Chong Realty, with an address on Stockton Street. Almost next door to Henry Lee's funeral parlor. Convenient. I could waste a lot of computer time trying to hook the Realtor to Lee, but what good would that do me?

I tried calling Maurence at his shipping office in Oakland. I was channeled from the receptionist, who had a sultry, well-modulated voice, to a secretary with a snappy, "it's almost quitting time" tone, and finally to a Miss Hayward, who communicated in short, blunt sentences.

"Who did you say you were?" she asked, after I'd introduced myself.

Technically the charge would be 538d of the California Penal Code. Impersonating a police officer. I prefer to think of it as more of an acting job, like Gene Hackman or Clint Eastwood in the movies. 538d is a misdemeanor and can get you "imprisonment in the county jail not exceeding one year," according to the law books.

"Inspector Harris of the San Francisco Police Department," I said into the phone, my thumb and index finger pinching my nose shut to distort my voice in case Mr. Maurence's secretary was in the habit of recording incoming calls, which, in case you're ever tempted, happens to be another violation of the Penal Code.

"What do you wish to speak to Mr. Maurence about?"

"About a hit-and-run case. The deceased's name is Charles Nelson O'Hara."

That didn't slow her down a bit. "And what does Mr. Maurence have to do with your investigation?"

Maybe it was my imagination, or maybe it was a faulty connection, but I was sure I heard the distinctive click of a phone being picked up. "I'd like to talk to Mr. Maurence about that personally."

"I'm afraid that's impossible at the moment, sir."

I cut in quickly before she could ask for my phone number.

"We found a license-plate number written down on a piece of paper in Mr. O'Hara's possession. The license-plate number belongs to Mr. Maurence's 190E Mercedes."

There was a long pause. "I don't believe Mr. Maurence has had any dealings with anyone by that name, Inspector."

"But you can't know everyone he deals with, can you?"

Another long pause. Then a male voice, confident, unruffled, stately. "This is Lester Maurence. Can I help you?"

I went through the whole spiel, just as if Maurence hadn't been listening in earlier.

"I'm sorry, Inspector. The name doesn't ring a bell. When and where did this tragedy take place?"

I gave him the date, time, and intersection.

"Hmmm, I think I was in Sacramento that day. Stayed over all night. You say this man had my car's license plate written down?"

"Yes. Yours and a couple of others."

"Whose were they?" he asked quickly.

"I'm not at liberty to say, sir. You know how it is."

"Yes, yes," he agreed quickly. "Sorry I can't be of more help. But please feel free to contact me again if I can be of any assistance."

He broke the connection. Mr. Maurence wasn't as curious as he should have been. He should have asked more questions. Should have dug a little deeper. He was anxious as hell to end the conversation.

I sent my fingers back to skipping through the yellow pages, finding International Auto Leasing located down the peninsula near the airport. I was about to call when the doorbell interrupted me.

Jane Tobin's normal workday outfit was slacks, a knit turtleneck, and a corduroy jacket. She was now wearing a forest-green knit dress scooped just low enough in the front to draw your attention. The black Burberry trench coat I'd given her as a Christmas present was draped over her arm.

"You didn't forget about dinner, did you?" she asked, flecks of suspicion showing in her eyes.

"Not at all," I said, waving her in, wondering just where we were supposed to be going. "I've just got one phone call to make. Fix us both a drink, would you?"

While Jane made for the kitchen, I hotfooted it back to the office and checked the calendar. Blank. There are weeks when Jane and I dine together, either at a restaurant, her apartment, or my flat, five out of seven days. Then there are weeks when we don't see each other at all.

I called International Auto Leasing to stall for time. A woman with a breathless, caressing voice answered the phone.

"Hello, this is Mr. Adams of Financial Insurance in Los Angeles. I need the name of your liability carrier and your fax number."

The voice became less breathless, less caressing. "What's the problem?"

"Oh, a simple 642B report we have to forward to DMV on a UI claim. Your vehicle was a third party. Minor damage. It's our insured who's at fault. But you know how that is."

If she didn't, she would not admit it. She gave me her fax number, then said, "Central Insurance Company in San Francisco on Mission Street handles our claims. Do you want their telephone number?"

She gave me both the number and address, and I thanked her, then hung up. Jane Tobin was hovering over my shoulder, holding two icy glasses of white wine.

"What's a 642B?"

"Damned if I know, but it sounds good, doesn't it?" I accepted the glass and took a sip, then told her about Scratchy.

Her lovely face changed minutely: eyes narrowing a bit, eyebrows riding up toward her forehead, lips pursing. The reporter mode taking over automatically.

We moved into the kitchen and topped off our wineglasses as I told her what I'd learned during the day.

The phony Rolex intrigued her. I took it from my wrist and she gave it a long, hard look and did everything but bite it. "What are you going to do with this?"

"It belongs to Scratchy's heirs. If we ever find any." I showed her the printout on the Rolls-Royce license plate and the scratch paper with two notations. "Who do you think of when you hear the name Duke?"

Jane sucked her lower lip in for a moment. "John Wayne, Duke Ellington, Tim Holt's horse—"

"Tim Holt's horse?"

"Sure," she said confidently. Never get into a Trivial Pursuit game with Jane. Especially if it involves money.

"Duke was the name of one of the dogs in *Swiss Family Robinson,* and—"

I had to bite. "Who was the other dog?"

"Turk."

I checked it out later. She was right. "Anyone else?"

"Duke Mantee, Bogart's character in *The Petrified Forest,* the English gentry, Duke University. That's about all I can come up with."

"I think we can safely rule them all out. Duke has to be local. One of Scratchy's buddies. Maybe he knows about the watch. And a lot more. What about Shark?"

"Greg Norman, the Australian golfer, is known as the Great White Shark. That's about all I can come up with."

"Well, Scratchy definitely wasn't the golfing type." I told her my theory of Duke possibly being a loan shark. "But hell, I don't know when Scratchy put that paper in his bank. Could have been a couple of years ago when he made out his will. Maybe they're nicknames of old buddies of his."

Jane examined the paper. "Are you sure this is Scratchy's handwriting?"

"Yeah. It looks exactly like the handwriting on his will."

"Scratchy certainly was moving in some strange circles," she said. "Lester Maurence and Henry Lee. What's the connection there?"

"I really don't know if there is one. It could be just like Scratchy told me. People who were steady tippers."

Jane's grimace told me she wasn't having any of that. "A funeral-parlor Rolls pulling off the freeway and dropping coins into Scratchy's hat? Come on, Nick. No way."

I had to agree with her. It was a stretch. But strange things do happen in this life. "The cop handling the hit-and-run investigation isn't going to do anything but let the file get dusty, then bury it."

"What about the leased car?"

"I won't be able to find out who was driving the car until tomorrow."

"The money. The watch. Will you be able to trace them?"

"I doubt it."

"Maybe this Susan person will have the answers." Jane placed a finger on the rim of her glass and ran it around a couple of times. "You don't really feel like going to the Linwood party tonight, do you?"

That was it! The Linwood party. Bill Linwood, a loutish reporter for the Associated Press, who preferred to be identified as a "distinguished foreign correspondent." He had apparently tired of his globe-trotting and had settled down in San Francisco. Linwood had published a few nonfiction books along the way, but now he was turning his ink-stained hands to fiction, a six-hundred-page espionage novel, all about CIA bad guys plotting to take over the world. Again. Jane had done a column on Linwood's book, and he was chasing after her. She'd given me an advance copy of the book. Thirty pages were enough. Messrs. Deighton and Le Carré had nothing to worry about.

Maybe I was prejudiced because Linwood made it clear that he thought he'd have the inside track to Jane's affections if I was out of the way. She seemed to think he walked on literary waters. One of these days she's liable to run into a real Prince Charming and dump me. But her dumping me for Linwood would be a bitter pill to swallow.

"Well. He's really not one of my favorite people," I admitted.

"He's a hell of a reporter, Nick. He's worked all over the world. I know he was stationed in the Far East for a long time. He might know something about Lester Maurence and a possible connection with Henry Lee. I could pick his brain for you."

I wasn't sure I wanted Jane groping around in Linwood's brain. "Why don't we just stop by the party for a drink? Then we'll go out to dinner. How about Chinese?"

CHAPTER 6

◄►

The book party for Bill Linwood was held, appropriately enough, at John's Grill on Ellis Street. "Historic John's Grill" is the way the owners like to publicize the place. It was opened in 1908, and its main claim to fame is that Dashiell Hammett used to be a regular, when he worked around the corner for Pinkerton's Detective Agency. Hammett had Sam Spade dine at John's in *The Maltese Falcon*. Spade's favorite was lamb chops, sliced tomatoes, and a baked potato. A version of the meal is still featured on the menu. One of the tuxedo-clad waiters was wandering around with a drink tray. I grabbed a glass of wine, wove through the crowd, and partook of the usual cocktail chatter, keeping an eye on Jane as she made her rounds. She got Linwood's ear, got a little too close to his ear in my mind. I stopped to gab with a broad-shouldered man from the Mystery Book Store, who was flogging Linwood's book, *Balance of Evil*. A nametag on the bookseller's shirt showed him to be Bruce Taylor.

"How's the book doing?" I asked, fingering a copy and examining the photo on the jacket. Linwood looked like a Hollywood producer's idea of a foreign correspondent: shaggy brown hair worn in a lion's-mane style, square jaw, squinty eyes under tangled brows.

Taylor shrugged those large shoulders. "Hammett did better."

Hard to argue with that.

One of the things that surprises first-time visitors to San Francisco is that it's physically more of a small town than a city. Forty-nine square miles, several of those vertical. Take away a few areas where no tourist dares visit, then the bedroom communities of the Sunset, Parkside, Excelsior, Ingleside, and Outer Mission districts, and you carve that forty-nine square miles down to maybe eight or nine.

There are the must-sees: Golden Gate Park, the Presidio, the downtown shopping areas, parts of the blossoming Embarcadero, Fisherman's Wharf, Nob Hill, North Beach, and Chinatown.

When I was a wee lad, Broadway, from roughly the 400 block at Montgomery Street to the 800 block at Powell Street, was a dividing mark, like a river, separating the Italian-dominated North Beach on one side from Chinatown on the other.

Now that river is at low tide. Chinatown has spilled across and into the Beach. Mahogany-skinned roasted ducks hang from hooks in storefronts next to delicatessen windows curtained with salami and mortadella. Tea shops have sprouted up alongside espresso coffee shops. The old paesanos don't like it, but they have no reason to gripe. A great many of them have sold their properties at inflated prices and migrated to the suburbs.

The heavy-duty section of Chinatown remains Grant Avenue, south of Broadway. The street is filled with restaurants and exotic stores selling pearls, jade, camera equipment, and carved statues of large-bellied gentlemen with leering smiles on their faces.

The cross streets are a little less touristy: sidewalk vendors selling newspapers and magazines in the various Chinese dialects, along with Asian editions of *Playboy* and *Penthouse*. Bakeries, laundromats, wonderful dusty-windowed herb shops with jars full of mysterious-looking leaves, beans, and twisted roots.

If you wander into the alleys, you can hear the sewing machines humming in the sweatshops, walk by the tiny garage-front kitchens where they make fortune cookies.

There are markets with the best fresh fruits and vegetables in town, as well as tanks filled with live fish, turtles, and snakes.

Wooden cages house frightened rabbits, chickens, and ducks. There are always rumors about places that sell exotic animal parts: bear paws, rhino horns, elephant genitalia. Even cats and dogs. I choose to disbelieve the latter; though, truth be told, I don't remember ever seeing a dog or cat wandering free in the area.

As exotic and exciting as Chinatown is, it has also become one of the most dangerous areas in the city. Not so much for the camera-toting tourists. They don't want to lose that market. But dangerous for the people who live and work there.

Take a stroll down the 600 block of Jackson Street. There'll be clusters of young Asian males, from fourteen up through their early twenties, congregating on the sidewalk. They often gather in front of a bar called Red's, reputed to be a hangout for the local bad guys. These young men usually dress alike, in jeans and black jackets. You'll see a bulge under their arms, or in their pockets. It's not what you think. No guns. Not in public, anyway. The bulges are cellular phones. If any known FBI or DEA agent or member of the local gang task force wanders by, those cellular phones pop out as fast as Alan Ladd's six-shooter did in the movie *Shane*.

The gendarmes are tracked, their positions relayed to the gang's headquarters, and the cops are kept under observation until they leave the area.

Any tourist-type person who spends too much time on the street has his picture taken, and the photograph is entered into a log as a "possible law enforcement agent."

San Francisco has been relatively clear of organized crime for years. In the old days, if a Mafia type came to town, select members of the Bureau of Inspectors would meet him, greet him, and escort him to the train station, with a one-way ticket out of town.

There's a famous story about Mickey Cohen, a notorious Los Angeles gangster, coming to San Francisco trying to muscle his way in with the locals. A bookie, quite happy with the way things were being run on the home front, tipped off the cops. One of the cops slapped Cohen around a bit and sent him home.

Another of the cops supposedly showed Cohen's girlfriend around town for a few days.

It was a simpler town in those long-gone days of the twenties, thirties and forties. The chief of police, always an Irishman, was picked at a boardroom meeting at the once mighty Hearst newspaper, the *Examiner*. The Catholic archbishop was always in attendance at those meetings.

The McDonough brothers, who ran a bail bond shop at Clay and Kearny, also operated most of the betting parlors and houses of prostitution. Drugs weren't much of a problem back then, except in Chinatown.

If you are a member of the male sex and are in town for a visit, an interesting spot is the men's room at the Big Four Restaurant in the Huntington Hotel atop Nob Hill. There are the usual furnishings, but on the wall, in the small anteroom before you get to the porcelain, is a map showing Chinatown in the twenties. Colored dots are splashed all over the map, each dot specifying a different house of sin: Caucasian prostitutes, black prostitutes, Asian prostitutes, opium dens, gambling dens. The number of these little dots is staggering. How could they all stay in business? Where did their clientele come from? Maybe there's an identical map in the women's lounge. I'll have to ask Jane.

For dinner, we selected a place with a bit of a rugged history. It was back in the late 1970s when a gang, numbering at least a half-dozen by most accounts, trooped by the restaurant's front windows with guns out. That's what saved several of the patrons, because when the gang members burst in the front door, they did so with their weapons firing. Those who weren't already hiding under the tables were directly in the line of fire. Five people died, seventeen were injured. The reason behind it was a dispute over which gang was entitled to run the very profitable fireworks business.

Even after all these years, everyone in the Golden Dragon seemed to be monitoring the front windows and the pedestrian traffic on Washington Street.

The Dragon was reputed to be a favorite restaurant of Henry

Lee's. He wasn't in attendance tonight. If he had been, I don't know that I'd have said anything to him.

Jane Tobin plowed her way through more than her share of the rice soup, smoked-tea duck, mu shu pork, Szechuan beef, steamed rice, and tea.

"Linwood kind of clammed up when I mentioned Henry Lee," she said, between spoonfuls of pork. " 'Heavy duty' was about all he'd say."

"What about Lester Maurence?"

"He wouldn't shut up about Maurence. Linwood knew Maurence when he was working out of Hong Kong. He thinks he was once connected with the CIA."

"Bill Linwood thinks Madonna, Magic Johnson, and the pope are connected with the CIA."

Jane took a sip of her beer, licking the foam from her upper lip. "If they are, it'd make a hell of a story. What are you going to do about Scratchy, Nick?"

"I don't know. Maybe we're reading too much into all of this."

Jane made a clicking noise with her teeth. "Well, maybe he just found it in the street, or swiped it."

"Could be," I agreed. "Then he just hocked it for the cash. But he was boasting to Father Tomasello that there was more money on the way."

We had the obligatory fortune cookies for dessert. We cracked them open and read the messages. Mine said, "Appetite comes with eating." Jane's read, "Money is the root of all evil. Take up gardening."

Fortune-cookie messages reached their zenith years ago with the line "Help, I'm a prisoner in a Chinese fortune-cookie factory." It's been downhill ever since.

We decided to stroll the streets a bit. I pointed out the gambling dens to Jane.

"How do you know they're gambling dens?"

"The lights over the entrance. The stairs leading down. The Chinese have a proverb, something about money traveling in a downward direction." We stopped in front of a rusty iron gate leading to well-worn cement steps, leading to another iron gate some six steps from the first. You could just see the floor of the basement den. Dirty green tile. The cuffs of pants. Shoes shuffling in and out of sight.

"Not very exotic, is it?" Jane asked.

"Nope. Basic stuff. Old tables and chairs. Beer from a refrigerator. The den is probably linked to a neighboring cellar in case the cops come a-calling. They play poker, fantan. A lot of money changes hands."

"If they're so easy to spot, why don't the police shut them down?"

"Easier said than done. By the time the cops get through the gates, all the chips have disappeared, all the bad guys have scooted through a hidden door into the next building. They're careful with the chips. They're as good as U.S. greenbacks in Chinatown. You can use them to pay your rent, buy your food, whatever."

Two youths in black jackets and jeans brushed by us, their eyes hard, arms outstretched, hands curled, as if to scoop water. Or throw a karate punch.

Jane's hand tightened on my elbow. "Let's get out of here."

We weaved our way through the streets and alleys, ending up on Pagoda. The entrance to Henry Lee's headquarters didn't look like much. A weather-blistered wooden door. Iron-barred windows. Six stories of smoke-blackened bricks.

The glistening car parked in front of the building stood out like a diamond in a pile of coal. A Rolls-Royce. Cream and brown. Vanilla and chocolate, with full-side whitewall tires. Either the cholesterol from dinner was kicking up my red blood cells or I was just plain excited. The license plate on the Rolls was the same number Scratchy had left on my answering machine. This was the Rolls listed in DMV files as belonging to the Stockton Street Mortuary.

I peered at the dark-tinted windows, but couldn't see anything other than my reflection. I walked around and looked at the front of the car. The famous Rolls hood ornament glistened under the yellow glow of the streetlamp.

The chrome was all brightly polished, the paint gleaming from a recent wax job. I bent down and examined the tires. They appeared to be brand-new, the tread thick, with tiny rubber nipples sprouting along the side.

Suddenly the driver's side door popped open and I struggled to get up, lost my balance, and landed on the seat of my pants.

"What the hell you doing?" demanded an Asian dressed entirely in black: shoes, pants, shirt, jacket.

I dusted off my hands and got to my feet. "Just admiring the car. It's a beauty."

He was of average height, his face round, a thin, droopy mustache under a nose that looked as if it had taken more than its share of punches. His hair was slicked straight back from his forehead. He swiveled to look at Jane, then snapped his fingers, and another Asian, younger, shorter, but also dressed all in black, exited the passenger door of the Rolls.

"You shouldn't be here," Droopy Mustache said, his voice nasal, maybe because of the bashed-up nose.

I grabbed Jane's arm. "We took a wrong turn. How do we get back to Grant Avenue?"

The two men exchanged glances. Droopy mustache nodded to the younger one, who climbed back into the Rolls. "Down to the end of the block. Turn left." He opened the car door. "And stay away from here."

"Not very hospitable, was he?" Jane said, as we hoofed it down the street.

"The Rolls," I said to Jane. "It's Henry Lee's. The license plate Scratchy called and asked me to run."

CHAPTER 7

◄►

The first thing I did the next morning was get to work on the computer.

Well, actually, the first thing I did that morning was to kiss Jane Tobin's bare shoulder, but let's stick to business.

A while back I mentioned that if you wanted to be a private eye, you first needed to learn the intricacies of computers and fax machines.

The computer you know about. Fax machines. Amazing devices. They've only been around about as long as the microwave oven, and like the microwave, once you've got one, you wonder how you ever got along without it. Especially in a business like mine, where you have to play games at times.

I called the number the leasing company's clerk had given me for the Central Insurance Company and got the name of the claims manager, Neil Hartman.

Thus armed, I cranked up the computer and printed an impressive-looking fax lead sheet for the Central Insurance Company, showing its address and phone number.

The letter was short and sweet:

> Re claim #AC64432812
> Claimant: Pine vs. International Auto Leasing
> Vehicle plate: 2AAGW466
> Please fax all forms re above unit directly to Neil
>   Hartman at 555-0678.
> Very truly yours,
> Neil Hartman

The claim number and the plaintiff's name were pure smoke and mirrors. The telephone fax number belonged to one of those private mail services where they sell stationery, print business cards, wrap and ship your packages, provide mailboxes and mail forwarding, and send and receive fax messages.

I keep an account there, for times like this when I don't want my fax number on a document. I called and told them to expect a report to a Mr. Hartman of Central Insurance, and to fax the report to me as soon as it came in.

Rather elaborate, you think? Much easier just to walk into International Auto Leasing and use some type of pretext like the TV PIs do? Or flash my old police badge, tell them it had something to do with a criminal matter? To use one of Mrs. Damonte's favorite English words: nopa.

Nowadays businesses, be they small car rental firms, giant insurance carriers, or just little mom-and-pop grocery stores, have all learned a single lesson: Don't release anything to anyone.

The reason? Civil lawsuits. Release any personal, medical, or employment records without the involved parties' permission, or without benefit of a subpoena, and you leave yourself wide open for a big damage claim.

It's gotten so bad, especially in personnel matters, that almost everyone is "released due to economic conditions." No one gets fired anymore, they all get "released" etc. and the complete personnel files are either locked up or destroyed.

Even if the "released" party got drunk, kicked the boss in a vulnerable area, and dropped lighted matches in the wastebaskets, by the time his personnel records are sanitized, none of this would be shown, making the next company to hire this lunatic vulnerable to more of the same.

I faxed the bogus request to International Auto Leasing, and then got to work on two civil cases that held no excitement, but did help bring a few shekels into my bank account.

It was lunchtime when I finished. Mrs. Damonte must have been reading my mind. The doorbell rang and she was there, elfin grin on her careworn face, pungent, spicy smells drifting up from the platter in her leathery hands.

Mrs. D's hands are the only part of her showing any effects of the sun. She wears a big straw hat whenever she's outside, and her usual getup of a black mourning dress covers everything from her ankles to her neck.

She handed me the platter without a word and trooped back downstairs to her flat.

I inhaled the aromas drifting from the *fitascetta,* a red-onion dough-ring pizza with tomatoes and rosemary. Nice of her, you say. True. But the tomatoes, onions, and rosemary all come from "her" garden in the back of the flats. In addition to paying very little rent, Mrs. D pays no gas, electricity, or water, so technically, the pizza cost her little other than the flour, salt, pepper, and olive oil involved. She always seems to drop off these wonderful presents just before rent day.

I called out a "thank you" to her retreating back and carried the pizza inside. I washed it down with an Anchor Steam beer.

After cleaning up, I checked the fax machine. No response to my request to International Auto Leasing. Maybe they were too smart to fall for the gag. Maybe they called the claims manager to check first. I'd just have to wait.

I called Father Tomasello and asked if he'd found anything new about Scratchy.

"Nothing yet, Nick. How goes the fight on your side?"

"The ticket was for a fake Rolex, Father. But an excellent fake, with a good six ounces of real gold in it. That's where Scratchy got the money, from pawning the watch."

"Do you have any idea how Scratchy got the watch?"

"Not yet. But I'd like to hold on to it for a while."

"Certainly, Nick. Do as you see fit. Anything on this Susan person?"

"Not yet. I'm trying to find out where Scratchy was spending his nights. Any ideas?"

"Ummm. I know he used to sleep out in Golden Gate Park, but that was some time ago, before the rowdies moved in. I don't know that Scratchy had any close friends, but I'll ask around."

"Ask about the names Duke and Shark that showed up on that piece of paper too, Father."

"I will indeed. Keep in touch, Nick."

I spoke silently to the dead. Scratchy, you scruffy scoundrel, what did you have or know that was of value to anyone? I ran a thumb across the Rolex's crystal. The pawnbroker was right. It would fool a lot of people.

The man who had taken over Scratchy's "territory," the off-ramp at Eighth and Harrison streets, looked, if possible, even more downtrodden than Scratchy himself: a wedge-shaped, rubicund face, scraggly, nicotine-colored hair, skeletal body wrapped in a shapeless olive-drab knee-length parka.

"Hi," I said. "How's it going?"

He edged closer to the freeway, fear flooding his bloodshot eyes. He held up his cardboard sign, an exact duplicate of Scratchy's "Vet Will Work for Food," over his head as if it were a shield.

"Take it easy, pal. I'm not a cop. Just a friend of Scratchy's."

His arms relaxed a little, the sign dropping to waist level. "Scratchy didn't have no friends."

"Sure he did. Father Tomasello, for one. He asked me to check around about Scratchy. Scratchy left some money in his bank at St. Matthew's."

His eyes turned inward, like a blind man's. I tried to guess his age. Impossible. Thirty-five to sixty, and I wouldn't want to bet on the high or the low. "How well did you know Scratchy?"

"Just a little," he conceded, pointing the sign toward the traffic waiting for the off-ramp's light to turn green.

"Looks like a slow day." I took a five-dollar bill from my money clip. He eyed it suspiciously before snatching it away and stuffing it into his coat pocket.

Clouds of foul-smelling exhaust fumes drifted over us as the light turned green and a big diesel rig lumbered onto Harrison Street.

"Look, what do you say I give you a twenty to go with that five, and you take a half hour off and we can go someplace and have a bite to eat. I'll buy you lunch. Okay?"

His name was Harry. He wouldn't give me the rest of it, and the someplace he picked was a workingman's bar on the corner of Seventh and Howard streets.

Harry wasn't at all interested in food, though he certainly

looked like he needed it. I tried ordering him the luncheon special, a hot roast beef sandwich, but he said he'd already had lunch. A drink he wouldn't mind. Harry's choice of poison was bourbon, a brand I'd never heard of, fished from the well by a formidable-looking fleshy-faced bartender in a leather apron, who, before reaching for the booze, made a point of asking Harry if he had the money to pay for his drink.

I slapped a ten-spot on the washed-out mahogany and asked for a Coke.

Harry's hand was shaking badly with the first shot, but calmed down after he gulped down the second. The bartender was there in a flash to drizzle more of the bourbon into his glass, scooping up another dollar and a half from the change left from my ten-spot.

"So tell me about Scratchy, Harry. When did you last see him?"

Harry's bloodshot eyes hadn't cleared up any, but his brain had. He turned crafty. "What was that you were telling me about Scratchy leaving some dough in Father Tom's bank?"

"Money and this." I pulled back my jacket sleeve, and Harry's red-rimmed eyes drooled at the watch. He took a sip of his drink, spilling a few drops on his fingers. He licked them up like an anteater. "I wish I knew where he got it, but I don't. I never seen Scratchy with any kind of watch. If he had one like that, he'd be afraid to wear it, I can tell you that."

"How about a guy named Duke? He ever mention a Duke?"

"Nah."

"Shark? That name ever pop up?"

Another "Nah."

"Susan. How about the name Susan? Did that ever come up?"

Harry shivered, like a man with a hard chill. "Susan? No. I don't ever remember nothin' like that."

"When was the last time you saw him?" I asked again.

"I'm not sure. Few days before he got killed, I guess."

"You're not sure?"

He smiled for the first time, flashing a row of uneven, tartar-stained teeth. "I don't keep a diary. You know what I mean?" His crescent-shaped eyebrows rose toward his forehead. "You work at the kitchen, don't you?"

"That's right."

"Tell Father Tom we're getting tired of turkey. Be nice to have some beef once in a while."

"I'll be sure to pass the word along. Now, what about Scratchy?"

"He's dead. That's all I know." He drained his glass, setting it down with a loud enough bang so the bartender would take notice.

I slipped another ten-dollar bill from my pocket, holding it above his empty glass. "If you can tell me where Scratchy was sleeping, this is yours. If not, I walk out of here with it in my wallet."

"He moved around a lot," Harry said, staring at the money as if it was an answer to his life's problems.

"I already knew that," I said, pulling the bill back a few inches.

"But I'm pretty sure he was holed up in some alley. Behind South Park."

"South Park Street? Which alley?"

"Shit, man. I don't know. Some alley there. Behind this place that dumps out a lot of boxes. Scratchy burrowed himself into them boxes."

It sounded like Scratchy, but it could be a place Harry was sleeping himself. Or a place he remembered from the past. A place he'd made up for a chance at the ten-dollar bill. "How do you know about this place?"

"I saw him over there one night. Tried joining him. He kicked me out." He rubbed a chafed hand across his chin. "Scratchy could be a mean bastard. Wasn't much on sharing."

I passed him the money. "Think you can show me this spot?"

"Sure." He looked around nervously for the bartender. "We got time for another drink?"

CHAPTER 8

◄►

South Park is one of the city's hidden gems. And located just a block away from where Scratchy's body had been found. Back in the 1850s an Englishman named George Gordon got a little tired of all the villains along the waterfront and Portsmith Square, so he bought up some acreage south of Market Street. He put in an oval garden some five hundred feet long and seventy-five feet wide, running between Second and Third streets, and began building homes. The new houses attracted the movers and shakers of the times: bankers, merchants, doctors, shipping magnates, brewers.

Legend has it that in order to help him get over his homesickness, Gordon imported English sparrows from London, to remind him of Berkeley Square.

South Park has gone through a lot of ups and downs since then. Mostly downs. But it was on the rebound. Gordon's garden was now an official city park, full of thirty-foot towering sycamore trees, a kiddies' area with slides, swings, and a sand pit with orange, red, and blue dicelike boxes with holes for the youngsters to climb through.

There are benches situated under the shade of the broad sycamores. Public barbecue pits. Stretches of grass big enough for the passing of Frisbees and footballs.

The buildings circling the park are a mixed bag. Wood-framed duplexes and fourplexes with bay windows and graceful millwork. The Hotel Madrid, which years ago had a reputation as a whorehouse, now chopped up into forty-eight units. Coffee shops, a couple of well-reviewed, upscale restaurants. Old brick two- and three-story residences now housing a mixture of attorneys, architects, and landscape engineers. Small manufacturing plants with warped doors.

The park was filled with an eclectic group of bike messengers on breaks, suit-and-tie businessmen grabbing brown-bag lunches. Well-dressed women who sat alone on the benches, heads tilted back to catch a few rays. Kids running everywhere. All in all, a nice scene.

Harry spoiled the mood. He growled, spit, and blew his nose, without benefit of a handkerchief.

"It was back here," he said, running his coat sleeve under his crimson schnozz.

I followed him into a small alley named after Jack London, then to another alley, Varney, which runs parallel to South Park.

There was the usual array of pickup trucks, garbage cans, and Dumpsters filled with debris. A squad of pigeons were picking their way through the garbage.

"Ain't here no more," Harry said.

"What ain't?" I asked, sensing there was no point in demonstrating my superior knowledge of the English language.

"The boxes. Wooden ones. Cardboard ones. There used to be a pile of 'em. And a big Dumpster. Used to be right over there." He kicked at a choleric-looking pigeon, who gave him a beady look, then took flight, settling on a telephone wire almost directly overhead.

I took two quick steps away from Harry and kept a wary eye on the bird. "You're sure this was the place?"

He went through the nose-blowing routine again. "Sure I'm sure. Scratchy's pad was right there, against the wall."

I wandered over to the spot he'd indicated. The building was two stories of old brick, the wall protruding out some fifteen feet beyond that of its neighbor. Some repair work had taken place on the wall recently, a space roughly six feet high and half that in width. The bricks here were new, with mortar oozing out from between them.

There was just the one back entrance, a battleship-gray corrugated-steel roll-up cargo door which took up most of the width of the building.

Harry was shuffling from one foot to the other, as if he had to find a men's room. "That Dumpster box used to be over there," he said, "by where the boxes was. By those new bricks." I passed him the promised ten-dollar bill. He shuffled away, his feet barely raising themselves above the pavement.

I walked around to the front of the building on South Park. There was just one entrance, a standard-size door made of metal and painted the same gray as the cargo door in the alley. I bent down and examined the hardware. A deadbolt was centered over a Schlage Company Primus model door lock. Schlage sells a lot of them to sensitive government installations, banks, and museums. Expensive, but efficient as hell. Whoever worked behind those doors valued his privacy. No doorbell. The building's address numbers, 77, were painted in the same color as the door and barely visible. I couldn't see a mailbox. The windows were covered by filigree iron bars, and the glass was a silver color. Nothing to indicate who or what might be inside.

The building to the north housed a pair of flats. No one answered the bell at either unit. To the south was a dusty-colored wood-framed building that appeared to owe its life to the fact that the places on each side were keeping it upright. A faded black-on-white sign showed the name Barker Industries.

The front door was open. A drowsy-looking woman of forty with dark, loose-waved hair was slumped over an old electric typewriter. A small white plastic oscillating fan sat on a table alongside the desk, ruffling the pages of the desk calendar.

"Hi. I'm trying to get in touch with the people next door. Do you know what time they come in?"

Before she could open her mouth, a portly character in a baggy blue suit hurried up to me. "What do you want?"

"Next door. I'm trying to contact them. Do you know when they come in?"

He walked to the door, peeked out into the street, then turned on his heels and gave me a nervous smile. "No. Who are you?"

I tried looking over his shoulder into the back of the building.

He moved in front of me to block the view. "Who are you?" he asked again, his voice turning hard.

"A friend of the people next door."

He kept the smile on his face, but was moving slowly toward me, shepherding me to the door. "I never see them. You want to leave your card, just in case?"

"No thanks."

He closed the door as soon as I passed the threshold. I could hear him shouting at the woman, "Keep the damn door closed. I don't want no one coming in here, you know that!"

I waited a minute. There was silence, then the clattering of the typewriter.

I walked back to my car, wondering what he was hiding. If he hardly ever saw his neighbors, why ask for my card? What was Mr. Barker manufacturing behind those dusty walls?

There were three pages waiting for me in the fax machine's tray when I got home. The first page was a bill from the private mailing shop for services rendered. The other two pages were from International Auto Leasing, addressed to Neil Hartman at Central Insurance Company.

The Toyota 4×4 was a long-term lease, to a firm named HKI Inc. The address, good old 77 South Park, San Francisco. The lease had started almost eight months ago. A. Dunhill was listed as president of HKI Inc. His illegible signature was scrawled across his typed name at the bottom of the page.

There was a phone number shown for HKI Inc. No residence address or identifying information on Mr. Dunhill. If I really was Claims Manager Neil Hartman, I'd call down to International Auto Leasing and chew some butt.

I dialed the HKI Inc. number. The phone rang four times, then there was a series of clicks, then a one-word message: "Now."

Short and not very sweet. I said a few hellos, waited a minute, but no one said anything. I hung up and tried again, getting the same long response time and the same canned reply.

HKI Inc. wasn't listed in the telephone directory. A. Dunhill certainly was, but only as Alfred Dunhill, the famous clothing, jewelry, and tobacco store. I somehow didn't think it was the same person. There was no sense running computer checks on A. Dunhill. Without a full name, middle initial, date of birth, or Social Security number, all I'd get would be reams of filings and a large database bill.

I tried the business name. There were two firms listed under HKI Inc., both in Southern California. One had gone out of business three years ago. I called the second firm, which turned out to be a manufacturer of sporting goods equipment. The courteous receptionist assured me that they did not have an A. Dunhill in the firm and had never had an office in San Francisco.

I tickled the right keys, got into an assessor base, and ran 77 South Park. The property had been purchased just a little less than a year ago by A. Dunhill. Mailing address for the tax bill, 783 Market Street, San Francisco.

All this computer time was beginning to cost me real money. And I had no client to bill, so I decided to start doing things on the cheap.

The terrible things happening to the economy have hit the public libraries as hard as everyone else. There was a time when you could call your local library and ask for a crisscross check on an address, and they'd look up a street number and give you the listed tenant and telephone number. No more. To pick up a few extra coins, the library has established a 900 service. In California, you dial 1-900-420-0707. The charge is a dollar a minute, which, by the time you've received the desired information, usually turns out to be much less than you'd pay through a computer database for the same material.

I called. They answered. I was given the tenant for 783 Market Street. Mail Service Inc. A private postal box. The nerve of the bastard. Mr. A. Dunhill played it awfully close to the vest.

I carried a pad of foolscap paper to the kitchen, made a cup of espresso, and dunked one of Mrs. D's homemade rock-hard *biscotti,* twice-baked cookies, into the inky brew while I tried to put the picture together.

I wrote down the three names developed from Scratchy's license-plate list:

1. Henry Lee—Chinatown godfather
2. Lester Maurence—supervisor, shipping magnate
3. A. Dunhill—Man of mystery
Connection????

I then tallied the costs of the number of the data checks I'd made so far. The total came out to just under two hundred dollars. Not a fortune, but what did I have to show for it? A fake Rolex that cost me $650 to get out of hock.

I reached for a handkerchief to blow my nose and suddenly thought of Harry. Between drinks and the money I'd slipped him, I'd thrown another forty-five dollars into the pot.

If I wanted to learn anything more about Mr. Dunhill, I'd have to stake out his place on South Park and catch him coming into the building, or I'd have to take it a step further and check him out through my money guru, a man with access to information not available on any legitimate databases.

He could no doubt dig up some information on Dunhill, but it would cost. A lot. And what if, after all that, I found out that he was legit? That Scratchy had just jotted his license number down because he wanted to know who his kindly landlord was?

As for Lester Maurence, I knew where he lived, but what good was that?

Henry Lee was not easily approachable.

I refilled the espresso cup and leaned against the sink, thinking about Scratchy. Not a friend. Not even an acquaintance. So why did I feel like I owed him something? Maybe it was those army medals. He'd paid his dues and hadn't gotten much for it. Except a bad habit. Like a lot of the men, boys really, who had ended up in those Vietnam jungles, and turned to drugs to help to get them through the dark, terrible nights.

The phone rang, dragging me from my thoughts. It was Jane Tobin.

"I did a little digging, Nick. Pulled some of the stories from the newspaper library on Maurence and Henry Lee. Guess who turned up?"

"Not Scratchy," I said incredulously.

"No, no, it was—"

The other phone line rang. I put Jane on hold and found myself talking to Father Tomasello.

"Nick. I've found Susan. She's Scratchy's daughter. Susan McCord. She lives in St. Louis. I just got through talking with her. She's coming out for the funeral, which will be the day after tomorrow. His veterans' benefits will pay for the funeral."

I was impressed. "How'd you find that out, Father?"

"The people at the Vets Administration. She was listed on his papers. They ran her down."

"That's great, Father. I'd like to meet her."

"I'm glad you feel that way, Nick. I was hoping you'd pick her up at the airport."

"When is she getting in?"

"She's making the arrangements now. I'll call and let you know. And Nick, thanks very much."

I got back on the line with Jane and passed on the information from Father Tomasello.

"He does nice work," Jane said. "Better than some private eyes I know."

"He's got better connections. Tell me who turned up in the newspaper articles."

"Well, there was an Associated Press story about secret triads taking control of organized crime in the United States. Story ran about two years ago. Henry Lee is listed as the head man in the Bay Area. There's a diagram showing who's who in Hong Kong and New York. There's a picture of Lee. His nickname is Papa. And there's a picture of his top gun. Willie Marr. Nickname Pork Chop. Guess what? He's the guy who got out of Lee's Rolls-Royce and kicked us off the street last night."

"You're sure it's the same guy?"

"Oh, yes. That's not a face that's easy to forget. It's him, all right. Guess who wrote the story? Your favorite author. Bill Linwood."

CHAPTER 9

◄►

I probably would have dropped the whole thing right then and there, but that was before they almost killed Mrs. Damonte.

Jane and I had planned to go out to dinner to Capp's Corner, a nice old-fashioned Italian spot just down the street from my flat. I changed the venue and we ended up at the South Park Café, at a window table with a view across the park that took in the entrance to HKI Inc.

We never spotted the mysterious Mr. A. Dunhill, but one mystery did get cleared up. The grumpy Mr. Barker came in with his secretary. He'd obviously had a few drinks at the office and was slobbering all over the woman's neck. His eyes almost popped out of his head when he saw me, and he grabbed the woman by the arm and dragged her out the door. He came back moments later, face flushed, hands rolled into fists.

"You're working for my wife, aren't you?" he demanded in a slightly slurred voice.

"No," I answered, scooting the chair back from the table in case he decided to throw a punch.

Barker glared at me, then at Jane. His shoulders were hitching up and down and he rocked back and forth on the balls of his feet like a prizefighter waiting for the bell to ring.

"Listen," I reasoned with him. "I have no idea who you are and I couldn't care less if you're having problems with your wife. My friend and I are enjoying a quiet dinner. Why don't you just get out of here?"

He continued the rocking back and forth on his feet routine, then put his hands knuckles down on the table and leaned close to me. The smell of stale gin caused me to wince. "If you're lying, buddy, I'm gonna kick the shit out of you." He straightened up, adjusted his tie, and strode jauntily out of the restaurant, as if he'd just knocked Mike Tyson out of the ring.

Jane dipped a fork into her sautéed red snapper. "What was that all about?"

"He's got the business next door to HKI Inc. I stopped in to talk to him. Apparently he's playing footsie with his secretary. He's a little touchy, isn't he?"

"Footsie? Isn't that a little dated, Nick?" She swiveled her head to see Barker hurrying to catch up with his secretary. "Whatever does she see in that man?"

"Love is blind, or so the saying goes. Did you bring those printouts on Maurence and Lee?"

Jane passed the stories over to me. Maurence's numerous printouts were held together by a rubber band.

"Nothing in there to link Maurence to Lee, just general background stuff—millionaire politician on the rise, that kind of stuff. Look at the Lee material."

I took her word on the Maurence stories and turned to the material on Henry Lee. There were a half-dozen articles indicating that Lee was a powerhouse in the Chinese community and that there were rumors of criminal connections throughout the United States and the Far East. The Linwood story was bylined out of New York two years ago and concentrated on the triads, with a heavy emphasis on the New York and Hong Kong Head Dragons. Lee got his share of ink. I had to admit that Bill Linwood had done a good job.

A connecting diagram with pictures of the leaders in the major cities and photos and descriptions of their top lieutenants accompanied the article. Sure enough, there was a picture of the man we'd seen get out of Henry Lee's Rolls-Royce last night. Willie "Pork Chop" Marr. The nickname had supposedly come from the injuries he'd inflicted on his enemies. "He chops them into raw meat," one of Linwood's sources had told him, a source "who chooses to remain anonymous."

There was a brief history of Marr's criminal record: a half-dozen arrests on assault charges, all dismissed, and two on homicides, also dismissed. Just the type of man Henry Lee would have behind the wheel of his Rolls.

Lee himself had never been arrested in the United States. But, in Linwood's words, "Federal law enforcement agencies believe Lee to be the head of the West Coast triad and second in America only to New York's triad leader, Louis 'Lucky Louie' Wong. Together the two men allegedly control over seventy-five American-based triads, stretching from New York to New Orleans to California. The Head Dragon remains Peter 'Crazy' Chu, in Hong Kong."

"Don't you love those nicknames?" Jane asked, her fork spearing a piece of swordfish on my plate. "Papa, Pork Chop, Lucky Louie, Crazy Chu. They sound like they're out of *Guys and Dolls*."

"Somehow I don't think even Damon Runyon could have done anything with a name like Pork Chop. Too bad there wasn't a Duke or Shark in there."

Jane's eyes were searching for a dessert cart. "So what are we going to do now, Nick?"

I maneuvered the remains of the swordfish out of her range. "I don't really know. All this stuff is juicy and fascinating, but where does it lead us?"

She reached for a piece of sourdough bread now that my fish was out of reach, tearing off a finger-size piece of the bread and pointing it at my wrist. "That watch. The watch and the money Scratchy got for it. And he was expecting more money, according to what he told Father Tomasello. Remember the old maxim 'Follow the money.' "

What an opening. "Speaking of that, who's buying dinner tonight?"

I had scheduled a business trip to Mendocino County the following morning and saw no reason not to go. A pleasant drive to a beautiful area of the state on a rather strange case.

If you've watched *Murder, She Wrote* on TV, you've seen the Mendocino coastline, some 160 miles north of San Francisco, all rugged beaches and swirling waves from the blue Pacific. In the show, Cabot Cove is located in Maine, but Hollywood knows how to save a dollar or two on travel expenses, so they journeyed up to the Fort Bragg area for outdoor shots.

A shot was what brought me to the area. The insurance company I was working for insured a small mom-and-pop store that sold everything from canned goods to fishing bait and tackle to gasoline.

One wintry day when the place was closed a young man had broken into the store. He was spotted, and a CB radio posse of locals took off after him. He was wearing camouflage combat fatigues and had reportedly brandished a large-blade military-style knife. He was chased along the cliffs and took refuge in a small cave. The posse, including our store owner, tried to coax him out of the cave from the cliff above. Someone, supposedly the store's owner, threatened to shoot him, and then fired a rifle shot into the air.

The burglar, who turned out to be a sixteen-year-old with mental problems and a Rambo fixation, promptly dove into the Pacific Ocean. Only he didn't come close to reaching the water, landing on a pile of jagged rocks some sixty-five feet below.

Now the boy's mother was suing. A complicated case. My job was to interview those who had been at the scene, including a deputy sheriff, who wanted nothing to do with me. He was being sued, too.

I worked through the day and night. The next morning I called home to check for messages. My phone didn't answer. I was sure I'd set the answering machine.

I called Mrs. Damonte's number. Not working. Alarm bells were ringing. I tried Jane Tobin, catching her in her office at the *Bulletin*.

She was all excited. "Nicky! Where the hell have you been?"

"Working. What's the problem?"

"Your flats. There was a fire. Mrs. Damonte almost died. She's in the hospital."

It took me some five hours to get back to the city, thanks to the usual traffic and road repairs. Mrs. Damonte had been taken to St. Francis Hospital on Post Street.

The hospital's gift shop was closed, so I arrived empty-handed. Mrs. D looked like a fragile old doll in the narrow hospital bed. For once she wasn't wearing black; her tiny body was wrapped in a green gown. Two of her cronies sat beside the bed. Both in their late seventies, both with iron-gray hair done up in a bun. Their dark, deep-curtained eyes stared at me the way the peasants did in Milan when they strung up Benito Mussolini toward the end of World War II. At least Il Duce had made the trains run on time. I had performed no such social service. And I was presumed responsible for Mrs. D's injuries.

She looked up at me and nodded her head, blinking her eyes as if she'd just stepped out from a dark room into the sunshine. Her thick gray hair was always worn in a tight bun, but now it cascaded down to her shoulders. For the first time in my life I saw her looking vulnerable, fatigued, weary.

"Ecco qui," she said with little enthusiasm. You're here.

"How are you?" I asked, moving to the bed and reaching for one of her tiny hands.

The two women got up from their chairs and left the room without spitting at me.

"I won't die," Mrs. D proclaimed, her soft tone showing a steely insistence.

"What does the doctor say?"

Her face tightened sharply. Doctors were not Mrs. D's favorite people. She figured the less she saw of them, the better off she was. "He wants me to stay here another day. Maybe two."

I questioned her about her injuries, but she wasn't giving out much information. "Swallowed too much smoke," was the best I could get out of her.

Her friends peered in from the doorway, waiting for me to leave. I patted Mrs. D's hand. "I'll go now. You call me when you're ready to come home."

Her thin lips turned downward. *"Che casa?"* she asked. What home?

"I haven't been to the flats yet. I came right over to see you. Is there much damage?"

"Tutto." Everything. She asked for a pencil and paper. I gave her my pen and notebook and watched while she scribbled a name on the pad. She switched to her fractured English to make sure I'd get the message. "He fix. You call him. No one else."

I studied her writing. Ed Dallara. A contractor. No doubt a friend of Mrs. D's. No doubt she would be skimming off at least ten percent of whatever Dallara charged.

Having been a policeman and worked as a private investigator for a few years, I've grown somewhat accustomed to seeing damaged property: homes, offices, warehouses gutted by fire or bombs. But it's never quite the same when it happens to your own place.

The destruction to the front of the flats put me into a state of shock. The front windows to Mrs. Damonte's, the lower unit, were boarded up with raw plywood. The edges of the stucco around the plywood were blackened by smoke. The fire had scorched the area leading up to the front steps. Her front door was boarded over also, the frame ringed with more smoke damage. The fire had not spread up to my unit. I went inside, poured myself a stiff drink, then went down the back stairs and used a key to get into Mrs. D's flat.

The smell of wet wood, plaster, and lingering smoke assaulted my nose. The laundry room and kitchen had been spared, but the rest of the place was a mess: walls scorched, upholstered furniture and carpets still soaked from the firefighters' hoses. I wandered through the rooms in a bit of a daze. The main damage was to the front room and the hallway, where the walls and ceilings were covered with thick black soot. The light was poor, but I could make out small burn marks on the floors, as if someone had tramped out hundreds of cigarettes.

There was a pounding noise coming from the boarded-up front door. A man's voice called out: "Are you Mr. Polo?"

"Yes."

"Inspector Joe Haley. Fire department. Arson squad."

I tried opening the door, but the boards had been nailed in from the outside. "Go on upstairs. I'll be right there."

Haley was a tall, lean, good-looking guy, with sandy-colored hair. He was wearing a gray-and-white herringbone tweed sport coat and dark slacks.

We shook hands, and he handed me one of his cards. "Someone said you used to be a cop," Haley said.

"Used to be, yes."

"Ever work any arson cases?"

"A few. But just on the sidelines. If they were connected to a homicide or a robbery."

Haley nodded his head. "Let's go down and take a look. I'll show you what happened."

I took Haley down the back steps and into Mrs. D's flat. He walked directly to the front room, unclipped a small flashlight from his belt, and rotated the beam between two large dark blotches on the carpeting. "Ignition points."

"What the hell are all these little black marks?" I asked, stooping down to touch the carpet.

"Firecrackers," Haley said, narrowing the flashlight's beam and focusing on the carpet. "Didn't you know?"

I stood up slowly, blowing air through my lips in a steady stream. "I don't know a thing, Inspector. I just got here."

Haley walked to the windows and tapped the wood. "Came directly from the street. First they threw in some rocks to break the glass, then the accelerant, plain old gasoline in whiskey bottles with cotton wicks." He pinched his nose between thumb and forefinger. "The old Molotov cocktail is still a favorite. The fireworks, that's kind of a new twist, though. They threw bags of them in. The bags were weighted down with rocks. Must have made a hell of a ruckus. Lucky they didn't frighten that poor old lady to death."

"Yes," I agreed. "Quite lucky. Any suspects?"

"No. Neighbors heard the fireworks go off. Then a car burning rubber. But no eyewitnesses. We received the nine-one-one call at ten minutes after three in the morning."

I placed both hands on my knees and slowly straightened up.

"No doubt it was arson, Mr. Polo. Do you know how our investigations are handled?"

"Yes, I think so. The fire department establishes cause, then the cops working out of the Arson Task Force chase the bad guys. Who's working this one?"

Haley paused, digging his toe into the carpet. "Sergeant Holt."

"Walter Holt?" I asked, knowing the answer and feeling like I was really on a losing streak.

"Right," Haley conceded. "Gas Can Holt."

CHAPTER 10

◄►

Fire Inspector Haley was a plain Coca-Cola man. I poured myself a double Jack Daniel's and we sat at my kitchen table discussing the fire. Haley took notes: name of insurance company, estimate of damage to personal property, that kind of thing.

I had no idea what little golden nuggets Mrs. D had sprinkled around her flat. As a child I had always harbored thoughts of shoe boxes full of gold coins and cash hidden away in the back of her closets. But Mrs. D was smarter than that. What money she had was squirreled away in a confusing clutter of stocks, bonds, and mutual funds. She studied the stock market and financial news with the same care and determination that she used in her gardening; weeding out the bad, planting anew. One of her weekly jaunts was down to the nearby bank on Columbus Avenue, where she had the interest posted on her accounts, then checked her safety deposit box to make sure nothing had been burgled. I got a quick peek into that box years ago. Mrs. D had asked me to escort her to the bank, then to a coin dealer on Montgomery Street. She'd taken a hand-sewn green felt bag from the box, then clutched it dearly to her chest as we went to the coin dealer. I didn't get to count the number of Krugerrands she'd sold to the dealer, but there had to be at least twenty. This was back in those crazy days when gold was pushing inevitably toward a thousand dollars an ounce. It never got there. Mrs. D cashed in when it was in the mid eight hundreds. Shortly thereafter, the precious metal plummeted to a much less precious price.

I had asked her why she was selling out. How she knew that

gold was going to drop through the floor. It was a typical Mrs. D answer—there were too many *sciocci,* fools, buying now. It was time to get out.

I told Haley I'd have to check with Mrs. Damonte on her losses.

Haley scratched his chin thoughtfully. "I saw her briefly at the hospital. Nice old lady."

"Indeed," I agreed. "Tough, too."

"Yep. Good thing she's tough." Haley told me of Mrs. D's rescue. I had had a fire detector and burglar alarm system put into the flats, at Mrs. D's urging, a couple of years ago. As soon as the window glass was broken, the alarm went off, and the police and fire departments were automatically notified. The nearest fire station was only a couple of blocks away, on Powell and Broadway. They had arrived within minutes.

"Had to break in the front door to gain entrance," Haley said. "They found the old lady on the floor in the hallway, trying to crawl to the back exit, I guess. She'd inhaled quite a bit of smoke, but didn't need artificial respiration. Just a good shot of oxygen."

Haley picked up his now almost empty glass and swirled the melted ice cubes around. "Who do you think did it, Mr. Polo?"

"I haven't a clue. What about you?"

Haley drained the last droplets of the Coke from the glass, and I went to the refrigerator to get him another.

"The firecrackers," Haley said in a puzzled voice. "That's a new one on me."

"I never heard of anything like it, either," I said, handing him the Coke.

Haley snapped the top open and took a swig directly from the can. "My job is to determine the cause of the fire, the place of origin. Was it an accident? Spontaneous combustion? Or arson? All I can tell you right now is that the fire here was definitely arson. But the firecrackers, they didn't really add much to the fire damage. The noise they created actually probably helped to alert Mrs. Damonte to the fire. All I can figure is that their purpose was to scare the hell out of whoever was inside the building. Has Mrs. Damonte got any enemies that you can think of?"

"No. I was the target. Whoever did it just screwed up. Hit the lower unit rather than the upper one."

"Why would you be the target?"

Firecrackers certainly made me think of Henry Lee, but I had no real way of tying him into the attack. "I've made a few enemies over the years, but I can't give you a name."

"Well, I wish I could help you more. All I can say is that it was definitely arson. We've got the remains of the bottle bombs, remnants of the fireworks, and the rocks they threw through the windows. No prints on anything, of course. I turned all the evidence and my report over to Inspector Holt. Not much more for me to do."

He stood up, and I shook his hand. "I knew Holt years ago," I said. "You mentioned a nickname for him. Gas Can. That's a new one to me. There were other nicknames for Holt when I knew him."

Haley grinned. "I can imagine. He got the Gas Can handle from a case he worked on. Happened to be driving by a place on Vallejo Street that was just torched. He saw a guy run out of the building, get in his car, and drive away. Holt chased him for a few blocks, lost him, but got the license number. Ran the plate and found the guy at his house. There was a gas can in the guy's car. Holt arrested him. The guy confessed, made bail, then fled the country. Came back about a year later, turned himself in. The DA prosecuted. Holt testified. The guy walked. Not guilty."

"Not guilty? He confesses, skips out, and you've got the gas can, and he still isn't convicted?"

"Apparently Inspector Holt made some mistakes in his reports, in his handling of the evidence, and in the transcribing of the confession. Seems he never sent the flammable liquid found in the can for examination, never saved it for evidence. There were rumors that the gas ended up in Holt's gas tank. So the guy walked. Ever since then Holt's been known as Gas Can to us firemen. What was his nickname back when you knew him?"

"Two Hats."

Haley cocked his head to the side and raised his eyebrows.

"When I knew Holt, he was working out of Missing Persons. He had two hats," I explained. "One he'd wear, the other was always on his desk or in his desk drawer. He'd come into the office in the morning, open the drawer, put the hat on his desk, and then take off. Go to the movies, out for a long, long breakfast, a longer lunch. Someone would ask for Holt and his partner, a nice guy by the name of Al Gasio, would say, 'He must be around somewhere. His hat's still on his desk.' "

Haley shook his head in wonderment. "Why did his partner put up with him?"

"Holt was married to Gasio's sister. Besides, it was easier to work a case by yourself than to drag Walter along with you."

"Things haven't changed much," Haley said, as he started for the door.

The odor of acrid smoke permeated my entire flat. I opened a few windows, but it didn't do much good. I went back to the kitchen and filled the coffeepot with water. The phone rang. Jane Tobin, all worried and curious. Which made two of us.

"How bad is it?" Jane asked.

"Mrs. Damonte's place is a mess. Water in the plaster, carpets ruined, smoke damage all over. The fire department did a good job stopping it before it spread upstairs, but my place smells like an old barbecue pit."

"Oh, you can't stay there tonight, Nick. Why don't you come over here?"

My thought exactly, but, being a gentleman, I was glad I had finessed her into making the offer. "See you in half an hour. I'll stop and pick up something at a deli."

I hung up and started for the bedroom to pack an overnight bag. The phone rang again. I picked it up, expecting Jane to give some explicit orders on what she wanted from the delicatessen, but the voice certainly wasn't hers.

"Good idea, going over to your girlfriend's place," a strange, reverberating voice said. "Stay away from me, Polo, or next time you and her are going to be right in the middle of the fire."

He banged down the receiver and I was left listening to the dial tone. Even though the voice was distorted, I was sure it was a he. I slammed my receiver down, missing the cradle on the first try. I hurried to the bedroom and took my .32 Smith & Wesson revolver from the nightstand, then grabbed the flashlight and went to the basement. The bug had to be in the basement. Unless it was some damn exotic laser thing. I was betting on the basement. The junction box. The water from the fire department's hoses had worked its way through the floor in Mrs. Damonte's flat, into the plasterboard ceiling of the basement. The utility meters and hookups for gas, electricity, and the telephone were all located just inside the garage doors, near the mailbox.

I examined the garage doors first. No sign of forcible entry. The firemen had gained access simply by going through the interior door leading from Mrs. D's kitchen to the basement. There was no need for them to force the garage doors. The utility companies had done a good job of restoring service after the fire. That's probably how Vibrating Voice had gotten in. An old burglar's trick. Dress up like a tradesman, then right after a fire, push your way through the barricades with a toolbox in your hands. The more enterprising burglars are usually responsible for the fire in the first place.

I opened the telephone company's cable box carefully. There it was. Sticking out like the proverbial sore thumb. A miniature FM transmitter, the size of a quarter. Just in case I was too stupid to pick it out from the maze of wires and connectors, Vibrating Voice had taped a single firecracker to the transmitter.

Most bugs of that size have a range of a mile or less. Usually much less, which means whoever was listening when Jane had called was probably parked nearby. Waiting to see what I'd do next.

CHAPTER 11

◄►

I zigzagged around the block, barely missing a cable car clattering down Mason Street. When I was sure that no one was following me, I made a quick pit stop on Columbus Avenue, running into Molinari's Delicatessen and picking up some cold cuts, cheese, asparagus frittata, and ravioli, and a slab of onion-topped *focaccia,* a flat, rectangular, pizza-dough-type bread.

Jane Tobin was waiting anxiously for me in her apartment. When I told her about the line tap on my phone, that beautiful anxious face took on a green tinge of panic.

"What the hell is going on, Nick?" she demanded, her nose twitching at the smells coming from the Molinari shopping bag.

I unloaded the food on her kitchen table and gave a brief summary of my meeting with Fire Inspector Joe Haley.

"The phone tap was nothing exotic, but it certainly would have picked up my discussion with Haley."

"You mean it works even when the phone is hung up?" she asked, opening the ravioli container and transferring the contents to a dish.

"Yes. It uses the telephone as a microphone. Picks up everything."

She swiveled, the dish of ravioli held precariously in her hands. "All the phones? Including the one in your bedroom?"

I nodded agreement and pulled a chilled bottle of Pinot Grigio Italian white table wine from her refrigerator. "Right. Every phone in the flat."

Jane slammed the microwave oven door closed on the ravioli. "Bastards. How long has that damn thing been in there?"

"I wish I knew." I dug an old-fashioned waiter's corkscrew from a drawer. "But I think it was put in after the fire. So you're safe. No one recorded your cries of ecstasy the other night."

She crossed her arms across her chest and glared at me.

"All right. My cries of ecstasy."

Her stern features melted a bit. "How is Mrs. Damonte?"

"She looks pretty good." The cork made that wonderful popping sound as it came out of the bottle. I filled two glasses and handed her one. "She'll probably be released from the hospital tomorrow." I sampled the wine. "Her place is a wreck. It'll be two to four weeks before she can move back in."

"Where will she go?" Jane asked, with real concern in her voice.

"I'm hoping she'll move in with one of her friends. Hoping and praying, in fact. But my bet is that she'll insist on moving into my place." The microwave timer pinged, and Jane brought the ravioli to the table.

"Do you think that's safe, Nick? Your place? Those people may come back."

"I don't know if it's safe or not. I doubt if they'd try and hit my place twice. I'd feel a lot safer if Mrs. Damonte were somewhere else. But knowing her, she'll want to get back to the flats as soon as possible. I'm going to hire some security people, just in case."

"It must have something to do with Scratchy," Jane insisted. "It just has to."

I couldn't disagree.

Jane started piling wafer-thin slices of *prosciutto di Parma* on her *focaccia*. Prosciutto. Italian ham. They make it in the good old U.S. of A., Canada, and Switzerland. But it's worth going for the real McCoy, even if this McCoy goes for about twenty dollars a pound. The meat comes from Lambrea pigs raised in the Po River Valley area and fed a diet of pure grains and the whey from Parmesan cheese. Then the hams are cured in the fresh mountain air of Parma for more than a year.

Jane divided the ravioli into almost equal portions and cut the frittata into wedges. "What I can't figure out," she said, spooning sauce over her plate, "is how they found out about you."

That was troubling me, too. "It had to be one of my phone calls."

"What phone calls?"

"I called Lester Maurence at his office. Used a pretext. The old police inspector line. Told his secretary, then him, that I was working on Scratchy's hit-and-run."

"How'd he react?"

I considered the question a moment before responding. "Too casual. Not interested enough. He didn't even ask my badge number, or work number."

"But how could he trace the call to you?"

There were only two slices of prosciutto left, and I grabbed one. "It's not hard to do."

"I thought that the phone company decided it was illegal to use caller identification in California."

"They did. Officially. But there are ways. You ever call an eight hundred number, maybe for something you saw advertised in a magazine or on TV, and have the person on the other end greet you by name?"

She nodded while lathering some Camonzola cheese, an obscenely rich combination of Brie and Gorgonzola, on a piece of *focaccia*. "I guess so. Never paid much attention, really."

"Well, as soon as you're connected to an eight hundred number, the board on the receptionist's desk lights up with your phone number. A database is activated instantaneously, and if you happen to have a listed number, your name and address will pop right up."

"That's not right," she protested. "How the hell can they get away with that?"

"They're paying for the call."

"So Maurence had an eight hundred number? And you called? Knowing what you know?"

"No, he didn't have an eight hundred number. And I doubt if he'd try something like that. Being a businessman, he could find himself in all kinds of legal trouble if he started tracing all his incoming calls. Besides, a business like his, he must get hundreds of calls a day."

"So? Who does that leave?"

"Well, I made a quick call to the Stockton Street Mortuary, and that's always a possibility, but I'm betting on the mysterious A. Dunhill. I called HKI Inc. twice. He's got an answering machine. I didn't leave a message. But when I called, it took quite a long time to get connected. I'm betting he had what they call a rollover set up from his regular phone number to an eight hundred line. You dial one number and it automatically rolls over into the eight hundred line, thus letting you ID the caller's number."

"The man on the phone. The one who warned you away. What did he sound like, Nick?"

"Disguised his voice. It had a bottom-of-the-barrel, echo sound. I think he was a Caucasian. There was a humming noise in the background. Probably held a vibrator to his throat."

"Vibrator?"

"Yes. One of those penis-shaped devices that are advertised in the Sunday papers. You always see a woman using it on her neck or feet in the ads. They get most of their workouts on other parts of the body." I leaned forward and leered. "Wouldn't have one hidden in your dresser drawer, would you?"

She used her sauce-stained spoon as a slingshot, sending droplets of tomato sauce in my direction. "With a hunk like you around, Nicky dear, who needs an imitation? Where did you learn about such unusual uses for vibrators?"

"Obscene phone callers use the technique. Distorts the vocal patterns, so if the call is recorded, there's no way to ID the voice. What I don't understand is why he bothered to disguise his voice in the first place. Why do that unless he was afraid I would recognize it? He was specific. 'Stay away from me.' Not us. Me. And he tipped me off about overhearing your call to me, so he wanted me to find the bug. He put it in the most obvious place, then tied a firecracker to it, just to make a point."

"So what do we do now?"

"We. I'm afraid that's the correct word. Whoever tapped my

phone heard you. Heard your voice. It wouldn't take much effort on his part to find out who you are. Where you live."

Jane was wearing a silk cognac-colored T-shirt. She ran her hands down her arms as if to rub away goose pimples. "I don't like this, Nick."

"Neither do I."

"So what are we going to do now?" she repeated.

I sampled the frittata, a combination of eggs and vegetables, sort of like an omelet, but baked. Good. But when you're used to Mrs. Damonte's version, not too good. "We've got two choices. One, play turtle, pull our necks back into our shells, and hope they leave us alone."

"If we back off, will they leave us alone?"

"There's no guarantee, but it'd make sense. They made a mistake in firebombing Mrs. D's unit rather than mine. I figure they just didn't bother to check. It was a warning. If they'd wanted to burn the place down, they'd have done a better job."

Jane grimaced and burrowed a hand through her auburn locks. "Damn. I keep thinking of that dear little lady in bed. Waking up to those firecrackers. It must have sounded like the St. Valentine's Day Massacre to her. What's the second choice?"

"Go after them. Continue the investigation. I don't know how much help we'll get from the police. The man handling the arson investigation is no prize. The hit-and-run inspector figures Scratchy was just a bum. Not worth much of an effort. So, we're pretty much on our own." I reached for the wine bottle. "What's your opinion?"

"Screw 'em," she said bluntly.

I spilled some wine into her glass. "I wish all reporters were as eloquent as you."

The next morning was a busy one. The first order of business was a call to Podestà Baldocchi Florists to order two dozen long-stemmed roses delivered to Mrs. Damonte as soon as possible. Then a call to her contractor friend, Mr. Dallara. He was available to get right to work on the job. I arranged a meeting with him for eleven at the flats.

I dropped Jane off at the *Bulletin,* once again zigzagging around streets looking for a tail. Nothing there.

The fire department's arson squad was located in a small building on Howard Street. Firemen work twenty-four-hour shifts, from noon to noon, so Joe Haley was at his desk.

"I guess you want to see Inspector Holt," Haley said, rising from his chair and walking over to an industrial-size coffeepot.

I accepted his offer of a cup. It tasted as if it had been brewed sometime early yesterday.

Haley saw my reaction. "Too strong?"

"No," I said between puckered lips. "Before I see Holt, there's something you should know." I told him about the bug on the phone and the possibility that someone had listened to our conversation in my kitchen.

Haley narrowed his eyes and scratched a thumb across his chin, trying to remember if he'd said anything he might live to regret. He chewed it over for a while, then said, "Shit."

He was almost as eloquent as Jane Tobin.

Haley led me up the back stairs to Inspector Walter Holt's office, a square box of a room, crammed with two desks and several putty-colored four-drawer file cabinets. The limited floor space was taken up with cardboard boxes like you get at the supermarket, filled with folders, newspapers, and magazines. The corkboard walls were littered with thumbtacked cartoons, calendars, and a glass-enclosed picture frame showing Arnold Palmer striding down a lush green fairway.

Walter Holt sat in a high-backed maroon imitation-leather executive chair, his feet up on his desk. He turned, gave me a small nod, then went back to his phone conversation.

Haley gave me a goodbye wave and took off.

Since there were no other chairs in the room, I leaned against the wall and eavesdropped. Holt was talking to someone about a golf game.

"Yeah, yeah, we got about three openings left, but I gotta have the money by next Tuesday."

This went on for a couple of minutes before he finally hung

up, but no sooner had the receiver hit the cradle than the phone rang again. More golf talk.

It gave me time to study Holt. It had been a good seven or eight years since I'd last seen him. He hadn't changed much. Lantern-jaw face, wattled neck. His sparse hair was carefully arranged to cover an expanse of waxy scalp, with untidy strands of gray hair settled about his ears.

He was wearing dark blue slacks with a slick polyester sheen and a white drip-dry shirt that hadn't dripped long enough. A blue-and-green rep tie dangled at half-mast from his collar.

Holt ended the second conversation, stood, and held out a hand. I'd forgotten how tall he was, six foot three or four. He moved with his neck bowed, as if embarrassed by his height. His hand was marshmallow-soft.

"Sorry to keep you waiting like that." There was a flash of recognition in his eyes once he took a real look at me. He snapped his fingers. "Polo. For Christ's sake. Nick Polo. How you doin', Nick? Retired, right?"

Almost right. I'd quit the department after my parents were killed in an airplane crash, leaving me what I thought at the time was a small fortune. "Right," I agreed. "How about you, Walt? When are you going to pull the plug? You must have more than thirty years in now."

"I do, I do," he said, bobbing around, peering out in the hallway, then lowering his voice as if whispering trade secrets. "Thirty-one years. But this place is the best hideout in the police department. Away from the Hall of Justice and the chief's office. Nobody bothers you. I'm handling the department golf tournaments this year."

That was part of Holt's MO. Helping out at functions, be they banquets, golf tournaments, or retirement parties. Anything that had nothing to do with police work, but was done on police time. The arson investigator's job had always been a place where the brass stuck people they didn't want to deal with. There was no captain or lieutenant working directly over the detail, and since it was several blocks from the Hall of Justice, the arson investigator could go weeks at a time without being seen by the powers that be. Holt was right. It was a hell of a hideout spot.

I gave him my business card. "Someone firebombed my building, Walt. You're handling the case. What have you got?"

The friendly smile faded from his homely features. "Oh, yeah. Now I remember. Green Street. Haley said something about it." He dropped my card into his shirt pocket. "That was kind of goofy, wasn't it? Those firecrackers. What do you think? Kids foolin' around? Something like that?"

"No. No kids. It was done on purpose, Walt."

Holt's eyes darted nervously toward the telephone. I hated to spoil his golf game.

"Someone put a bug in my place. I think it was done right after the fire. By whoever was responsible for the fire."

"Bug?"

"Unlawful, surreptitious audio monitoring device."

Holt's face crumbled inwardly, as if I'd hit him a good one in the balls. "Shit," was all he said.

It seemed like a popular response.

CHAPTER 12

◄►

Walter Holt reluctantly agreed to return to the scene of the fire with me. He had apparently given up his old Kojak-style felt hat, the one with a feather in the brim, and now topped his dome with a tweed English cap, the type you'd expect to see on the driver of an MG roadster.

Holt stared at the telephone connector box with despair-glazed eyes.

"You're sure it's some kind of a bug, huh?"

"Positive. Are you going to have the crime lab out to look at it? Check it for prints?"

The suggestion seemed to cheer Holt up. "Good idea. Let them worry about the damn thing."

Damn thing. I like that technical talk. Holt went up to his car to call in a request for the crime lab.

The contractor recommended by Mrs. Damonte showed up. Dallara was a tall, hardworking type in his fifties, dressed in faded jeans and a khaki shirt with extra pockets, the pockets loaded down with pens, pencils, tape measure, and small tools. He took a quick look at the basement, then went upstairs to examine Mrs. Damonte's flat.

Fifteen minutes later, the insurance adjuster arrived, a short, nervous man with a killjoy face. He had an elaborate 35mm camera, complete with zoom lens and a battery-pack flash-strobe. Flashes of light from his camera broke the basement gloom like quick shots of lightning.

Dallara came back to the basement. He and the adjuster circled each other warily, like two heavyweights waiting for the bell to ring, each sure that in some way the opposition was going to throw a sneak punch.

Holt informed me that the crime lab was busy and wouldn't be able to respond until the afternoon. He was in a hurry to get away, and I saw no reason to stop him.

The adjuster gave me his business card, which showed his name to be Richard Hines. After a brief nod and a wary shake of his head, he trudged upstairs to survey the damage.

Dallara was much more cheerful. And why not? He stood to make some rather decent bucks. The adjuster would be doling those bucks out, and adjusters tend to treat each dollar as if it were their very own.

"We're going to have to rip all the plaster off the walls and ceiling in the lower unit," Dallara said, pulling a small notepad from his pants pocket. He began scribbling something on the pad. "Walls, ceilings, redo the flooring. Paint throughout. Smoke damage to the exterior—have to paint the entire front. New glass, new molding. Fire department destroyed the front door. New door, hardware, lock. Lot of smoke got into the kitchen. There may be some fixture damage. I'll have to check that out." He glanced up from his notepad. "Then there's the rugs, furniture, clothing. Not my department, but I've worked on jobs that adjuster has handled before, Mr. Polo. You'll have to stand firm with him or he'll try to screw you. Don't let him try to cut costs."

"Mrs. Damonte recommended you."

Dallara closed his pad with a snap and put it away. "Yes. She's gotten me a few jobs."

"I'll let the adjuster deal with her."

Dallara rubbed his hands together as if he were standing in front of a fireplace. "Then you shouldn't have any problems."

Mrs. Damonte's two cronies were back at their posts, hunkered down on chairs bracketing the bed. They stood up as soon as I entered the room, but this time there were no sneers. Maybe it was the two dozen roses I'd had delivered. They were in a pair of matching vases alongside the bed.

The color of Mrs. D's cheeks was almost a match for the roses. "You're looking much better," I told her sincerely.

She raised a hand and rotated it back and forth slowly. *"Finora tutto va bene."*

So far so good. "Have you seen the doctor this morning?"

She had. She'd be released that afternoon. Now came the touchy part. "The flat needs quite a bit of work," I told her. "Your contractor friend was there this morning. He thinks he'll be able to get started tomorrow. But it will be a couple of weeks before he's finished. Then we'll have to get some new furniture. New rugs."

She lay there patiently, knowing exactly where I was leading the conversation. I looked out in the hallway at her two friends, standing there in their heavy woolen coats, shoulders hunched, deep in conversation. Probably talking about dirty old me.

"Have you thought about where you're going to stay while the flat is being worked on? How about your friends? Will they put you up for a while?"

Her hand sneaked out from under the covers again, made a small fist, then the thumb popped out and she gestured toward the ceiling. *"Di sopra."*

Upstairs. My flat. It was my turn for a softly muttered "Shit."

I spent the rest of the afternoon tidying up my flat in preparation for Mrs. Damonte's return—rearranging the one and only bedroom for her convenience, piling linen on the front room couch for myself.

She'd also given me a list of chores to be done: plants watered, vegetable garden policed for small, multilegged critters foolish enough to trespass into her domain.

The crime lab finally made an appearance and examined the phone box, dusting for prints, taking measurements, and photographing everything in sight. The technicians took the bug, saying they'd turn it over to Inspector Holt. I managed to get a good look at it before it disappeared into a zip-lock bag. Nothing exotic—a standard model that could be purchased and assembled from dozens of security equipment manufacturers, or put together with components purchased from any full-line electronics outfit.

John Henning, a good friend and the man who'd taught me the dos and don'ts of being a private investigator, had been an electronics genius. Before he'd been murdered, he'd shown me the basics of that particular black art. His will had named me as his main beneficiary. Among the things I had carried away from his basement were several of his homemade gadgets, including three basic types of transmitter or bug detectors. I dug all three from an office file drawer and went through my unit, Mrs. D's, and the basement. I found nothing. But if they'd tried it once, they might try it again. One of John Henning's gadgets was a "bug monitor." If you unscrew the mouthpiece of your telephone receiver, you'll see a round, poker-chip-size perforated microphone disk that will drop into your hand if you turn the receiver over. I replaced the disk in every one of the phones in the office, kitchen, and bedroom with one of Henning's monitors. It looks exactly like the phone company's disk, but in effect constantly monitors the phone line for any taps. If anything abnormal comes on-line, the monitor begins howling as soon as you pick up the receiver.

I went back to my housekeeping chores. The phone rang as I was changing the bedsheets. It was my Uncle Dominic.

"Nicky," he said, "I heard about the fire. Are you all right?"

"Yes. I'm fine, Uncle."

"Let's talk. George's place," he said, then broke the connection.

Uncle is always very cryptic when talking on the phone. He has to be. Uncle's a bookie.

We were both only about two blocks from "George's place." Washington Square Park.

I don't know how the park got named Washington. It couldn't be after George, because sitting smack in the middle of the large sunny park lawn, ringed by Italian cypress trees, is a statue of Benjamin Franklin.

I stood alongside the park's other statue, Haig Bitiglia's bronze of three valiant firemen, one holding a fire-hose nozzle, another with a horn to his mouth, and the third bearing the weight of a woman presumably rescued from a burning building.

The statue was given to the city by Lilly Hitchcock Coit, as a "tribute to the firemen she dearly loved."

There are legends about just how much Lilly loved firemen. In 1929, Mrs. Coit left a hundred thousand dollars to the city fathers to erect the famous fluted white column, known as Coit Tower, atop Telegraph Hill. The tower was built by Arthur Brown, Jr., the same genius responsible for City Hall. It was reportedly designed to resemble a fire-hose nozzle. Skeptics say it's more of a phallic symbol.

I looked up toward Filbert Street, past the dominating twin spires of SS. Peter and Paul Church, toward Coit Tower. It was silhouetted against a glorious blue sky dappled with puffy, snow-white clouds. Whatever old Lilly had intended it to be, it fit just right.

"Come sta?" Uncle Dominic said, a wide grin on his handsome face. "You're looking good, nephew."

"And you, Uncle." He gave me a bone-crushing handshake. Uncle had gone through most of his adult life with the nickname Pee Wee. He stands just over six feet in height, with a drill sergeant's erect back and broad shoulders, chiseled Roman features. But my father was a few inches taller, so Pee Wee came into being. But not from me.

I can't remember seeing Uncle when he was not dressed in a suit. Today's version was a tan gabardine model that looked as if it'd just come from the dry cleaner's press.

"Tell me about the fire," he said, his eyes roaming the park's green shadow-checkered wooden benches. Several old paesanos recognized him as we strolled by and bobbed their heads in respectful nods.

We had circled the park on the wandering macadamized path twice before I was through with my story. Two men in dark suits trailed discreetly behind us. I left nothing out.

Uncle pointed to a vacant bench. "Let's sit and think this thing out, Nicky."

We sat quietly for a minute or two, watching a couple of

seagulls fighting with pigeons for scraps left by the brown-bagging crowd.

Uncle laid one hand across his chest, as if getting ready to recite the Pledge of Allegiance. "Do you think it's safe for Mrs. Damonte to return to the flats now?"

"I don't think there's a problem, but who knows with these people? I'm going to hire some security guards for a few days, just in case." I noticed the two dark suits had pulled to a halt some thirty feet away.

Uncle saw my interest. "Do you know much about my business, Nicky?"

"Only that you're successful."

He laughed. "If you mean I've never been to jail, you're right. There are two kinds of bookmakers in this town, Nicky. Anglo and Asian. I've never had any trouble with either, yet.

"The Asians all operate under the umbrella of Henry Lee. His people are *menefreghisti,*" he said heatedly. (Polite translation: people who don't give a damn.) "They will kill you and your children if you don't pay. There have always been rules here. Someone doesn't pay, you simply cut him off. No breaking of legs, threats to the family, none of that is necessary. And you don't interfere in another man's territory. You do your business. I don't bother you. You don't bother me. So far, Lee has left me alone. I think this is because he's been too busy with his other interests. Prostitution, drugs, smuggling, extortion. But there are rumors. Rumors that he wants to expand his bookmaking operation. I know it's happening in New York. The Asian gangs are making a move. *Fari vagnari u pizzu.* They're beginning to dip their beaks everywhere, Nicky. A small independent like me, I wouldn't stand much of a chance against them. If Lee's people are behind your troubles, you're going to need help. Lots of help."

CHAPTER 13

Uncle Dominic's first idea of help was money. I declined. "No need, Uncle."

He stared at me for a long while, then nodded his head. *"Ostinato.* Stubborn, like your father. Listen, when someone tries to harm my nephew and Mrs. Damonte, it's my business. I like that woman very much. So, if you need money, don't hesitate." He hooked a thumb toward the two men who had been following us around like lapdogs. "I want them to stay at your place."

I started to protest. He grasped my hand firmly, his other hand going to my elbow. "You said you were going to hire some security people. Take them. They're cousins of some friends of mine. From the old country. One can stay inside, the other in a car out front." Uncle stretched his legs and crossed one gleaming brown shoe over the other. "And you'd be doing me a favor. I don't know what to do with them. Their English is *va bene.* They prefer Italian. A dose of Mrs. Damonte will do them both some good." He waved and the two men came over. "This is Gino," Uncle Dominic said, gesturing to the shorter of the two men, "and this is Delio."

Both men appeared to be in their late twenties or early thirties, dark-haired, dark-complected, with stubbled beards that would require two shaves a day. They looked enough alike to be brothers, but there were obvious differences. Gino was broader through the shoulders, and his eyebrows went across his face without a break. Delio was the better-looking, his face thinner, his hair carefully parted. His suit was hand-tailored, a red silk handkerchief spilling over the breast pocket. I could smell his aftershave lotion. Uncle went into rapid Italian and told Gino and Delio of their new duties. Gino kept his eyes on the pavement, Delio looked at me suspiciously through half-closed eyelids. Uncle Dominic ended by wrapping his arm around my shoulder, advising me to be careful and informing them that I was his family. The last of his family. "This Henry Lee, he is dangerous. We must all be careful."

For a minute I thought we were all going to nick our fingers with a knife tip and join blood.

The expression on Delio's face made it plain he wasn't all that thrilled about guarding me and an old lady. But he didn't say anything. Gino did the talking, his eyes still on the ground.

"What time do you want us at your home?" he asked in Italian.

"How about seven o'clock?"

Delio looked at his watch, and his mouth turned down at the corners. I had a feeling he was going to have to break a date.

I hadn't been entirely truthful in telling Uncle Dominic that money was not needed. I was going to need quite a bit of it. My checking account had swollen up, thanks to the checks I'd deposited the other day, but that was about to change.

I headed straight for the Hall of Justice to see Paul Paulsen, making a quick stop at the pay phone located just fifteen feet from the entrance to the Homicide detail. A single booth, no neighbors, a shelf big enough to rest a notepad on, and an accordion-style door that closed nice and tight. For someone who uses pay phones as often as I do, this is about as good as it gets.

I used my credit card to call a Southern California number. The man who answered the phone was, for lack of a better name, a money guru. A former federal bank examiner who had gone into business for himself. His business was finding out about your business. Or whoever's business you pay him to dig into.

He grunted unintelligible one-syllable replies as I gave him my request. Anything and everything available on HKI Inc., and especially A. Dunhill. I gave him the South Park address and the Market Street private post office.

"That could run into a lot of money, Polo," he admonished. "Hold on a second."

I held. I counted. Eighty-two seconds later he came back on the line, his voice perhaps a drop more deferential. "It's okay. You can handle it." He read off the current amount in my checking account. To the penny.

"I need this in a hurry."

"You know, I like you, Polo," he began with silky reasonableness, "but you're really a Mickey Mouse account for me. I hear from you, what? Fifteen or so times a year? Usually small-time stuff. But you're interesting, Polo. I'll give you that. Interesting. Call tomorrow morning."

I opened the door for fresh air, then closed it and made another call. This time to a contact at the phone company. More of the same. Anything he could pull up on HKI or Dunhill: toll calls for the past three months, and the application sheet, which is a gold mine of information. It can contain bank account numbers, former addresses, references, even Social Security numbers if the applicant is foolish enough to fill out that line on the form. I told my source I needed the information in a rush.

He informed me a rush was expensive. I said an hour. That made this rush twice the cost of a normal rush. My bank account was dwindling fast. At this rate, I'd have to take Uncle Dominic up on his offer of money.

I exited the booth and traipsed down the hall to the door marked "Homicide." I cracked the door just enough to see who the receptionist was. When I saw Jean Gorham sitting behind the desk, I opened the door all the way and went in. Jean is one of those all too rare individuals: a civil servant who is not only civil, but dedicated and hardworking. We chatted for a few minutes about old friends, then I asked if I could use her phone for a local call. I could. I did. I called the number for HKI Inc. The same gargled collection of line clicks, then the one-word message—"Now." I hit the disconnect bar with my forefinger, then punched the redial button, wondering how Mr. A. Dunhill was going to feel when he traced the calls to the Homicide detail.

I thanked Jean, then walked down to the General Works detail. Paul Paulsen put a finger to his lips as soon as he saw me. His eyes wandered to the window of the lieutenant's office. Three men were in the office. I recognized one as Lieutenant Mike Bracco, one of the good guys. The other two were strangers to me.

Paulsen turned his back on me, and I did a quick about-face and headed for the basement cafeteria. A half hour later, Paulsen came down and stuck his head in the door. He spotted me, then did a quick about-face and disappeared. I caught up with him by the stairway and followed him out onto Bryant Street.

"What's the problem?" I asked, almost jogging to catch up with him at the traffic signal on Sixth Street.

"I'm not sure," Paul said with a slight air of disgust. "Those two guys hammering on Mike Bracco are from Internal Affairs. Butler and Flann."

"What are they after? Who are they checking on?"

"I don't know," Paul said, glancing over his shoulder. "But they give me the creeps." We crossed Sixth and headed toward the Flower Mart Café. Paul didn't say a word until we were seated at a booth.

"Just coffee," he told the waiter.

Now I was scared. If Paulsen didn't order at least a piece of pie or cake to go with his coffee, he was really worried.

I ordered a tuna melt sandwich. "There's nothing they could go after you for, is there?" I asked hopefully.

Paulsen gave a rueful smile. "Just those little goodies I pull off the computer for you from time to time, Nick. I'm telling you, it's getting ridiculous. You order a report, a plate, a driver's license, you have to log in with your badge number."

"What kind of guys are the Internal Affairs cops?"

Paulsen drummed his fingers nervously on the tabletop. "Ben Butler hasn't been around long. I don't know much about him, but I hear he's not a bad guy. Russ Flann's a different story. You don't know him?"

"No," I admitted. "Should I?"

"Well, he was around when you were in the business. Flann's a strange cat. A real loner. In Narcotics for a while, then he landed in Internal Affairs. Most guys don't last long in Internal Affairs. Flann seems to like it. If he gets you in his cross hairs, he doesn't let go."

The waiter, a cadaver-thin number with bushy sideburns down to his jawbone, put the two cups of coffee on the table with a clatter, spilling coffee onto the table. He came back with a dishrag and a full pot of coffee, filling the cups with an unsteady hand.

"I hope I didn't get you in trouble," I told Paul earnestly.

"Nah." He shrugged. "What was it I got for you? The hit-and-run report? The rap sheet I ran on Scratchy—what the hell was his right name?"

"Charles Nelson O'Hara."

"Yeah. O'Hara. Hell, I can tell them I was doing a favor for Father Tomasello. That should do it. What was the rest of the stuff? The license plate was just a funeral parlor. Right?"

"Right," I agreed reluctantly. "A funeral parlor owned by Henry Lee. And Paul, the other night someone threw a firebomb into what I believe they thought was my place, but they hit Mrs. Damonte's flat. I was out of town. Along with the firebomb they lobbed in a bunch of firecrackers."

"Jesus," Paulsen said, letting out a whoosh of air. "How's Mrs. Damonte? Is she okay?"

"Yes. She's fine. She gets out of the hospital in a couple of hours."

Paulsen picked up his coffee cup with two hands. "This Scratchy guy asks you to run some plates that turn out to belong to Lester Maurence and Henry Lee. Then your place gets torched. He banks some cash from hocking a phony Rolex that's worth about a hundred times more than this plastic digital piece of crap I'm wearing. What's the connection?"

"I wish I knew."

Paulsen put his cup down untouched.

"Do you know much about Henry Lee?" I asked.

Paul picked his cup up again. He took a slurping sip, then sighed. "Henry Lee. Papa. He's got everyone in Chinatown scared shitless. Protection, bookmaking, whores, the whole banana. We've never gotten close to him."

The waiter came with my sandwich, looking as shaky as ever. I had a laundry list of data checks I had planned to ask Paul to run for me: HKI Inc., to see if there were any vehicles registered to the company. The 77 South Park address, for incident reports. That was all out the window now. Maybe the two guys from Internal Affairs were fishing for something, or someone, else. Maybe, but it was one of those coincidences that make you leery of coincidences.

I gave Paul more bad news, telling him about the bug on my phone line. The look on his face told me that I had ruined his appetite for the rest of the day. Maybe the week. "Guess who they've got handling the arson investigation?"

Paulsen gave an indifferent shrug.

"Walter Holt."

His face almost broke into a smile. "Walter Holt? Two Hats? Is he still in the business?"

"He's still drawing a check twice a month. The fire boys gave him a new nickname—Gas Can. Seems he misplaces them from time to time. Same old Walter. He says the Arson detail is a hell of a hideout."

Paulsen interlocked his fingers and stretched his arms out in front of him until the joints cracked. "Maybe I should talk to Holt. A hideout might be just what I need."

CHAPTER 14

◄►

Paul Paulsen was in a hurry to get back to his office. I watched him leave, then picked at my food, leaving half the sandwich and all the French fries on the plate. Not the kitchen's fault. The news of a possible Internal Affairs investigation involving Paul had ruined my appetite, too.

One of the pluses in eating at the Flower Mart Café is that it's located right in, you guessed it, the Flower Mart, where a dozen or more growers sell their goods to commercial accounts and drop-in customers at bargain rates.

Our fumble-fingered waiter was sitting on a bench outside the front door, sucking deeply on a cigarette. No wonder he'd been nervous—he had been close to a nicotine fit. He blew out the smoke quickly, then inhaled another heavy drag.

The florists were getting ready to close for the day, so there were bargains galore. I loaded up on yellow roses, sweet-smelling purple chrysanthemums, marigolds, and snow-white Shasta daisies for Mrs. Damonte's homecoming.

I used the pay phone outside the Flower Mart Café to call my telephone company contact. The phone was located on the building's outer wall, very near where the heavy-smoking waiter had been sitting. There were a half-dozen cigarette butts ground into the cement, and I wondered as I dialed how many were the waiter's.

My source sounded cheerful. That's because he gets paid no matter what he turns up. What he turned up on HKI was damn near nothing. The phone company has stopped logging local calls. Just too much action even for their massive computers, so they charge a flat rate on calls within the designated dialing area.

Toll calls are different: each and every toll call is listed with the date, time, minutes, city, and number called, and the charge.

HKI Inc. had no listed toll calls for the past two months, which was as far back as my source dared to go.

The application for installation of service was just as bad: A. Dunhill had not supplied a Social Security number or date of birth. The billing address was simply 77 South Park. To make matters worse, Mr. Dunhill paid his bill with traveler's checks. Very clever of him. Remember the old TV ad with Karl Malden staring at you from under a hat and over his nose, strongly advising, "Don't leave home without them." Something Mr. Malden didn't mention. The damn things are impossible for nosy people like me to trace.

Mrs. Damonte was waiting impatiently in her hospital room. The floor nurse insisted that she be taken out of the hospital in a wheelchair. She sat stone-faced in the chair as we took the elevator down to the business office. She studied her bill carefully, scrutinizing every item, complaining wildly about the price of the room, the doctor, the aspirin, the Kleenex. I looked at the bill and blanched. I didn't blame her a bit. Although she wasn't going to have to pull a single dollar from her sewn-up pockets to help pay the damn thing. Someone else was. You know that someone. In fact, you are that someone. The taxpayer.

The sight of all the flowers in the backseat of my car brightened Mrs. D up a bit. She settled in among the foliage, gave the hospital a final glance, and said, *"Grazie al Dio!"* Thank God.

Mrs. D seemed no worse for wear when we got home. She stalked the corridors of her burned-out flat, issuing orders to the contractor, Dallara, and making life miserable for the insurance adjuster, Hines, who was finishing up his damage report.

I went to my office and found the answering machine stocked with messages, most pertaining to open investigation files. There was one call from Jane, very cryptic—"Call me about tonight."

I handled the clients' requests, then called Jane at the newspaper.

"How's Mrs. Damonte?" she asked.

"Back to normal, harassing the hell out of the insurance adjuster."

"She's staying at your place?"

"Yes. It's getting a bit crowded. Uncle Dominic is having a couple of his friends house-sit for a few days. How about dinner?"

"Where?"

"A picnic. A late-evening picnic. On South Park Street."

Within the boundaries of the City and County of San Francisco you can buy revolvers, semiautomatic pistols, semiautomatic rifles, hunting rifles, target rifles, shotguns of varying bores, crossbows, black-powder muskets, machetes, bayonets, commando daggers, throwing knives, Mace, and spray canisters that shoot pepper-based agents. The last are reportedly for canine attack, but they work equally well in a human's eye.

All of these you can purchase legally, though there may be some waiting periods involved. Illegally, you could add just about anything you want to that list until you get close to nuclear weapons.

But the city's elected officials, in their desire to keep the citizens safe, have banned the sale of BB guns. Makes us all sleep a lot better at night.

Mrs. D has an old Red Ryder lever-action job she uses to ward off any enterprising birds and cats with an eye on venturing into her vegetable garden, but it didn't have enough firepower for what I had in mind.

So I had to drive to Daly City, the first town south of San Francisco, to make the purchase.

BB guns, or air guns as they're called now, have come a long way from the ones I remembered as a kid. Whether they're better or worse is a good question. They have handgun models that now look exactly like a .38 revolver or .45 automatic. Long-barrels that look like Uzis and assault rifles and fire off cluster rounds from shaving-can-shaped clips.

I settled for an old-fashioned-looking pistol, a Benjamin single-shot hand-pump model that shot .177 caliber pellets.

Jane was in charge of rations for our little bivouac, and while I did the armament shopping, she stopped at a nearby deli and picked up a rotisseried chicken, potato salad, a bag of Famous Amos chocolate-chip cookies, and a screw-top bottle of wine from some vineyard in Modesto. If the wine was no good, we could use it for target practice, she reasoned.

There is now another covenant to add to those well-known universal laws: never play poker with a guy named Doc; never play chess with anyone with no vowels in his name; never eat at a place called Mom's; and never, ever buy a screw-top jug of wine made in Modesto.

"It's really not that bad, Nick," Jane protested, after taking a tentative sip.

"Scratchy would have loved it," I said, emptying my glass out the car's window.

We were parked in Jane's VW convertible alongside a fire hydrant on the north side of South Park Street, which gave us a view of the front of HKI Inc.

The little VW's top was up, as it is some three hundred days a year. San Francisco is not a convertible town.

"What now?" Jane asked, toweling her hands off and then breaking away a leg from the chicken.

I turned the engine over and edged away from the curb. "Now we do a little fancy shootin', partner," I said, circling the park until we were adjacent to 77 South Park. I reached over, rolled Jane's window down, and advised her to lean back. I pumped the pellet gun's handle a dozen times, loaded in a pellet, and fired at the building's windows. A pane of glass broke, and I revved the engine and drove back to our parking spot by the fire hydrant to wait.

Jane poured herself a full glass of the wine. I settled for a chicken wing.

"Shouldn't there be bells or lights or something?" Jane asked.

"If the building's alarmed, it must be a silent system." Most alarm systems are connected to a phone line, which, when the alarm goes off, signals the monitoring station, which in turn notifies the police department, or the fire department in the case of a heat sensor or smoke alarm. The alarm system at my flats, the one that may have saved Mrs. Damonte's life, is hooked up to a phone line that is controlled by a satellite, and the red light that shows up at the alarm company's monitoring station is in the city of Chicago. Right. Chicago, Illinois. The technician who installed the system assured me that it was quicker and more reliable than using a local monitoring station. Hard for me to believe, but then I'm still amazed at such old-fashioned gadgets as radios.

If Mr. A. Dunhill had a system, he wasn't getting much response. No police. No fire department. No alarm-company truck. Not after ten minutes. Not after twenty.

"Are you going to eat your cookie?" Jane asked, her fingers flickering over the picked-clean chicken carcass.

"It looks like there's no alarm," I said.

Apparently she took that as a "no, I don't want the cookie," response, because she began munching away on the last Famous Amos in the bag.

I was thinking of the door on 77 South Park, trying to determine the best way to breach the Schlage lock, while I searched for the carton of potato salad. Suddenly Jane said, "The lights went on."

I snapped my head up and looked across the street. She was right. "Someone must have come in from the back alley," I said.

I slid out of the car. "Stay here. See if anyone comes out front. I'll check around the back."

Jane's words were muffled by the cookie. I crossed the park and hurried down the alleyway. There was a dark green 4×4 parked in front of the roll-up door leading to the rear entrance of 77 South Park. The license plate was caked with mud. The roll-up door was closed. The side door was shut tight.

I hugged the wall of a three-story brick building and waited. He, or she, would have to come out sooner or later. It was almost fifteen minutes later when the door rolled up with a clatter. The building's interior lights were clicked off. A medium-size figure, a man's, barely visible in the darkness, exited the door, his head swiveling left and right, looking up and down the alleyway. I couldn't make out his features. He turned back toward the building and pointed a hand toward the door, and it rolled down. He gave the alleyway another long look. I pulled my head back, counted to five, then took another peek. He was walking to the 4×4. He opened the driver's door. The car's interior lights went on, and I got a look at his face: tight-skinned, pug nose. His hair was blond-white, and long enough to curl over the collar of his dark windbreaker. When he smiled, which was seldom, the first thing you'd notice were his canine teeth, which looked like fangs. Baby-vampire teeth.

He ducked into the 4×4, raced the engine, and drove away slowly. I waited until he was out of sight, then ran back to Jane's car.

Jane looked worried. "Well, no one came out front. How'd you do?"

I reached for the wine, taking a swig right from the bottle. "He came out the back. I recognized him. Al Davis. An ex–San Francisco cop. I worked with him for a short time. He quit long before I did." I took another hit of the wine. "Rumor has it he left to join the CIA."

CHAPTER 15

◀▶

"Shouldn't we try and follow him?" Jane asked, piling the remains of the dinner into the brown paper bag.

"He'd spot a tail. He'll probably park somewhere close by and wait to see if someone makes another try at the building."

"So what are we supposed to do?"

"Want to neck?" I asked, half seriously. Believe me, if you ever have to work a stakeout, it is well worth bringing along a friend to help while away those lonely hours.

Jane had another suggestion. "Why don't we just go into the café there and have a drink?"

There are times when I'm disappointed at the lack of romance in her soul.

We sat at the bar, which gave us a view toward HKI Inc.'s front door, and had a glass of wine. Napa Valley chardonnay, thank God. I tipped the bartender a dollar for use of the house phone for a local call. If Davis was hanging around, I wanted to scare him away. For a while.

The police department communications operator had a calm, steadying voice.

"The burglar alarm at 77 South Park Street has been ringing for fifteen minutes," I fibbed. "I'm right across the street, and it's driving us crazy."

She asked for my name.

"Robert Mondavi," I replied, scanning the chardonnay bottle's label.

The black-and-white patrol car cruised by some ten minutes later. Two uniformed officers checked the front and back, and minutes later got into their car and drove off.

"You haven't told me anything about this Mr. Davis," Jane said, declining the offer of another glass of wine.

"He's a real case. Come on, let's get out of here."

I kept a lookout for the dark green 4×4 as we left the area. "Davis and I went through the police academy together. It was hate at first sight. We never did get along. Little things— popping off in front of the rest of the guys, calling me a dago, wop, that kind of stuff."

I made a U-turn on Howard Street and headed back toward South Park. "He was a little older and had been a cop of some type, something federal, before joining the San Francisco Police Department, so he was way ahead of everyone in our class. He finally pushed me a little too hard. Remember, I was young and dumb then. I challenged him. We had a fight in the academy's gym."

"A fistfight?" Jane asked.

"Yes. No dueling swords or pistols. An old-fashioned knock-'em-down, kick-'em-when-they're-down fight."

We were back on South Park. There was still no sign of the 4×4. I pulled to the curb and cocked and loaded the pellet gun again.

Jane watched with an amused grin on her face. "And I suppose you taught him a lesson. Did you hurt the big bad bully, Nicky?"

"I could have. Could have broken his knuckles if someone hadn't dragged Davis off me. He beat the living hell out of me. He was a judo-jujitsu, karate type. He went right into undercover work after graduating from the academy. Narcotics. Then he went into the Intelligence detail. It used to be a freewheeling job then. Shortly after that, he left. The rumors were he went into the CIA. Good place for him. He was spooky, all right. Then he came back to the department. This was a few years back. Nothing really unusual about that. Several cops had taken military assignments and continued paying into their city pension plan, then, when they had enough time in the military to retire, they came back, finished up a couple of years of duty, and retired with a full pension from the city. I guess the

CIA is considered the same as military time served. The ultimate double-dipping. Davis didn't stay long, though. There was some stink about him stealing files from the Intelligence unit."

"I don't remember any of that. I was covering the sports beat at the time, I guess."

"They kept it very low-profile. I just remember it because of Davis."

"Can I try this time?" Jane asked, reaching for the pellet gun as I slowed down in front of Barker Industries.

I handed her the gun. "Shoot low, Sheriff. They're ridin' Shetlands."

Her forehead wrinkled in confusion. "You want me to shoot at the place next door?"

"Exactly."

She dutifully took aim and scored a bull's-eye. No bells, no alarms. If Barker Industries had a security system, it was silent also.

I took the gun and reloaded quickly, working the pump handle a half-dozen times, then moved the car forward twenty-five feet and put another pellet into HKI Inc.

There was the sound of breaking glass, and I drove off. Some blackguard had taken our fire-hydrant space. I drove up to Second Street and backed into a warehouse loading dock.

The fog had penetrated the park trees and spread like a fine gauze down to street level. We exited the car and huddled in the doorway of a multiunit apartment house some hundred yards from the entrance to HKI Inc.

Ten minutes later, the green 4×4 stopped in front of 77 South Park. Davis played his spotlight across the front of the building, centering the light on the broken window. He played the light over the doorways of the neighboring properties, then got out of the vehicle and approached the front door slowly, flashlight in hand. He examined the damaged window, running the light beam up and down the building, then checked the flats on his left, and finally Barker Industries. He played his light around Barker's broken window, then walked over to the park, stopping at intervals, examining the ground, the trees, the empty benches. He crossed over to the east side of the street and disappeared into the café, popping out moments later, standing on the pavement, looking up and down the street.

Jane pressed herself against me. "What do we do if he starts walking this way?" she asked in a hushed whisper.

"Shoot him."

"I'm serious, dammit!"

Davis started walking up in our direction. He'd spot us if we left the doorway now. He might even recognize me before we could get back to Jane's car.

I took out my wallet and extracted my concealed-weapons permit, a wallet-size ID encased in plastic. I used it to slip the lock leading into the apartment lobby.

Jane's toes almost clipped my heels as we got inside, closing the door behind us. There was a small hallway leading to a single elevator. The elevator's door was open. We slipped inside. I kept my finger on the "door open" button, pressed my head to the opening, and squinted, one-eyed, at the front door. Jane ducked under my arm and did her version of the one-eyed peeper.

"He's at the door," she whispered softly.

I could see Davis. He hadn't changed all that much, just gotten older. Like everyone else. He was wearing a black jacket, the collar pulled up. The wind had blown his strawlike hair down in front of his face and over his ears. He stood so close to the window that his breath dulled the glass. He shook the door's handle. Jane grabbed my arm. I could feel the pressure of her fingernails digging through my sport coat.

"Relax. He's just rattling doors like a beat cop."

Davis gave the door one last push, then swiveled around on his heels and continued on his foot patrol.

Jane straightened up, leaned against the elevator wall, separated her hair with her hands, and looked at me from between her fingers. "What will he do now?"

"Give the neighborhood a quick toss. Then take off."

She gave her surroundings a scornful glance. The elevator was a five-foot-square box, the walls paneled in a cheap wood veneer decorated with scratches and the usual graffiti. The carpet was a black, gray, and brown tweed. Someone had spilled something sticky on it recently. At least I hoped it was spillage.

"And what are we supposed to do in the meantime?" Jane said irritably.

I thought I'd give it one more try. "Want to neck?"

I called Paul Paulsen the next morning at his office. He was very abrupt, saying nothing other than that he'd meet me at the creamery.

I then called the money guru. It was the first time I'd ever heard him sound humble. Well, not humble, but less than totally arrogant.

"Problems, Polo. I'm not pulling anything out of that address. Nothing on this Dunhill guy, either."

"He pays his phone bills with traveler's checks," I told the money guru. I read off the information I'd gotten from the phone company application. "Can you do anything with that?"

"Traveler's checks. Your friend is very cautious. I can find out where they originated, but any kind of a detailed trace is just about impossible. Even for me," he added modestly.

"I've got a little more information. I saw someone who just might be Mr. Dunhill last night. I recognized him. Former San Francisco cop. Quit to go into the CIA. That was about ten years ago. His real name is Al Davis. Alan is the first name, as I remember."

The less than totally arrogant voice turned icy. "CIA? You didn't mention that, Polo."

"I didn't know until I saw Davis. I'd like to know if he's still with the agency."

"So would I, Polo. So would I. Where are you calling from?"

"A phone booth in the Mission District."

"Good. Stay with the pay phones. Call me back tonight."

I hung up and walked back to the booth at the rear of the St. Francis Fountain & Candy Store. Not many places you can tag as a Fountain & Candy Store, but the St. Francis certainly qualified. It had been doing business at the same location, 2801

Twenty-fourth Street, since 1917. The neighborhood had gone through quite a few changes over the years, from Irish to Russian to its present makeup, Latin. Lots of South American influence in the storefronts: bakeries, restaurants, bars, bookstores, all with a bit of a salsa flavor. Except for the St. Francis. It's like stepping into a time machine and turning the clock backward. You expected to see kids wearing beanies slide in on old-fashioned metal roller skates screwed onto their thick brown shoes, pull a coin from their pressed corduroys, and ask for a nickel's worth of peanut brittle, butterscotch, or animal-shaped sweets, all handmade in the back kitchen and displayed across the counter in apothecary jars.

I had ordered a chocolate milk shake, which was waiting for me when I got to the booth. The shake was quicksand-thick. I pulled the spoon free and took a loving lick.

"Looks good," Paul Paulsen said, sliding into the booth.

I was facing the front door. "Keep an eye open. See if anyone familiar comes in," Paul said.

"You think someone may be following you?"

"I don't know what the hell to think. Internal Affairs put me through the ringer." He signaled to the waitress and called for a vanilla milk shake and a liverwurst sandwich.

I heaved a sigh of relief. At least his appetite was back.

"What were they after?" I asked when the waitress retreated with her order book.

"They played their usual games. At first, they tried to make me think that it wasn't me they were investigating, but someone else in the detail. But the questions kept coming back to the computer. Who was using it for 'materials not relevant to department investigations'? That's the way they phrased it."

His milk shake came, and he buried his lip in the thick brew, coming away with a vanilla mustache.

"I don't know what got them started, Nick. The rap sheet on Scratchy, the hit-and-run report, or the history on the Rolls-Royce. Somebody pulled their chain. They had to have the computer tagged so that anyone pulling out certain information would send up a red flag."

"How'd you handle it?"

Paulsen's eyes became slits. "I took your advice on Scratchy. Told them that he was a St. Matthew's regular, a buddy of Father Tomasello's. They backed off a bit. Butler and Flann. Dr. Death and Dr. Doom. Butler, he played the good guy to Flann's bad guy. Flann plopped your name into the stew."

"What was his interest in me?" I asked.

"He wanted to know if you were the one who requested the rap sheet, the hit-and-run report, and the history on the Rolls-Royce. I said you and I had discussed Scratchy, but the rap sheet and the hit-and-run stuff was my idea. A favor to Father Tomasello."

"Did they buy it?"

Paul took another sip of his shake, adding a layer to his mustache. "I don't think so. They pressed me hard about the Rolls's history. I told them it cut me off when I was driving to work. That if I still had a tag book, I'd have pulled it over and written the driver up. I just ran the plate to see who it belonged to. They didn't buy that, either."

"Did they mention Henry Lee's name?"

"No. And I played dumb. Said when I found out it belonged to a funeral parlor, I just forgot about it."

"Do you remember a guy named Al Davis? Used to work undercover Narcotics. Then the Intelligence detail?"

"Secret Agent Al? Sure, I remember him. A real nut case. When he worked Narcotics, they called him the Great White Narc. Then he went into the Intelligence detail, then over to the CIA. Or so the rumors went. He left the feds and came back into Intelligence for a short time, just a few months, then quit." Paulsen tossed a quick glance over his shoulder and lowered his voice. "There were all kinds of rumors about him taking a pile of files with him when he left the last time. All on floppy disks. The DA was scared to go after him. Davis had everybody bullshitted with that CIA crap."

"I saw Davis last night. He's tied into this. He's running some kind of business out of a small warehouse on South Park." I told Paulsen about the stakeout.

Paulsen pushed his half-finished milk shake across the table. "Davis and you never got along, did you?"

"Not at all."

"This is getting serious, Nick. Too damn serious. Last I heard about Davis, he had just disappeared. There was an intradepartment investigation, but nothing came of it. He'd just vanished off the face of the earth."

"He's alive and well, Paul. I guarantee it. Can you ask around about him? Check his personnel file?"

"Hell, I'm afraid to open my desk drawer, much less dig into any files," Paulsen said, lifting up the bread on his sandwich and reaching for the pepper shaker. "What the hell do you want out of his file?"

"Something with his signature on it. A picture. Anything available."

"Why the signature?"

"I've got a copy of the lease on the 4×4 Davis is driving. I want to check the A. Dunhill signature on the lease against Davis's."

Paulsen took a bite of the sandwich and considered the request. "Al Davis. He's the one you had the fight with at the police academy, isn't he?"

"Right. And he beat the hell out of me."

"Looks like he's trying to do it again," Paul said.

CHAPTER 16

◄►

The Central Intelligence Agency is listed in the book by the telephone number only. No address. I called the number. The bland-voiced woman who answered listened patiently to my spiel.

"I'm a former San Francisco policeman. We're having a reunion. One of our class members, Alan Davis, left our department and joined you people. I was wondering if there was some way for us to get ahold of him."

"Leave a number and I'll have someone contact you," she said. I imagine she said that to a lot of callers. I hung up without leaving a name.

While I had contacts in most of the federal security services, I drew a blank with the CIA. I made a few calls. More blanks.

Jane Tobin had a suggestion. "Why don't you try Bill Linwood?"

"His book was all about the CIA being the bad guys," I protested. "What kind of connections would he have?"

"Bill's been around. Don't ever underestimate him, Nick. He has all kinds of contacts. It's worth a try."

Maybe she was right. I didn't have anyplace else to go. My money guru hadn't turned up much of anything. HKI Inc.'s traveler's checks had originated in Hong Kong. Period. Finale. End of trail. He was not anxious to pursue it any further. Not only was the gruffness gone from his voice, but, unless it was my imagination, I'd swear there was a little fear in his blunt assertions.

So, that left Linwood. Jane set up the meeting for me, but didn't tag along. Linwood's place was a small Victorian on Twenty-fourth Street in the Noe Valley section of the city. The house was painted in one of the standard Victorian patterns: olive green, with black and white trim around the windows. A copper-colored shoulder-high photinia hedge shielded the front of the house from the street.

The front door was old and weather-beaten and covered with a thick layer of varnish that emphasized its hard-earned nicks and scratches.

I rang the pearl-buttoned doorbell. It was opened almost immediately. Bill Linwood stood there smiling at me. He was wearing khaki chinos that had faded to white along the permanent-press creases on the legs and a bruise-blue denim shirt that looked as if it had been stolen from the Marlboro Man's saddlebags. His hair had been combed in a casual, carefree style and sprayed carefully into place.

"Hello, hello," he said cheerfully as he looked past me. The smile faded. "Where's Jane?"

"She couldn't make it," I said, striding into the house. The hallways were honey-colored pine planks of random widths. The eggshell-colored walls were dotted with framed photographs of my host in various settings. Most seemed to show him in a trench coat, gazing at the cameraman from under his shaggy eyebrows, the look on his face expressing something between exhaustion and exhilaration.

There was music coming from the back of the house, a radio or CD player. A piano playing Cole Porter. Porter was losing.

Linwood gestured to the living room. "Be with you in a minute," he promised, then walked hurriedly down the hallway. The music died moments later.

I followed his directions. A black floral art nouveau rug covered most of the room. The walls were done in beige mohair. Twin oversize sea-green leather couches faced off against each other, separated by a bronze-ribbed, glass-topped coffee table.

In the middle of the coffee table sat an ancient Royal typewriter that could have been in a museum. Next to the typewriter was an oblong rosewood box with inlaid brass appointments.

The ceiling was parchment-colored and covered with a map

of the world, giving the appearance of a beautiful old globe that had been flattened out. I was staring at the Bering Sea when Linwood entered the room.

"Jane coming along later?" he asked hopefully.

"No. She got tied up. You know how it is."

He did. But he didn't like it. He plopped down in one of the leather couches, semaphoring with his arms for me to follow suit.

"Like the typewriter?" Linwood asked, his tone indicating that he was sure I did.

"Interesting."

"Picked it up in Cuba years ago."

"Oh." I think he expected more from me.

"Can't prove it, of course, but I know for sure that it was Papa's."

He confused me for a moment—I thought he was talking about Henry Lee. Then it registered. "Hemingway's?"

A smile danced across his lips.

"I thought that Hemingway did all his work in longhand," I said, reaching out to run my fingers across the typewriter's keys.

"True. True. But his wife wrote, you know. And she helped him with some of his manuscripts, so you never know. Got it from the son of their housekeeper. Carlos. Hell of a good kid." He leaned forward, elbows on his knees, fingers laced together in front of him. "Jane tells me you need some help with the Agency."

"I'm trying to run down an old buddy. He was in my police academy class. Joined the CIA, for some foolish reason."

"Why do you want to find him?"

"Class reunion. I'm in charge of rounding up the lost souls."

Linwood leaned back and digested this. Apparently, it didn't go down well. He shook his head from side to side, then grabbed one of those three-by-six-inch wirebound notebooks that every reporter always has tucked away within grabbing distance, along with a Parker stainless-steel pen. "Name?"

"Alan Davis."

"What did he do in the police department?"

"Narcotics. Intelligence."

Linwood stood up, brushed the seat of his pants, and strode over to the far wall, staring into a mirror in a carved and gilt rococo frame. He watched his mirror image, directed his conversation to it, as if it were a different person. "This man, a private investigator, an ex-policeman, an ex-con, comes and asks questions about a CIA agent, former policeman who worked Narcotics and Intelligence. Tells me it's all for some jolly reunion dinner where they can all get drunk and tell war stories. What am I to make of that?"

"Are you talking to Dorian Gray, or me?" I said, giving him a full five points for bringing up my ex-con status.

Linwood swiveled on his heel and faced me. His dour expression deepened into great furrows of distrust. "If you want me to help, you'll have to do better than this, Polo. I—"

A phone rang somewhere in the back of the house. Linwood excused himself gruffly. "Be back as soon as I can."

I ran my finger over the typewriter Linwood had bought from "Carlos." The keys were sticky and really had to be pushed hard before they moved.

Linwood came back a few minutes later, carrying two opened bottles of St. Pauli Girl beer in his hands. He handed me a bottle. "Look, Polo. Who do you think you're kidding? If you want my help, you're going to have to level with me. Does this have something to do with what Jane was asking me the other night at the party? About Lester Maurence and Henry Lee? Is there some kind of connection?"

"Not that I'm aware of. Be interesting if there was, though, wouldn't it?"

"Do you smoke?" he asked.

"No."

Linwood leaned over, opened the rosewood box on the coffee table, and extracted a long, fat, dark cigar. I had the feeling that if I'd answered yes to his smoking question, Linwood never would have revealed what was inside the rosewood box. He pulled a penknife from his shirt pocket, carefully snipped off the cigar's end, then dug through his shirt pocket again, this time coming out with a battered Zippo lighter. I was afraid he'd start telling me the cigars were from Fidel Castro and the lighter was a gift from Walter Cronkite.

He got the stogie going and blew out some smoke, waving it away from his face with a hand. "Do you have any idea where Davis worked when he was with the CIA?"

I sampled the beer. "I'm not sure, but I think he operated out of Hong Kong."

Linwood stood and went back to talking to himself in the mirror. "Interesting. Very interesting. Hong Kong. Lester Maurence and Henry Lee certainly are no strangers to Hong Kong. Now this Mr. Davis of yours. I could look into it. As a favor. To you. And Jane. Have her call me in a day or so," he said, gazing deeply into his own eyes.

Some men look good in an apron. I happen to be one of those men. Maybe because I wear one so often. Gino, Uncle Dominic's man, definitely was not the apron type. He had on one of my favorites, a sturdy denim job with a large front pocket and towel ring. He was standing on a small stepladder, pulling glasses and cups from Mrs. Damonte's cupboard.

He peered down at me, narrowed his eyes, shook his head, and went back to his chores.

Mrs. D herself came rambling by, wearing a black dress, which covered her from neckline to ankle, her hair back in its customary bun, her tiny feet encased in a pair of black tennis shoes. She gave me a hard look, then began complaining about the insurance man, the contractor, and poor Gino. Nobody was moving fast enough to suit her.

There was a lot of construction dust in the air. The plaster was pulled away from the walls in the front room and living room, exposing bare studs. Two coveralled workers with surgical-type face masks were sweeping and vacuuming up the debris. Others were pounding nails, installing pipe. An attractive young woman in tight Levi's and a bright orange T-shirt, a tool belt circling her waist, was standing on a ladder, pulling electrical wire to the junction box in the center of the front-room ceiling.

Delio, Gino's cousin, was chatting her up, circling the ladder like a shark waiting for fresh meat to fall from a boat. When he saw me, his mouth puckered into a smirk. He turned his back my way, protecting the lady electrician from any possible unwanted advances. Other than his. I hoped she'd drop a tool or two on his slicked-back hair.

Mrs. D was instructing one of the surgical-masked sweepers on just how to do the job properly. It looked like a good time to leave, so I did, walking up the stairs to my place.

The answering machine had two messages, inquiries on an insurance case in the works. I made the necessary calls, then wandered into the kitchen.

Mrs. D had something wonderful cooking in my double ovens. I peeked at the top oven first. A hand-shaped loaf of black rosemary bread. To get it dark, she toasts bread crumbs, *briciole,* and adds the crumbs to rye flour, along with molasses, ground ginger, and crushed rosemary.

The lower oven contained a chicken-shaped clay pot. Inside would be a three-pound chicken stuffed with garlic, lemons, and whatever herbs she'd decided to pick from the garden.

There was one more clay pot, a small round one, the top crested with a replica of a head of garlic. This is where Mrs. D and I have a disagreement. She likes to cut her garlic bulbs off at the top, drizzle olive oil over them, and let them bake for twenty to thirty minutes in the oven. Good, good, good, no doubt about it. Never eaten baked garlic bulbs? Give it a try. Smooth, no bite. Use them as you would butter—just smear them on pieces of bread. My choice is to cut the bulbs in half, coat them with olive oil, and zap them for three minutes in the microwave. The cloves pop out of their shells like bread from the toaster. But no microwave for Mrs. D. I think she'd prefer an open fireplace to the oven, but one has to compromise in this life. Especially if you've been around as long as she has.

I made a pot of coffee and thought about my meeting with Bill Linwood. It seemed a mistake now. Linwood might stick his nose in too far. Jane was right. He'd been around, and survived to tell many a story. But would he tell me anything he developed on

Davis? No, but he might tell Jane. To impress her, if nothing else.

The doorbell rang. The Ichabod Crane figure of Walter Holt was waiting on the stoop, hat in hand. He had company: the two men I'd seen in Lieutenant Bracco's office, inspectors Ben Butler and Russell Flann.

"Gentlemen," I said in a lukewarm welcome. "What's up?"

Holt waved a bony index finger at me. "You lied to me, Polo. You didn't retire. You got in shit. Went to jail."

"Not true, Walter. At least not in that order." I had quit the police department. The jail time came a year or so later, when I was working as a private investigator. A lawyer hired me to find a client of his, a drug dealer who had not shown up for a court appearance. I found him, OD'd on his own product in a motel room, his only companion a suitcase full of cash. We—the attorney and I—decided to save Uncle Sam the trouble and expense of counting and storing the contents of the suitcase, and split the money. He, no longer we, got cold feet and talked to the cops. I, not we, ended up in prison.

The two surgical-masked construction workers came out of Mrs. D's front door. They tugged their masks down to their necks, then each pulled a pack of cigarettes from his coveralls and lit up.

"Maybe we should go inside and talk," Butler said. He was in his early thirties, squat-figured, with a round Charlie Brown head. His partner, Flann, looked to be in his forties, with heavy features: thick lips, broad cheeks, and slightly protruding eyes covered by round metal-rimmed glasses. The glasses and the ballpoint pens clipped in the breast pocket of his tweed sport coat gave him a clerklike appearance. What was left of his hair was mottled gray. His face was ruddy and weathered, the top of his head smooth and pale, as if he wore a hat to protect it from the sun.

I folded my arms across my chest. "The place is a mess. I'd hate for you to see it like that."

Walter Holt waved his finger at me again. "And what about your uncle? The bookie? His people could have been involved in the fire. You never told me about him."

"Why would you suspect my uncle? Find a can of gas in his car, Walter?"

Holt left his arm pointing in my direction, but his finger wilted down, like a suddenly disinterested penis.

Flann fluttered his lips and shook his head. He had a low-key voice to go along with his image. "This isn't getting us anywhere, Mr. Polo. We'd like to talk to you about a friend of yours. Paul Paulsen."

The two construction workers were craning their necks, trying to pick up the drift of our conversation.

"If Mrs. Damonte sees you smoking on her stairs, she's not going to like it," I called down to them.

They took off down the steps in a hurry.

"What about Paul?" I asked Flann.

He took one of the ballpoint pens from his jacket pocket and clicked it rapidly. "He's been giving you confidential police information. That's a felony. He could lose his job and go to jail. You could join him, Mr. Polo."

Mr. Polo. Almost as bad as sir. "If I didn't think you were joking, I'd close the door on all of you and call my attorney. I don't appreciate being accused of a crime."

"Bullshit," Flann snorted. "You've been doing business with Paulsen for years. Rap sheets. DMV information. Reports. FBI checks. That makes it a felony, Polo. Confidential federal information."

"You said it better than I could, Inspector. 'Bullshit.' "

"You did ask Paulsen to run a check on Charles Nelson O'Hara, didn't you, Mr. Polo?" Flann asked patiently, probing like a dentist.

"Mr. O'Hara was a friend of Father Tomasello, of St. Matthew's Kitchen. He'd been killed in a hit-and-run. Father Tomasello was hoping to find the poor man's relatives. It was just a favor for Father Tomasello. Lots of people do him favors. The chief, the mayor, the governor. Even you'd do a favor for him if he asked, I'd bet."

"You'd lose that bet," Flann said, sliding his pen back into his jacket pocket. "You spoke to Inspector Davall in Hit-and-Run about Mr. O'Hara, didn't you?"

"He's the one handling the case."

Butler took a turn. "Why did you see Davall? What's so special about this O'Hara?"

"I'm just doing a favor for Father Tomasello. It's as simple as that."

Flann's turn. "This wasn't the first time that you had Paulsen run checks for you. Don't try and tell us that. We know you've been using him for years."

"No you don't. Because I haven't." I unfolded my arms and reached for the doorknob. "I know you boys have important things to do." I turned my eyes to Holt, who had a seasick look on his face. "And Walter here is busy working on the arson assault on my property. And to tell the truth, I have a few errands to run myself, so if you don't have any more questions . . ."

"Oh, we have lots more questions, Mr. Polo," Flann intervened smoothly. "Would you like to come down to our office? Would that be more convenient?"

"No to both questions." I stepped back into the flat and slowly started closing the door. "Call back tomorrow—maybe we can make an appointment."

Flann's voice throbbed with resentment. "You're doing this the hard way, Polo. We can be just as hard. You've done time. Hard time. Not much fun, was it? Or maybe you liked it. Maybe a pretty boy like you had fun in the slam. Well, you can always go back. We can get a warrant. For your arrest. For searching your place."

"I don't think so," I answered with more confidence than I felt. I closed the door, then quickly reopened it.

"Hey, wait a minute. Flann, you've been in Internal Affairs for a long time. Remember a guy named Al Davis? He left the department, joined the CIA, and then came back for a short stint. He stole some materials from the Intelligence unit's computers, then hightailed it out of the country."

Butler and Flann looked at each other before turning their attention back to me.

"He was in my recruit class. Big guy. White-blond hair."

Both Flann and Butler did the bouncing-eyes routine again.

"What's your interest in Davis?" Flann asked.

"I'm trying to find him."

They must have worked out a routine where they each asked one question, then turned the show over to the other one. Butler's turn. "What do you want with Davis?"

"Oh, talk about old times, that kind of thing. I heard he's back in town. Opened up a shop of some kind around here."

Flann's eyes narrowed. "You heard wrong. He died years ago. Over in the Philippines."

"Who told you that?"

Flann's face broke into a grin. "Confidential information, Mr. Polo. You wouldn't want us to reveal confidential police information, would you?"

I went into an Ollie North mode as soon as I'd watched Butler, Flann, and Holt disappear from view. Flann's threat about a search warrant was probably just that. A threat. But one I had no choice but to take to heart.

I have a standard routine with confidential information. Either "sanitize it," as they say in the movies, or simply run it through the shredder. Usually this operation is supposed to take place as soon as the information is received, or, if it's necessary for working the investigation, as soon as the case is closed.

I was behind in my purging chores, so it took me a good hour to pick through hard-copy files, turn the incriminating stuff into confetti, and then purge files from the computer. By the time I'd finished, it was past quitting time for the construction crew.

Mrs. Damonte had adapted well to my kitchen, but she was supplementing the larder with some of her own goodies: favorite dishes, knives, pots, a bone-handled garlic crusher that was almost as old as she was.

Gino had an apronful of freshly picked tomatoes, Bibb lettuce, cucumbers, radishes, and green beans.

Mrs. D had taken the rosemary bread from the oven. She cut off an end piece, brushed on some olive oil, and handed it to Gino, who stopped washing the salad fixings long enough to take a bite, close his eyes, roll them toward the heavens, and murmur a heartfelt *"Delizioso."*

Mrs. D asked if I was staying for dinner. She did not seem disappointed when I told her I had other plans. Neither did Gino.

CHAPTER 17

I had no idea of the whereabouts of Al Davis, former San Francisco cop and CIA agent. I did know where Henry Lee's office was, but avoiding Lee seemed like an excellent idea.

That left Mr. Lester Maurence. I drove by the front of his place at 310 Buena Vista Terrace. Buena Vista Terrace encircles Buena Vista Park, a thirty-five-acre hill of greenery just east of the famed Haight-Ashbury District that looks like it was discovered, and then left in its natural state. Actually, its natural state was a dull-brown, treeless hill. It was John McClaren, the same visionary who seeded the sand dunes into Golden Gate Park, who put in the oaks, Monterey pines, redwoods, Australian tea trees, and madrones that look so natural. At one time a goodly portion of the terrace was taken up by St. Joseph's Hospital. But St. Joe's went the way of so many of the old buildings and is now a massive condominium complex.

Many of the houses on the street are tall, stately homes, built when there was a need for servants' quarters, or even the infamous "Chinaman's room" in the basement. The rooms are small, scrubby, low-ceilinged dungeons, some with jail-like bars for doors, that were used to house the imprisoned housekeeper, and sometimes his entire family. They make dandy wine cellars, or so say those designers featured in the Sunday paper's real estate section. There was even a construction boom in "faux Chinaman's rooms" for a while.

Maurence's place was a newer addition to the scene, roughened concrete, a full four stories high, but squeezed into a twenty-five-foot-wide lot. A narrow stairway of brick-rimmed concrete snaked up to the second-floor entrance.

The doorway was framed by a black walnut arch. Directly above it was a bull's-eye window. The hardware was a shiny brass Schlage Primus lock, just like the one on the front door of HKI Inc. The chimes tinkled out a narrow version of the old Richard Rodgers tune "Getting to Know You."

The person who answered the door was definitely worth getting to know. She had long inky-black hair, with bangs that reached almost to her eyebrows. Her skin was a light coppery color and her face featured high cheekbones and amber eyes under peaked brows. She was wearing slim-cut white denim jeans and a matching white short-sleeved top with a sculpted neckline that rested just on, but almost off, her shoulders. A series of gold bracelets jangled on her wrists.

A look of surprise creased her beautiful features. "Oh, I was expecting a friend."

"I'm sorry I don't qualify. Is Lester in?"

Her hand was caressing the door's edge as if she were wondering whether to slam it shut or open it all the way. I flashed one of my I-just-flossed smiles. "If he's not around, I can come back later."

She studied me with her amber eyes. "You look trustworthy. What's your name?"

"Nick." That news didn't seem to excite her. She gave me a quick once-over, and I was glad I'd taken the time to shine my shoes and put on my best blue blazer and slacks. When you're dealing with the rich, and Maurence certainly fit into that category, it's best to put your best shoe forward. At least it gives them one less thing to sneer at.

"Are you a friend of Lester's?"

I had a feeling she knew most of Lester's friends. "No, not really. It's business."

She looked at her wrist. Apparently there was a watch of some kind buried among the bracelets. "He called. He should be here in a bit." She licked her lightly lacquered lips and made a decision. "You can come in, if you want."

I wanted. She closed the door behind me, then led me through a narrow white-walled hallway and into a very large room, done in ivory, with gold-filigree panels. Oil paintings in gilt frames of old sailing ships bucking heavy seas were sprinkled around the walls. The fireplace was marble and sat below a wall mirror that stretched almost to the top of the twelve-foot ceiling. A coffee table, holding glassware and a vase filled with a profusion of flowers, squatted in front of the fireplace.

Chairs covered with heavy tapestry materials were scattered around the room. The walls were abutted with small, intricately carved inlaid tables topped with more flower-filled vases. The chandelier dripped with pear-cut crystal, the size of the diamonds Richard Burton had frequently bestowed upon Elizabeth Taylor.

To the left of the fireplace sat a stone garden ornament of a lion at rest, paws stretched out in front of him.

"I didn't catch your name," I told her.

"Shy. Shy Celli."

"Unusual name." I asked her how she spelled it.

She told me, then said, "Please, sit down. What is your business with Lester?"

I reached into my pocket for a business card. "It's about something he may have hit with his car."

She barely glanced at the card before dropping it to the coffee table.

"I always wanted to meet a real private detective," she said, in a mocking tone.

"Now your wish has been granted. Disappointed?"

"Maybe just a little. I always pictured a man in a trench coat, with a squashed-in nose. Would you like a drink?"

"A glass of white wine would be nice."

"I'll be right back."

I nosed around the furnishings, studying the oil paintings. I could hear two people talking, not able to make out the words, but getting the gist that it was an argument.

Shy Celli came in first, handing me a frosted metal glass, filled to the rim with white wine.

"Les just came in. He'll be with us in a moment."

I had just enough time to take a sip of wine, then Maurence came pounding into the room.

"What's the meaning of this, Mr.—"

"Polo," I told him, while Shy picked up my card from the table and handed it to Maurence.

He was somewhere close to fifty, five foot six or seven, bristly eyebrows and a grooved face. His brown hair was splintered with gray; a neat mustache was tucked under his nose. He had a pained expression on his face as he studied my card. He looked like a man who had a pained expression much of the time. He wore dark gray slacks and a brass-buttoned yachtsman double-breasted dark blue blazer. "I wish you had called at my office for an appointment," Maurence said, slipping the card into his coat pocket. "What do you want?"

"It's about a man's death, Mr. Maurence. Charles Nelson O'Hara."

The pained expression vanished for a split second, then settled back into place. "I've heard that name before. The police called me about a Mr. O'Hara. Are you working with the police?"

"Sort of."

Shy had left the room for a short time. She returned, handing Maurence a cut-crystal tumbler filled halfway with a whiskey-colored liquid. Maurence dipped his nose to the glass and inhaled the fumes of the liquor before sampling it. "What's your interest in this O'Hara?"

"I'm working for his family, Mr. Maurence. We were wondering what his relationship was with you."

"Relationship? Are you kidding? What the hell would I have to do with such a man?"

"What kind of man do you think he was?"

"I believe they used to be called winos, vagrants, tramps. A beggar would be a kind description. What kind of a family does a beggar like that have?"

A beggar like that. I decided to give Scratchy some upper-crust kinfolk. "Charles was the black sheep, I guess. His brother is a wealthy stockbroker in New York. His son is an attorney. They're willing to pay a lot of money to find out just what happened to him. If you've never heard of him, what makes you think he was a beggar?"

"After this supposed police inspector called me, I made some calls myself. To the police department." He paused theatrically. "I'm not without influence there. They told me about this Mr. O'Hara of yours."

"Maybe he worked for you at one time. He wasn't always a beggar."

A smile stretched across Maurence's face, like an elastic band. "I think not."

"Maybe not here, in the Bay Area. Maybe in Hong Kong."

"O'Hara was in Hong Kong?"

"Yes," I lied easily, "after he was discharged from the army. Did his time in Vietnam."

Maurence swirled the liquor in his glass. "Which outfit?"

"Military Intelligence. You ever deal with them?"

Maurence pushed up his upper lip, causing his mustache to disappear. I took a sip of the wine. It was good, but there was something about drinking from a metal cup. It reminded me of a chalice, and the wine I used to sneak out from church after my duties as an altar boy were over.

"I dealt with a lot of people over there after the war. His name means nothing to me," Maurence said. He stood up and arched his left eyebrow, lowering the right at the same time. "The policeman who called me—his voice sounded quite a bit like yours, Mr. Polo."

"Really. What was his name?"

"He told my secretary his name was Harris. Strange. When I checked with the police department, they said there is no Inspector Harris."

"That is strange," I agreed. "Maybe she got his name wrong. I think Inspector Davall is handling the case."

"Just how did you get my name, Mr. Polo?"

"From Mr. O'Hara."

A pucker of wrinkles formed around his lips. "You'd better explain that," he said, though I'd already done that with the phony Inspector Harris call.

"Well, not your name, actually. The license number on your Mercedes. Why do you think O'Hara had your license number written down?"

"And you ran the number? And came up with my name?"

"Right."

Maurence took a step toward me, his voice dropping several notches. "I'm sure it was you who called my office. I don't like the kind of games you're playing, Polo. Get out of here before I throw you out."

"Why do you think O'Hara had your license number written down? There were other plates, too. Did your friends in the police department mention them?"

"Whose plates?"

"HKI Inc. A firm located in a building about a block from where Mr. O'Hara's body was found. Ever do business with them?"

"No. Get out of here."

"How about a man named Dunhill? That ring any bells, Mr. Maurence?"

"No. None at all."

"Dunhill uses another name sometimes. Al Davis. He was CIA in Hong Kong. I bet you knew a lot of those guys."

"Get out," Maurence screamed, putting his drink down and starting to take off his coat. I guess he was afraid he'd lose a gold button if we got into a scuffle.

"I'm going," I said, handing the wineglass to Shy Celli. "I can see my way out."

I sidled out of the room, keeping an eye on Maurence. He looked the type to come at you from behind. Just before I closed the door after myself I heard him shout Shy's name, then a loud, slapping noise. The door shut before I could hear any more.

"Unusual culture, isn't it?" Bill Linwood said, settling his haunches into the barstool alongside Jane Tobin.

"Bars, I mean," he added without being prompted. "How certain bars attract a certain clientele."

He waved a hand to the bartender. "Dirty martini, over here."

Dirty martini. Ever try one? Instead of vermouth, the bartender adds a dash of the juice from the olive jar to the gin or vodka. Never liked them myself, but to each his own. Linwood glanced down at our drinks and commissioned the bartender to replenish them.

We were in the N&N, a saloon located in an alley behind the *Bulletin*. Once a newspaper hangout, frequented by cigar-chomping reporters, printers wearing folded paper hats made from the morning edition, and drivers wearing Giants and 49er jackets, the N&N had gone through a conversion since adding those prosperous words "Bar and Grill" after the initials. This allowed them to upgrade the silverware and china, as well as the prices of drinks. The crowd had a much more yuppie feel to it now, but then reporters don't chew cigars anymore, hard-ink printers are being phased out by computers, and the drivers can find more congenial spots to argue sports bets, spots where the tariff for a draft beer is less than three bucks.

Linwood kept his preacher's voice on full throttle. "Yes, very interesting. I may do a piece on it sometime."

"Sounds fascinating," Jane said irritably. She was not in a good mood. An editor had slashed her story on the fistfight between two sports reporters on the *Bulletin*'s rival newspaper. She'd had two Gibsons and nothing to eat, other than the popcorn provided by the bar.

Linwood took no notice of her response, but continued in a voice that he obviously loved. "Cop bars. We're all familiar with them." He favored me with a glance. "Right, Nick? But not just cop bars. Each law enforcement agency seems to have its own private territory staked out. The Secret Service people hang out on a place on Stuart Street. The FBI does its off-duty imbibing at a seedy little place on Ellis Street. But the CIA—ah, they're a little different. They congregate at Roldan's out on Pierce, near Lombard." He risked severe injury to his hand by digging into Jane's popcorn bowl. "I was just out there. Ran into a few people I knew, Jane. Asked around about your Mr. Davis, Nick."

"Find out anything interesting?"

Linwood gestured slowly up and down with one hand like a conductor ordering the string section to lower the volume. "You have to be patient in these things, Nick. One of my sources knew Davis, all right. Apparently he left the Agency under less than honorable circumstances."

Getting information from Linwood was like pulling teeth. I felt like doing it the easy way—upper plate, then lower plate—but as he advised, you have to be patient in these things. "Did your contact say that Davis was in San Francisco?"

Linwood lobbed some popcorn into his mouth. "Didn't say he wasn't. Are you two going to tell me what this is all about, or am I going to have to guess?"

"I'm interested in this Davis, that's all."

"Bullshit," Linwood said irritably. He tapped a finger on his nose. "I've been around too long to be bullshitted." He picked up a cocktail napkin and began writing on it, drawing three straight lines, connecting them in a pyramid shape.

"Here we have your mysterious Mr. Davis," he said, writing Davis's name along one line. "Then there's good old Papa Henry Lee and Lester Maurence." He added the two names and held the diagram up to Jane. "A triad. That's what we have here, isn't it?" He dragged his eyes from Jane toward me. "You know what a triad is, don't you, Polo?"

"Nowadays it's usually connected to the Chinese Mafia."

"Indeed." Linwood sipped his drink, then said, "I know a lot about the triads. They make your Italian friends look like juvenile delinquents."

'Your Italian friends'? I felt my neck turn red and my shirt collar tighten, but before I could respond, Jane broke in.

"Was Maurence involved with the triads in Hong Kong?" she asked.

"My dear girl," he answered as if he was a teacher instructing one of his favorite students, "of course he was. Everyone was. You couldn't operate a shoeshine stand in Hong Kong without dealing with Peter Chu. He's the Head Dragon. Crazy Chu is his nickname. They all have nicknames.

"Chu is"—he again turned toward me—"what you would call the *capo di capi*. The don of dons. As powerful a figure as Henry Lee is, he stands at attention when he talks to Chu. But things are getting dicey in Hong Kong. No one knows just what

Beijing will do when it takes over. It's not only the banks and businessmen that are nervous. There's talk of New York, or maybe San Francisco, becoming the Dragon's new stronghold."

I was getting tired of Linwood's lecturing, but I asked another question. "When Maurence was in Hong Kong, was he running around with a woman named Shy Celli?"

Linwood chuckled. The dirty-laugh kind of chuckle. "Sweet Shy. She was one of Crazy Chu's projects. He fancied her as a singer. Set her up in a nightclub. Made sure the place was packed every time she sang there. People would come from everywhere—New York, San Francisco, Europe. All the triad leadership would fly to Hong Kong for her opening night." He plucked the olive from his drink and chewed it thoughtfully. "Beautiful girl. Couldn't carry a tune, of course, but she certainly had other talents. I couldn't keep my eyes off her voice."

"She was Crazy Chu's girl?"

"For a while, yes. He goes through them rather quickly. Once they reach twenty-one or so, he dumps them and acquires another, younger, one."

"I met Shy Celli," I told Linwood. "She's living with Lester Maurence."

"I hadn't heard that," Linwood said, as if it couldn't be verified as the truth until he heard it. "Very interesting, but I wouldn't make too much of it. Chu sets his old girls up well when he dumps them. No hard feelings either way. It's all a business arrangement from the start. Maurence wouldn't have made any enemies going after her. He may have strengthened a friendship."

"Maurence made all his money in Hong Kong," I said. "Shipping and real estate, according to the papers."

"Shipping and real estate. That covers a lot of territory, Polo. Like I said before, no one, absolutely no one, can operate in Hong Kong without doing business with Chu. He and the CIA scratched each other's backs constantly."

Jane plucked the onion from my Gibson. "Who do you have to screw to get a meal around here, fellahs?"

Though he had several years on me, I had to admit that

Linwood moved quite fast when he had to. "I know a charming little place down in the Mission. Real Tex-Mex food. They say peppers are an aphrodisiac, did you know that?"

"Never had the need," I piped in, "but if you're buying, let's go."

CHAPTER 18

◀▶

Maybe the chilies were too hot. Maybe the pork in the *carne asada* wasn't quite done. Maybe it was the tequila shooters and beers I'd gulped down at Bill Linwood's charming little Tex-Mex place. Or maybe it was Jane Tobin's deciding to go home alone, leaving both Linwood and me eyeballing her taillights as she disappeared around the corner. We shook hands and walked to our own cars, each wondering if somehow Jane had invited the other over for a nightcap.

It didn't help when I turned on the car's radio and KJAZ picked that particular moment to play a vintage Sinatra version of "The Gal That Got Away."

Gino had pulled the car-watch duty. He gave me a lazy wave as I drove into my garage.

Delio, ever resilient, had taken over the front couch, which left me rolled up in a blanket on the office floor.

Father Tomasello had left a message on my machine. Scratchy's daughter, Susan, was due to arrive at San Francisco International Airport at 7:15 A.M., Flight 61. "If you can't pick her up, give me a call, and I'll make other arrangements," the good father advised before hanging up.

The combination of all of the above didn't help the sandman sprinkle his magic dust in my eyes. I was in that never-never land of half asleep, half awake when the phone rang. The digital desktop clock showed it was 3:11 A.M.

Nobody ever calls with good news at 3:11 A.M. This was certainly no exception. I picked up the phone and mumbled a garbled "Hello."

"You just don't learn, do you, Polo?"

It was the old vibrating voice. He hung up before I could

respond. It had to be good old Al Davis letting me know he was alive and well. And that if he had anything to do about it, I soon would not be. Alive or well, that is.

I untangled myself from the blanket and went exploring. Delio was snoring away in the front room. I looked down to the street at Gino's car. All looked quiet. I tiptoed down the hallway to my bedroom and inched the door open a crack. Mrs. Damonte was snuggled in among the pillows. One eye popped open.

"Problema?" she asked, a small hand snaking out from under the blanket.

"No. No problem," I whispered. "Go back to sleep."

She struggled to a sitting position and asked who had telephoned.

"Wrong number," I said, and closed the door. I went back to the office, where the clock showed 3:20. I lay down and stared at the red digital numbers. The alarm was set to go off in less than three hours. A 7:15-A.M. arrival. God, what an untimely hour to land at an airport. What the hell time had Scratchy's daughter taken off? Since I was wide awake now, I decided to find out.

The United Airlines reservation and information clerk sounded bright and helpful. She told me that Susan McCord's flight was on time. It had left St. Louis at 11:30 P.M., San Francisco time, stopped in Chicago, and would arrive at Gate 61 at 7:15.

I lay there wondering what had brought Davis out of the woodwork to call me at this ungodly time. Maybe it was my conversation with Lester Maurence. Maybe he figured out I was the bad boy with the pellet gun. Davis had responded to HKI Inc. about twenty-five minutes after the first pellet went through the window. He had some type of alarm system that notified him of any problems at 77 South Park. A twenty-five-minute response time would give him a lot of leeway. He could be living damn near anywhere in the city.

Davis, Lee, and Maurence. What the hell was it that Scratchy O'Hara had had on them? What had he seen? What had he heard? How would he have gotten close enough to seasoned pros like that to see or hear anything in the first place? It had to be HKI Inc. Something about Scratchy sleeping in the discarded garbage in the alleyway. Listening to them discuss some plans. Something illegal. What was it he'd said when he called me? Something about his ship finally coming in. Maybe he'd meant it literally. One of Maurence's ships.

And the counterfeit Rolex. What part did it play in all of this? Would Scratchy's wine-soaked brain have known who Henry Lee was? Probably not, and he'd have had no idea who Davis was, so he wouldn't have been shy about going after more money. The hit-and-run accident was a natural. Who was going to waste time on a wino run down by a car in the wee small hours of the morning? And Duke. Who the hell was Duke? I'd swear I hadn't dozed off, but in what seemed like a matter of seconds, the alarm went off.

I found Mrs. D in the kitchen, dressed for the day ahead, the coffee made, her *cialda* cookie iron in hand, holding it over one of the stove's burners. *Cialde* are thin cookies made with the usual ingredients: sugar, eggs, flour, milk, and vanilla. They get their special taste from adding anise seeds, olive oil, and whiskey to the batter. Mrs. D makes them individually. Her cookie iron looks like a small squash racket: a five-inch-round cooking surface attached to iron rods with wooden handles. The cookie batter is poured onto one side of the iron. The top is clamped shut, then the iron is rotated over the stove's flame for a minute or so. When the cookie is done, it's taken out immediately and rolled into a cylinder.

A half-dozen of the tasty devils sat in a dish on the kitchen table. I sampled one, dutifully told her how wonderful it was, and headed for the shower.

When I got back some twenty-five minutes later, showered, shaved, and dressed in appropriate funeral attire, there were two full platters of the cookies on the table. Gino was wolfing them down as if they were peanuts. I grabbed a few of the *cialde* along with a coffee to go and headed for my car.

Parking at the airport garage is always an adventure. You couldn't follow the permanent, well-painted, brightly illustrated directional signs because they were covered by a confusing array of arrows and wobbly hand-painted signs advising different routes to take because of remodeling.

I bought a cup of coffee and a croissant from a small cafeteria dolled up to look like a French bakery and wandered down to the arrival gate for Flight 61. I had a twenty-minute wait. I took a bite of the croissant and did some people-watching, killing time putting jobs to the bodies slumped in the lounge chairs: stockbroker, saleswoman, mom and pop and kids doing the West Coast circuit, the kids outfitted in Disneyland hats and those silkscreened T-shirts they sell at Fisherman's Wharf: "I went to San Francisco and all my mom bought me was this shirt." You can't have everything, kid.

The St. Louis flight was on time. The passengers from the first-class section bolted off first, plowing their way through the multitude like thoroughbreds hurrying to the starting gate, fresh-faced, bright of eye, and in a hurry to get that job done and get back on another plane.

I wondered what Susan McCord would look like. The rest of the red-eye passengers came out of the gate appropriately red-eyed, yawning, stretching, scratching if they had a free hand.

I smiled politely at three women in the twenty-to-thirty-year age group, getting nothing but uninterested looks in return. I was getting worried. Maybe McCord had missed her flight. Or maybe she'd changed her mind at the last minute.

Two of the plane's flight attendants came into sight. A woman in her late twenties with a heart-shaped face was between them. She had glossy golden hair done up in braids that hung well past her shoulders. She was wearing a floral-print dress with a white bow at the throat and a white shawl draped around her shoulders. She was lugging a small black vinyl carry-on bag.

Susan McCord was young, beautiful, and very, very pregnant.

"Hi, you must be Mr. Polo," she said, flashing a contagious smile and extending a slender hand. "Father Tomasello's description of you was perfect. It's awfully nice of you to pick me up."

She had pale skin. I could see the outline of veins at her neck and forehead. "My pleasure, Susan. Do you have any more luggage?"

"No, just this."

I took the bag and escorted her to my car. She was full of questions about her father. Did I know him well? How had he died? What was he doing before he died? Had he remarried?

I fielded them as best as I could. "It was a hit-and-run accident. The police are still working on it. So am I. No suspects yet."

We got back to the car, and she stretched the seat belt to its limits as she settled into the passenger seat.

The traffic was bumper-to-bumper heading into San Francisco, so I took a side route. Susan had never been to the Bay Area, so I felt duty-bound to give her a quick tour. I drove up to Skyline Boulevard and took her past the green stretches of the Olympic Club and Lake Merced. She was fascinated with the hang gliders roaming the cliffs like lazy, overgrown gulls. I skirted the beach and drove down the straight-as-string Great Highway that bordered the Pacific Ocean. I could hear her stomach growling, so we stopped for breakfast at the Cliff House. She was as delighted as a small child as she watched the sea lions perform their circus tricks off the slippery rocks just outside the restaurant's window.

She continued to pepper me with questions. I responded with one of my own.

"Your father. Did he ever write to you?"

She dipped a piece of toast into an egg yolk, stirring the yolk around as if it were paint. "No. I haven't heard from Pop in years. When he came back—from Vietnam—he lived with us, me and Mom, for a year or so. But they were always fighting. Pop had problems. He got arrested a couple of times. Nothing real bad. Fights in bars, that kind of thing. Then he took off. I remember getting a postcard from him. He was living in Seattle."

"When was this?"

"Oh, in the early eighties, I guess. About the time Mom remarried. He came back once. He had a fight with Mom's new husband. A real fight. I remember hiding behind the sofa. They were punching each other." She gave a small smile. "Just like in the movies. Then Pop took off. I got a Christmas card a couple of times, but that was years ago."

"Did you know he was in San Francisco?"

She shook her head sadly. "No. You're a private detective, right?"

"Right."

She eyed me over the lip of her coffee cup. "I thought about hiring a detective to find Pop. I even called one up, but he wanted a lot of money. I couldn't afford it."

"Do you work, Susan?"

"Oh, sure, I'm a clerk at K Mart." She patted her stomach lightly. "Not much longer, though. It's getting close."

"How close?" I asked nervously.

She gave me one of those contagious smiles again. "Oh, two months. Seven weeks, actually. Terry wants me to quit work now, but I want to stay on as long as I can."

"Terry is—?"

"My husband. He's out of work. Has been for a long time. So things are kind of tight."

She began asking me more questions, pleading for anything I could tell her about her father. "I know he wasn't doing well, that he had problems. How did you come to know him?"

"He worked for me, off and on."

That perked her up. "Really? Pop worked for you? As a private eye?"

"Yes. Not full-time. I'm a small outfit. But I hired your dad when I needed him to work a stakeout. Things like that."

"God. I can't believe it."

It just goes to show you what you can believe when you really want to. I fed her some private-eye war stories, substituting Scratchy for the actual investigators involved. "Your father was a good person, Susan, but he did have a bit of a problem with his health."

"Drinking, you mean?"

"He was known to have a drink now and then."

She went back to the questions, this time inquiring about any benefits she might get from her father's estate.

"As far as I know, there's just the cash he left with Father Tomasello and his veterans' benefits."

Her smile crumpled a bit. "Dad was such a mixed-up guy. It's a shame, isn't it? The war. The war is what did it to him."

I asked that famous old question. "What exactly did your father do in the war, Susan?"

"He was a tunnel rat. Real dangerous stuff, huh? Climbing down in those holes. I've read a lot about it. The Cong set all kinds of booby traps. Cobra snakes, spiders, grenades." She rested her arms on her stomach and shuddered. "Can you imagine crawling down in those things? No wonder Pop had problems."

I nodded in agreement, my mind going back to the alleyway. The rear entrance of HKI Inc. New bricks, oozing with fresh-looking mortar. Maybe Scratchy had gone back to tunneling.

"Did your dad ever mention someone by the name of Duke? Or Shark? Do those words mean anything to you?"

"Duke? Shark? No. But I remember Pop had some colorful names for the guys in his army unit. Snakebelly, Dirtface, Wildman. I remember him telling me about them. But Duke and Shark? Could be, but I don't remember."

I unclasped the Rolex and held it out to her. "Your dad left a pawn ticket with Father Tomasello. This is what he pawned."

She took the watch in both hands as if it were a small, injured bird that had to be protected.

"It's not a real Swiss Rolex watch," I explained. "If it was it'd be worth around fifteen thousand dollars. The pawnbroker gave him six hundred and fifty dollars for it."

She pulled her eyes from the Rolex and blinked them at me. "You got it from a pawnbroker?"

"Yes. I paid off your dad's loan. The watch is yours, Susan, but I'd like to hold on to it for a few days. It may help me with my investigation."

"And it's worth six hundred and fifty dollars?"

"In gold alone. You could get more for it, but again, it's a counterfeit. The Rolex people would want to confiscate it, and the police would be interested in it too."

"You can keep it, Mr. Polo. Sure, you can keep it. But where did Pop get it?" she asked, passing the watch back to me.

"That's what I'm trying to find out, Susan. That's what I'm trying to find out."

It was probably a bigger shock to Mrs. Damonte than the firebomb and the firecrackers. I mean me, walking up the steps to the flats with a young pregnant woman. Mrs. D's mouth formed a worried O as her chin dropped toward her knees. I could read her mind as if it were an electronic cue card, flashing out the news to an anchorman. The son of a bitch got some poor girl pregnant. Now there's going to be an heir!

I introduced Susan to Mrs. D. Susan looked as if she could use a rest, and there was still three hours before the services for her father.

Mrs. D wiped her hands on her apron and shot off some quick questions in Italian, the foremost being "Whose baby?"

I told her the whole story while Susan McCord made use of the bathroom. Relief flooded through the network of wrinkles around her eyes. She was relieved, but not happy.

Susan was adamant about getting back to St. Louis as soon as possible. She was booked for a return flight on the red-eye, leaving at midnight.

Mrs. Damonte wasn't having any of that. Either the girl slept at the flat that night or she must fly out at a decent hour. I went to the office, called United Airlines, and found that for the sum of $220 I could get Susan upgraded to a flight leaving at seven in the evening with a fifteen-minute stopover in Denver. I dug my Visa card from my wallet and told the United clerk to book the flight. Before she took the order she advised me that I could further upgrade to first-class seating for another eight hundred dollars. Eight hundred dollars. I could get her a penthouse suite at the Fairmont Hotel for that kind of money. "No, I think we'll pass on that," I told the kindly clerk.

CHAPTER 19

◄►

Charles Nelson "Scratchy" O'Hara had limited his religious participation to his meals at St. Matthew's Kitchen. His will specifically ruled out a church service, and for his final resting place he had requested that his ashes be scattered in the Pacific Ocean. If nothing else, his request meant one less piece of baggage for Susan McCord to carry back to St. Louis.

The Neptune Society's columbarium is an impressive dome-topped, four-story, marble-skinned building located on, appropriately, a dead-end street in the placid Laurel Heights area of San Francisco. The building, which was constructed at the turn of the century, sits in the middle of a neatly trimmed lawn bordered by purple lacata plants. Well-branched cypress trees provide shady areas on the carpetlike grass.

Inside the columbarium the decorative stone-and-plaster walls are lined with small glass-covered vaults holding cinerary urns of all shapes and sizes: flat, round, many looking like they could be trophies awarded to the winner of a major golf championship. There was one in the shape of an old pirate's chest—the remains dating back to 1895.

The magnificent stained-glass windows and ceiling cast surrealistic shadows on the mosaic tile flooring as Father Tomasello gave a brief, nondenominational eulogy for Mr. O'Hara.

There was a bigger crowd in attendance than I had anticipated, the good father having hauled down some twenty or so of the better-dressed of his flock in the old school bus he uses for special occasions.

The good news was that Jane Tobin was there. The bad news

was that she came with Bill Linwood. Linwood was driving a cherry-red 1960-something Ford Mustang convertible that looked as if it had just come off the showroom floor. Another reason to despise the man.

After Father Tomasello concluded the service, we all trooped out to the lawn, where a buffet table had been set up by the St. Matthew's crew. It featured, to no one's surprise, lots of turkey, salads, and soft drinks.

I introduced Susan McCord to Jane, and they wandered away to participate in what, before political correctness came into being, was identified as "girl talk."

Linwood was keeping an eye on his convertible, which was now surrounded by a group of St. Matthew's regulars.

"Jane asked me to drop her off. Who's the deceased?"

"An old-timer who got run over in the streets."

"I'm meeting with someone today," Linwood said. "Ex–Company man. If anyone would know about your Mr. Davis, he would."

"You think there's a story in there, don't you?"

Linwood reached back and massaged the small of his back as if it were getting stiff. "Could be. I'm so damn busy pushing the book and working out the details on a movie deal that I don't have time to do it justice. I just might do a little digging, develop some leads, then give Jane a crack at it."

"These are dangerous people. I wouldn't want her getting hurt."

Linwood grinned sideways at the statement. "Rather chauvinistic of you, isn't it? I think Jane can handle herself."

"I do too. But I repeat. These are damn dangerous people."

"Got you scared, do they, Polo? I've dealt with these characters all my life. If they respect you, they leave you alone. After I interview my source, you and I are going to have a long talk. I want to know just what the hell this is all about. I can understand Jane's interest. She's a reporter. But you're a shamus, Polo." His eyes strayed over me as if he was a used-car salesman surveying a bumpkin who'd just walked onto the lot.

I tugged at my earlobe, and Linwood took a long look at my

wristwatch. Scratchy's wristwatch. He was the type to notice small details. Like gold watches.

"Someone is paying you for your time, Polo. I want to know who that is. Be ready to let your hair down."

Linwood figured he had scored the final point, so he swiveled on his heels and hurried over to his car to keep the onlookers from marking up the polish job.

I was surprised to see that one of the people admiring the Mustang was Paul Paulsen. Paul saw me, waved, and walked over.

"Man, what I wouldn't give for that baby," he said, throwing an admiring glance toward the vintage Mustang. "Whose is it?"

"Bill Linwood's."

"The writer?"

"You know him?" I asked.

"Read a couple of his books. The one on the Kennedy assassination wasn't bad. Better than most, anyway."

Another Linwood fan. Just what I needed. "What's up, Paul?"

"I called Father Tomasello yesterday. He told me about the service for O'Hara, and said he appreciated my running O'Hara rap sheet, and he'd back me up on it." His freckled forehead corrugated in a frown. "Let's go inside for a minute."

The columbarium was deserted now. Paulsen looked around at the recessed vaults lined with urns. "Hell, I was born and raised in this town. Never knew this building existed." His head tilted back, following the pillared walls to the ceiling. "Not a bad place to end up, I guess."

"What's happening down at the office?"

His forehead wrinkled up again. "Butler and Flann haven't been around for a while. I don't know if they're backing off or what. Lieutenant Bracco thinks I should take a few days off. I'm going to follow his advice. Go fishing. Get out of town."

"Butler and Flann threatened to come to my place with a search warrant. Go through my files."

"Bullshit. Probably. Would they find anything?"

"No," I said, but Paul could see that I wasn't all that confident. We both knew how even the sharpest of people had been caught with their file drawers down. That little scrap of paper, that forgotten scribbled note. How many times do you think Nixon scolded himself for not burning those tapes?

Paulsen looked down at the polished tile flooring as if at any moment it might break up under his feet. "I went in early this morning." He dug an envelope out of his suit jacket pocket. "Got into the record room. Clerks were all half asleep, waiting to be relieved. I picked this up. I didn't have to sign for it, so it can't be traced back to me. Don't hold on to it too long. Shred it, or burn it. But get rid of it."

There were three printed pages and a photograph. The picture was of a younger Alan C. Davis. His original San Francisco Police Department ID picture. He was smiling at the camera with those vampire teeth, looking as if he was about to pounce on the photographer's neck.

The printed material listed his date of entrance into the police department—his prior employment as a military policeman and a short stint with the Treasury Department, then the date he left the SFPD "for federal employment." Then his brief return to the department. For a total of three months. There was a department inquiry regarding "missing documents and computer disks from the Intelligence unit."

That was it. No further entries. No listing for mother, father, brother, sister, or spouse. His residence address was in the 2500 block of Gough Street, in San Francisco. I made a bet with myself that it would be an apartment building and that Davis hadn't been heard from in years. Later that day, I checked, and won the bet. The final document was Davis's resignation papers. I stared at the signature for a moment.

"Did you read this stuff?" I asked Paulsen.

"Yep. I brought Davis's name up with Lieutenant Bracco. Bracco was a sergeant in the chief's office at the time Davis allegedly took off with the Intelligence unit's confidential materials. Bracco said that the chief was ready to go after Davis. Apparently some of the material Davis hoofed off with was very sensitive. You know what type of things the Intelligence unit gathered up in the old days."

Yes, I did. They kept files on unions, radical groups and

organizations, and "high-profile" individuals, be they visiting celebrities or local and national politicians. Anyone with a name. I looked at Davis's photo again. "But they dropped the investigation."

"Like the proverbial hot potato," Paulsen agreed.

"Yes. Just about the time Lester Maurence was breaking into the political scene."

"It's getting a little complicated, Nick. Maybe you should come fishing with me."

"Yes. Maybe I should."

But I didn't. I was glad to see that Bill Linwood's Mustang was gone from the lot, and that Jane Tobin was still elbow to elbow with Susan McCord.

Father Tomasello came over and whispered some final words of condolence in Susan's ear. Her eyes were tearing when Tomasello left.

Jane and Susan piled into the back of my sedan, and I made like a guide again, giving Susan a quick grand tour of the city and depositing her back at the airport one hour before her departure time.

Jane and I stayed with her until boarding time and watched the plane taxi from the runway, giving a final wave out the concourse windows as the 707 lumbered down the tarmac toward its takeoff point.

"That's a real nice young lady," Jane said, an undertone of sadness in her voice.

"Sure is. Old Scratchy didn't know what he was missing."

"Did you talk to Bill?"

"Mr. Linwood and I conferred. He didn't have much to say. Apparently he'll tell you all, and you'll pass along the crumbs to me."

"Well, the first bit of crumbs are going to cost you," Jane purred amiably, learning forward a trifle for emphasis. "I'm starved. I just couldn't bear to eat another bite of Father Tomasello's turkey."

★

I hate to be redundant, but the freeways were jammed. One accident, added to the fact that the Giants were playing a night game at Candlestick Park, led me to take the Oyster Point off-ramp a mile or so north of the airport and head for the Pasta Moon Ristorante. You have to know where the Pasta Moon is, and really want to get there, to find it. Off the freeway, over some railroad tracks, along a road bordered by concrete-walled, windowless warehouses, and finally to a motel-restaurant complex alongside the Brisbane Marina. It's worth the trip. The dining room is all pastel walls, snow-white table linens, bowls of flowers, and a view of the marina.

I've never been able to enjoy rabbit, mainly because my parents raised them in our backyard. They were my buddies, my pals, my playmates, until they ended up in the oven. I used to hide in my room with my eyes squeezed shut and my fingers in my ears whenever my father was going out to slaughter one of the little beauties. But Jane assured me that the *coniglio in padella*, braised Sonoma rabbit with wild mushrooms served over soft polenta, was the best she'd ever tasted.

I sampled the polenta, and agreed. Thumper's distant cousin would not pass my lips, however. I had the house-made linguine with prawns. Thank God prawns weren't cute little furry things a kid could hold in his hand and pet.

Jane sponged up the remains of the rabbit sauce with a piece of bread. "Are you ready for your crumbs?" she asked, in between bites.

"What has your mentor got for me?"

Jane's eyes frosted at the "mentor" jab. "Bill's a damn good reporter, Nick. I keep telling you that, but you don't believe me."

"Convince me."

The frost stayed in her eyes and spread its way down to her throat. "He's been talking to some people in Hong Kong, to see if there's anything specific he can pin Maurence to. He found out Papa Henry Lee was back in Hong Kong last month. Maurence is still active in the shipping business over there. His freighters make regular dockings between Hong Kong and Oak-land."

"No telling what they could be carrying, is there?"

Her voice warmed a bit. "No. God, the opportunities are enormous. It could be anything."

"Even phony Rolex watches. The key is Al Davis and 77 South Park. Somehow, I've got to get in there."

"Well, I think the key is Maurence. I'm going to do some digging into his shipping company. There's something there, all right. I can feel it."

"Can you feel anything else?"

"You mean like your foot running up and down my ankle?"

"How can you be sure it's my foot?"

That got a light laugh and a smile. "Susan McCord told me what you did for her."

"Picking her up and showing her the town? It wasn't much, under the circumstances."

She dusted her hands of any remaining bread crumbs. "No, I mean getting her off the red-eye flight. Upgrading her. That was nice of you. Real nice."

"It was either that or Mrs. Damonte was going to give Susan my bed, which would mean Mrs. D would take the couch, which would mean I'd either share a carpet with one of the bodyguards, sleep in my car, or just walk the streets all night."

"There's always my place," she said softly.

I tuned my voice down to a confessional whisper. "Now why didn't I think of that?"

CHAPTER 20

◀▶

Diane Brecker had worked the Fraud detail for the San Francisco Police Department for close to fifteen years. During that time, she had become the department's handwriting expert. The department had sent her to all the right schools, and the FBI lab, and she'd testified in court more than enough times to qualify as an expert witness. The difference between a witness and an expert witness is about three hundred dollars an hour. A witness who gets subpoenaed to court gets a standard witness-fee check, somewhere in the neighborhood of fifty bucks.

The expert witness gets as much as the traffic will bear. When Diane retired, she went into private practice. The Rolex on her wrist looked like the real McCoy. I'd thrown some work her way on a couple of civil cases, so she greeted me warmly when I dropped by her office at the Flood Building.

"Nick, good to see you."

Diane was on the shady side of fifty, with a soft, oval face and a halo of blond hair. I showed her the rental agency form with the A. Dunhill signature and the Al Davis signature from the personnel records Paul Paulsen had pinched.

"Nick, these are no good," Diane said, leaning over her desk and running the papers under an incandescent magnifier lamp. "A fax copy and this other copy. They'd never hold up in court."

"I don't need it for court, Diane. I just want your personal opinion."

She waved the two documents slowly under the lamp, first one, then the other. Then she folded them, arranging them so the signatures were side by side.

"Well," she finally said, "the relative size of the letters and their slope and spacing are pretty close. But the capitals, the A and the D, and the characteristics of the end loops lead me to believe they were both written by the same person." She raised her head and squinted up at me. "I said 'lead me to believe,' Nick. No way I could testify to this. I'd need a lot more material."

"Diane, on a scale of one to ten, what have we got?"

"Seven. A heavy seven. Get me some more documents, more signatures for comparison, and maybe I can do better."

A heavy seven was pretty good. But Diane's request for more samples of the Davis-Dunhill signature made sense. So, I'd have to call on another expert.

Hootsie was sitting at a small table near the window at Caffè Trieste on Vallejo Street. Everyone was drinking some type of coffee made from the strong beans Trieste roasts and sells under its own name. Espresso, cappuccino, and latte are the local favorites. Almost everyone was reading something. Some had the morning newspaper. The paesanos were checking out the *Il Leone Sons of Italy* weekly. Others had their noses buried in paperbacks. Hootsie was no exception. His literary choice was the racing form.

Caffè Trieste had opened back in the mid-1950s, in the middle of the beatnik era. Legend has it that some of the movers and shakers of that time, Jack Kerouac, Lawrence Ferlinghetti, Ginsberg, et al., had done some of their best writing while camped in chairs at Caffè Trieste.

Things hadn't changed much over the years. Local poets still penned their hopes and dreams amid the sound of opera selections coming from the jukebox. No rock, no roll, no jazz. Just opera. On Saturdays, starting around noon, amateur and professional alike, sopranos and tenors, shoulder to shoulder, sang to, or sometimes against, the notes coming from the jukebox. Pavarotti had dropped in to blast the rafters. Nureyev had given impromptu pirouettes atop the mosaic-tiled tables.

Hootsie saw my shadow and raised his head slowly, hoping the shadow would move. When it didn't, his eyes finally inched up and spotted me.

"Hey, Nicky. Good to see you." He patted the empty chair next to him. "Sit down, sit down." He used his index finger to make the sign of the cross over his heart. "Swear to God, good to see you. How's Uncle Pee Wee?"

"He's just fine, Hootsie." I nodded toward his racing form. "How are the ponies treating you?"

The index finger made its journey again. "Swear to God, Nicky, I don't know what I'd do without your uncle. I been making bets with him over twenty years now. I hate to take his money sometimes." A cross of his heart, and another "swear to God."

Hootsie wasn't bragging. Not too much, anyway. Contrary to popular belief, there are a few people who can make money by betting the horses. Very few, but Hootsie's one of them.

Hootsie averaged about one "swear to God" every two minutes. His full name is Robert Montelongo. Hootsie's in his seventies, with thick, neatly combed hair just starting to be flecked with gray. A good-looking Mexican who looked and acted more Italian than most of the paesanos in North Beach.

He started to get up. "Let me get you a coffee. Something to eat."

"No. I'll get it."

I went to the counter and bought us both cappuccinos. At one time, Hootsie would have risen from his chair with the grace of a trapeze artist. But a broken leg, a crushed knee, and arthritis had turned his once-graceful movements into a painful limp. Hootsie, in his prime, had been the best cat burglar in the Bay Area. He had only done prison time once. That was after he quite literally fell into the arms of the law, dropping from a third-story ledge outside a Nob Hill mansion. Hootsie was so mad he tried to get Jake Erlich, then the best lawyer in town, to sue the owner of the house or the contractor. His theory was that if the ledge had been properly constructed, it never would have crumbled under him. "Swear to God."

I carried the coffees and some sweet rolls back to the table. "I need some help, Hootsie. Your help."

"Anything you want, Nicky. You got it. Swear to God."

After Hootsie was forced to give up his lucrative career, he looked around for a way to make an honest living. Not much out there in the business world appealed to him, so he decided to keep his hand in at his old profession, so to speak, and became a "security consultant."

Hootsie joined the other side and began telling legitimate businesses and wealthy homeowners how to protect themselves from people like him. Not only do these enterprises have trouble with burglars, they also spend an enormous amount of money retooling and changing locks because of honest mistakes, such as lost keys, mislaid security codes, and the like. Those fancy and very expensive electronic entry systems at the Fortune 500 businesses or the card keys now used by most of the top hotels can develop problems. Problems that in due time can be solved. But time is money to these people, and they want that door opened right now.

The old law holds true: Build a better mousetrap, and someone will find a way to set the mouse free. Or something like that.

Hootsie listened to my problem and told me he thought he had the answer. He even volunteered to do the job himself, but I declined his assistance. If anyone was going to go back to jail, it'd be me.

He brought his device, all bundled up in a narrow aluminum cylinder, to my flat, and we practiced on the front door. Hootsie was afraid I'd never get the hang of it. So were the various construction workers and Mrs. Damonte, who would stop their chores long enough to watch my bumbling efforts. We started by taking a thin sheet of plastic, spraying it with a film of WD-40, and sliding it under the door. Then I tried putting the tool to work.

Hootsie insisted I wear burglar gloves, also known as leather golf gloves. "Thin, flexible, you can deal cards with the damn things on."

Why not those surgeon's gloves the spies and burglars on TV wear? Fingerprints, Hootsie explained. "Guy goes in, does his job, leaves, peels off the gloves as soon as possible, and dumps them. Cops find the gloves, turn them inside out, and there are the prints. And what kind of excuse you gonna use if the cops catch you walking around with doctor's gloves? You were giving yourself a prostate exam? The golf gloves you can explain away as driving gloves, and if they drop out of your pocket as you're leaving the job, no damage done. No prints inside those babies."

I tried and tried, but couldn't get it to work. Hootsie would perform his magic and in moments my front door, deadbolt and all, would unlock and swing open.

I kept at it. And kept at it. It looked so simple when he did it. His device consisted of two pieces of thin tubing, double-hinged in the middle, with an inch and a half of the same-diameter tubing between the hinges. Each tube was made of flexible spun glass, with a hook on the working end.

Most deadbolts are positioned between forty-two and forty-five inches from the bottom of the door. Door locks are standardized at thirty-six inches from the bottom. Hootsie's little tool extended out to forty-eight inches. Each side of the tubing was connected to a pair of thin nylon cords, one cord about twice the diameter of the other. The idea was to slip one of the tubes under the door and manipulate it up the inner side of the door and past the deadbolt, slipping the cord around the bolt itself. You then tighten the cords, and if all works out, the bolt turns.

I just couldn't do it. Hootsie moved in and popped the deadbolt easily, then told me to give the door lock a try. Here an eight-inch strip of Velcro is attached to the edge of the tubing, which is adjusted to the height of the door lock. The same procedure—go under the door, maneuver the tubes, get the Velcro to fall over the knob, and tighten the cords. Under Hootsie's agile hands, the knob magically turned. It took him thirty seconds, tops. Thirty minutes of my efforts brought forth nothing more than an urge to kick the damn door in.

Hootsie called a beer break. I got a couple of bottles of

Rolling Rock from the fridge, and Hootsie began asking questions.

"I don't need to know where this place is that you're going to hit, Nick, but tell me what's inside."

"I don't know," I admitted.

Hootsie pulled a face and held up his index finger. "Burglar's rule number one. Never break in unless you know what's on the other side of that door. What kind of people are involved?"

"Rough. One's ex-CIA. Henry Lee's involved, and there's a connection to the firebombing of Mrs. Damonte's flat."

Hootsie squeezed his eyes shut as if his appendix had suddenly burst. "Jesus! CIA. Henry Lee's hoods. You think they might figure you'd try to get into this joint?"

"It's a possibility."

"Swear to God, Nick, you ain't cut out for this one." He crossed his heart twice. "Tell you what. I do the door. Anything happens, cops come by, we say you told me you owned the place, lost your keys."

I didn't like it, but unless I wanted to practice with his break-in tool for a week or more, it seemed to be the only way to go. I agreed to let Hootsie open the door, then take off. He had one more question.

"These rough guys. Think they might play games? Set up a trap?"

"It's a possibility, I guess."

"He guesses," Hootsie snorted. "Amateurs. God save me from amateurs. You got any basketballs?"

"Basketballs?"

"Yeah, you know." He made a dribbling motion with one hand. "You ain't got none, better pick up a couple. Swear to God."

I went shopping. When I came back, Hootsie was in the kitchen watching Mrs. Damonte assemble a couple of her standbys: minestrone soup and *baccalà*. *Baccalà* is made from those cardboard-stiff codfish you see in delicatessen barrels. They look as if they should be used for firewood, but when Mrs. D gets through with them, soaking them overnight, then dicing the fish, sautéing them in olive oil with peppers, onions, tomatoes, parsley, and a little bit of red chili pepper, they're sheer heaven.

Jane stopped by just in time for dinner (not an unusual happenstance), and Delio wandered in, took one look at Jane, kissed her hand, and told her simply, *"Son il tuo schiavo."* I am your slave.

I translated for Jane. "He says you have nice table manners."

Delio was a bit like Mrs. Damonte. He knew a lot more English than he let on. He gave me a look, the kind that hunters give to deer the day before hunting season starts.

Mrs. D apologized for the simple meal, explaining that telling painters how to paint, electricians how to make lights work, and carpenters how to pound nails didn't leave her much time for kitchen chores.

Mrs. D had somehow found time to make a *cassata,* a colorful mold of chocolate and vanilla ice cream combined with a center of whipped cream seasoned with maraschino liqueur and candied fruit. Jane was fascinated with Hootsie, especially after she learned of his colorful career. By the time the *cassata* was served, Jane had several pages of her trusty notebook filled with Hootsie's exploits.

After Hootsie finished his dessert, he went out to practice with his break-in tool some more.

I left Jane to ward off Delio's smarmy advances and gave Mrs. D a hand with the dishes.

When I was through, I found Jane settled on the couch in the front room. Delio was nowhere in sight.

"I have to go out," I told her. "Where's Delio?"

"He started drooling out some Italian that didn't need any translation and I told him to bug off."

Jane had started her career in journalism as a sports columnist at the *Bulletin.* Her dressing-room exposure to horny, towel-clad professional athletes had made her an expert in the "bug off" department.

"Poor Delio. You probably broke his heart."

"Not for long. His type has a heart that heals quickly, believe me."

I believed her.

Jane said she had an appointment to meet Bill Linwood at nine o'clock at the N&N bar. "He said he may have something for me."

"I'll meet you there."

"Be careful, Nick. You're going back to that place on South Park, aren't you?"

"Yep. Be careful yourself. I'll meet you at the bar."

The weather gods were cooperating. A chilly, low-lying fog had rolled in from the Pacific Ocean, dampening the sidewalks and cutting down on pedestrian traffic. The broken windows of HKI Inc. had been taped over. From the inside. There were no lights that I could see. I knocked on the door, then stood to the side, my hand resting on the butt of the .32 revolver in the holster at my belt. I wore a dark raincoat and a snap-brim rain hat.

I went around the back. No cars in sight. I knocked on the metal roll-up door, then backed away across the street. No response. I hiked back to the car, finding Hootsie squirming in his seat, like a second-string quarterback tired of his place on the bench.

"Is it a go?" he asked.

"It's a go."

Hootsie hopped out of the car and went to work immediately. He stood as far away as possible when he inserted the tip of his tool under the door, running it back and forth. "Sometimes they put a motion detector right behind the door." He looked up and grinned at me. "Sometimes they put other things there, too."

Hootsie had the deadbolt unlocked in less than a minute. He retrieved the tool, inserted the Velcro strap, and in seconds the door was unlocked.

Hootsie slapped his device back into its cylinder and hurried back to the car. "All yours now, Nick." He came back, a basketball under each arm. "You sure you don't want me to stick around?"

I buried the three-cell flashlight under my arm and reached out for the basketballs. "No. See you in a few minutes."

Hootsie got behind the wheel of my car and drove down toward Second Street. He suggested four minutes. No longer. "You stay inside longer than that, you're asking for trouble, Nick. Swear to God."

I watched him drive away, then turned to the back door of 77 South Park. I must have made an amusing sight. Grown man, flashlight under arm, camera with light strobe dangling around neck, two basketballs cradled to chest.

Hootsie thought the basketballs were the best. "Some guys use dogs, but they've got to be trained. Then if things don't work out, the poor mutt gets it. Who gives a damn about a basketball?"

The theory was that if there were motion detectors or traps, they would be no more than a foot above floor level. "So guys can't crawl under them," according to Hootsie.

I took a deep breath, dropped one of the basketballs to the floor, steadied it with a foot, then twisted the doorknob, stood to one side, and pushed it open.

No lights, no sirens, no bombs went off. I put one of the balls between my legs and turned on the flashlight. Bare walls, bare cement floor. A familiar smell. Cleaning solvent. The flashlight beam showed scrape marks in the cement floor. They looked recent—jagged cuts as if heavy equipment had been dragged around. I crouched down, took aim with the ball, and rolled it toward the back of the building, following its path with the flashlight. It rolled unimpeded until bumping to a stop against the metal door.

I heaved a sigh of relief. No motion detectors. No booby traps. "Use both balls," Hootsie had insisted. "Sometimes they set 'em so they don't go off until they get hit twice."

I stepped inside the building, closing the door behind me, then dutifully rolled the second ball toward the front of the building, my interest already on the east wall, where the new bricks were installed. Where I figured Scratchy had made his entrance.

There was a short burst. Maybe twenty shots fired. I dropped to the floor, my hands instinctively going to cover my ears. There was the smell of gunpowder, cordite, the sound of bullets digging into brick, ricocheting off the cement floor. I reached for my .32 revolver as I crawled backward toward the door, expecting more gunfire, expecting to see men with guns coming after me, but there was nothing. Nothing but that eerie silence that follows a moment of panic, as if time itself was taking a breather and the seconds were a minute long.

I scrambled backward, opened the door, rolled out into the street, got to my feet, and started running. A set of taillights was backing up toward me. I threw myself into a recessed doorway and aimed the barrel of the .32 at the car's rear window, my finger slacking off the trigger only when I recognized Hootsie through the glass.

He screeched to a stop, and I grabbed the door handle, yanked it open, and tumbled inside.

"I guess they figured you might be coming," Hootsie said, as he jammed the car into gear and punched the accelerator.

CHAPTER 21

◀▶

Hootsie may have been a first-class burglar, but a getaway man he was not. He took a looping turn onto Second Street, one foot on the gas, the other grazing the brake pedal. "Slow down, slow down," I said, patting him on the shoulder. "Pull over to the curb."

Hootsie followed orders and we changed places. "Look for a phone booth," I said, once behind the wheel. There was a Chevron service station just one block away. I parked next to the phone and dialed 911. The fact that the operator would automatically know where the call originated and that my voice would be recorded didn't matter now. The sound of all those gunshots would have alerted even the most blasé of neighbors. I could already hear the sirens of police cars and fire rigs racing to the scene.

I pinched my nose shut when the emergency operator came on the line.

"There's been a shooting at 77 South Park. No injuries, but the place is booby-trapped. Tell the cops and firemen to be careful. The place is booby-trapped."

The operator responded as calmly as if I were reporting a parked car blocking my garage entryway.

"Yes, sir. Your name, please?"

"Listen. There may be a bomb in there. Tell the emergency crews to be careful. This is not a joke!"

I hung up and hopped back into the car. Hootsie had some sage advice as he made the sign of the cross. "Swear to God, Nick. We could use a drink."

★

I gave Hootsie a rundown of what had happened at 77 South Park. When we got to the N&N we marched straight to the bar and ordered double bourbons.

Jane Tobin was sitting at the table in the corner playing one of her favorite games, liar's dice, with a man dressed in hickory-striped overalls.

Usually when playing liar's dice, the two players each use a dice cup and five dice. You shake out the dice, hiding them from your opponent, and bet against each other on the combined hands. Ones, also called aces, are considered wild, so if you rolled three fours and two ones, you'd have five fours. You then run out the string until someone calls the hand. The purpose is to get your opponent to overbid his hand. Say your opponent has one four, no aces. He challenges your call of six fours. But with your five fours and his one four the combined total is six fours, so you win. The stakes range anywhere from a round of drinks to whatever amount of cold currency you want to wager. I've seen games at private clubs where the bills are hundreds and the stacks reach shot-glass height.

All the dice boxes were in use, so Jane and her playmate were using dollar bills to play the game. The theory is the same. Your "hand" is the eight-digit serial number on the president's side of the bill. Once again, ones, or aces, are considered wild. There are all too many hustlers who secrete ace-filled dollar bills in their wallets for just such occasions. To keep the game legit, each player gets the bartender to break a ten or twenty-dollar bill into singles.

Jane had a neat stack of bills and three Amarettos over ice stacked in front of her.

Hickory-striped overalls was looking as solemn as a mortician as he sipped from a Bud Lite bottle. "Five fours," he said, looking at me suspiciously as I walked over, drink in hand.

Jane called him. "I haven't got a single four, Rudy," Jane said, holding her bill under her opponent's nose.

Her vanquished opponent used a tobacco-stained finger to flip his dollar toward her cash pile. "Got to get back to work, Janey. I'll get you next time."

unted her loot. "Bill Linwood called. He can't make

," I said, with all the disappointment of Opie when
Sheriff Andy told him he couldn't go fishing.

"Bill sounded funny. Said he had some information on Al
Davis, but he wouldn't tell me what it was. He wants to meet
with both of us tomorrow at his house. Lunchtime."

"Good," I said. "Come on, we've got to get out of here."

Jane slid her winnings into her purse, then gave me a hard
look. "You don't look so hot. What happened?"

"That's what I want to find out."

We stopped at the bar and I ordered another drink for Hootsie. He was trembling like a dog after a long run. He raised his
glass in a toast, crossing his heart with his free hand. "Swear to
God, Nick, I'm getting too old for this stuff. It's a good thing we
brought the basketballs."

I swore to God in agreement with him.

"Basketballs?" Jane inquired testily. "What are you two talking about?"

"I'll tell you in the car," I said, laying a twenty-dollar bill on
the bar for Hootsie's drink and cab fare home.

There were a half-dozen black-and-whites, the bomb disposal
van, and several gleaming red fire rigs surrounding South Park
Street. We parked on Third Street and, after I threw my raincoat
and hat in the trunk, hoofed our way to the action, Jane telling
me in locker-room dialogue what she thought about my commando assault on HKI Inc.

I looked around for a friendly face among the cops and firemen, but couldn't see any.

A bulky motorcycle officer in glistening black leathers held up
a beefy hand when we got close to the front entrance of 77
South Park.

"Hi, Danny," Jane said confidently. "Heard the call come in
over the radio. Anything good?"

The cop was in his early thirties, barrel-shouldered, his chest

puffed out thanks to a bulletproof vest. He tilted his uniform ca
back and smiled. "You back on the night beat, Jane?"

"Just in the neighborhood," she answered. "Thought I'd
check it out."

Danny Boy gave me a curious glance, then turned his attention back to Jane. "Goofy damn thing. Someone set up a
machine gun in there to an infrared beam. Something set it off—
shot the hell out of the place and cut a basketball to pieces."

Jane looked at me and shook her head at the mention of the
basketball.

"Good thing no one was in there," the cop continued, "or
he'd be shredded meat."

"Was there just the one weapon?" I asked.

Danny Boy's glance was more than curious this time. "Who
are you? You got business here?"

Before I could play any flash-the-badge games, Jane jumped
in. "He's with me, Danny. What about the weapons? Just the
one?"

"That's what they tell me. But it'll have to wait until the
bomb squad and the lab get through."

"Can we get in to take a peek?" Jane asked.

Danny Boy considered the request for a moment, then said,
"Let me check."

He disappeared inside HKI Inc., and came out moments later.
"Boss says no one in until the lab is through." He gave Jane a big
smile, then said, "Sorry." As if he actually meant it.

We waited in the warmth and comfort of the South Park Café,
Jane making the rounds of the gathering neighbors and customers, then crossing the park, notebook in hand, to pump the cops
and firemen.

I had one coffee brandy, then switched to straight caffeine,
watching the crowd dissipate, wondering if Al Davis would
drive by to see who he'd caught in his net.

Jane came scurrying back into the restaurant, face flushed.
"Have you got your camera?"

"It's in the car."

"Well, get it. It's our ticket inside."

I got the camera and played Casey Crime Photographer to Jane's Brenda Starr. Somehow Jane got Danny Boy to extend us an invitation.

The inside of 77 South Park was a bare concrete floor under a twenty-foot ceiling. A desk stood inside the front door. A small refrigerator and a portable stove were along the west wall.

The crime lab technicians had done their dusting and taken their photos, but Jane had persuaded Danny to let us see the weapon before it was tagged, dismantled, and transported back to the lab for further examination.

The weapon itself was one of those all too efficient rifles that can be purchased legally as a semiautomatic weapon, the "semi" meaning that the trigger has to be pulled each time to fire a bullet. Modifying them into fully automatic killers doesn't take much skill. It's one of the reasons metal shops are the vocational choice of many of the imprisoned population.

I took some pictures, getting down on my knees for a closer examination. This particular killing machine was an old Charter Arms AR-7. A banana-shaped clip that looked as if it could easily hold fifty cartridges hung from the bottom of the weapon, which was encased in a crude wood frame made of two-by-fours. The gun itself was no more than two feet long. A square, fist-size box was mounted to the top of the barrel with bands of metal plumber's tape. Two wires protruded from the box, one going to a car battery on the floor, the other to a three-inch metal device screwed directly to the rifle's plastic stock. A small metal bar at the end of the device had a cigarette-size hole in it, enabling it to be slipped over the rifle's trigger. A piece of electrical wiring held it securely to the trigger.

"What the hell is this thing?" Jane asked, her face wrinkled into a sneer.

"The gizmo on top is an infrared security beam. The thingamajig hooked up to the trigger is probably an electric door-lock actuator. Simple, really. Anything that moves across the light beam activates the weapon."

Jane stood up and folded her arms across her chest. "Where the hell would someone get a system like this?"

"It's not hard. It would just take a trip to an electronics dealer and a hardware store."

Jane was skeptical. "How do you know about such things?"

"I can thank Uncle Sam. Unattended snipers is what the army calls them, though theirs are much more elaborate."

Jane went to question a crime lab technician, and I edged away from the weapon, studying the building's interior. Most of the walls were bare, the age-darkened original timber studs skeletonlike against the brick walls.

I found the spot where the new bricks had been installed. Nothing special. A quick patch job. The codes would have been pretty lenient at the time the building was constructed. Just slap up a frame, fill in a wall of double-lined bricks on a cement foundation. The studs were spaced sixteen inches on center. Plenty of room for a man of Scratchy's size to squeeze through, once he'd tunneled his way past the bricks. A partition wall of moldy Sheetrock framed by two-by-fours had been strung up some two feet past the bricks, so the area was pretty much out of sight. Scratchy could easily wiggle in, then, when he wanted to leave the building, wiggle out and loosely replace the bricks so he could come back the next day. Or night.

That had to be it. Scratchy had had a temporary home here. But what had he found in this barren old building? What had he heard?

There were a half-dozen or more wooden pallets stacked near the rear doors. Nothing else. Just the deep scratches in the dirty concrete.

I took some photos of the brick area, then worked my way to the front of the building. Jane was enveloped in a cluster of police and fire officials. No one was near the gray metal desk adjacent to the front door.

The desk was ordinary. A laminated top over metal legs. Four drawers. All open. The crime lab technicians had gone through them the way a burglar would. Start at the bottom and work your way up—that way there's no time wasted closing one drawer to get at the next. The top two drawers were empty. I nudged them partway closed with a knee. The drawers below were empty also.

The desktop was bare. No blotter, no phones, no answering machine, and I'd bet no fingerprints for the lab boys.

The small refrigerator's enamel was worn through to bare metal in spots. I used a handkerchief and cracked the door open. Nothing but a light bulb and some food crusts. A Coleman two-burner camp stove hooked up to a small butane tank sat on a wobbly-legged stool next to the refrigerator. My handkerchief came away black with grease when I ran it across one of the burners. Not much, but to someone like Scratchy it would look like Betty Crocker's kitchen.

A partition wall of unpainted plywood jutted out some eight feet. No door, just a plastic, egg-yolk-yellow shower curtain hanging on a piece of steel pipe. As I pulled the curtain back, the curtain rings made a rasping sound against the metal rod, drawing the attention of a uniformed cop, who started walking toward me. There was a bathroom behind the curtain—single toilet, single basin, a small molded-fiberglass shower. The cement flooring was stained white from the solvents used to clean it.

"Whaddya think?" the cop asked. He was young, nervous-looking, with tight lips and hollow cheeks.

"Looks like somebody cleaned this place up in a hurry. There's a stove, a refrigerator, but no pots, pans, forks, not even a coffeepot."

"Too bad they left that damn machine gun," the cop said, taking off his uniform cap and fanning away a fly.

I looked around for the basketballs. They were both gone, the survivor and the one that had been shredded by the shots. I wondered what the crime lab would make of them. I wondered what the crime lab would have made of my remains if I hadn't followed Hootsie's advice and rolled that second ball.

CHAPTER 22

◀▶

Jane Tobin was in a hurry to get back to the *Bulletin* and submit her story on the events at 77 South Park for the paper's morning edition. She made it clear that my company wasn't needed for the moment. We made a date for tomorrow to see Bill Linwood.

I spent the night on the couch by the front window, the .32 revolver within easy reach. Churchill was quoted as saying, "Nothing in life is so exhilarating as to be shot at without result." Easy for him to say. Exhilaration was not among the emotions coursing through my nervous system. Fear, confusion, terror, maybe, but definitely not exhilaration.

Had that infrared setup been put there especially for me? Or was it standard operating procedure for Al Davis to leave his little sniper tool in position every night before leaving the office?

And he had definitely left the office. For good, from the looks of the place. Everything taken from the desk, even the refrigerator emptied out. Those scrape marks on the cement floor. The busted-up pallets left behind. What had been on those pallets? What had caused the scrape marks? Heavy boxes. Of what? Phony Rolex watches?

The police would be in the hunt now, looking for Mr. A. Dunhill, the owner of the property. They wouldn't have much more luck than I had. Probably less. Would they be able to pin the Dunhill name to Davis?

The sound of Mrs. Damonte banging around in the kitchen brought me out of a troubled sleep a little after seven in the morning. I padded into my bedroom, stared longingly at my bed, showered and shaved, then pulled a shirt, pants, and sport coat from my now totally jammed closet. I was back in the kitchen in time for Mrs. D's morning special. It was ricotta pancakes this morning, along with garlic sausage and coffee. I dug in quickly, before the construction crew showed up. We talked about the construction project. Things were going well. New Sheetrock was up, and the hardwood flooring had been dried and sanded and was ready for refinishing. The hapless insurance adjuster, Richard Hines, had been battered down by Mrs. D's demands and had taken the easy way out, doing what he should have done in the first place—giving her everything she wanted.

Gino wandered in while I was on my second helping of pancakes. He was rumpled and grumpy. He cheered up when I told him he had worked his last tour of duty. Then he looked at the sausage and pancakes and his expression told me how much he was going to miss Mrs. Damonte's cooking.

The coverall commandos began showing up, so I carried a cup of coffee into my office and got to work on the phone. I called several security guard services before I was satisfied—arranging for two guards, in separate marked patrol cars, to be on duty twenty-four hours a day starting as soon as possible. After last night, I wanted some high-visibility watchmen to replace Gino and Delio at the flats.

Bookies and stockbrokers have a lot in common. They both handle heavy volumes of money and, if they work on the West Coast, they have to start work early in the morning. Much of the action, whether stock market quotes or point spreads, originates in the East, a three-hour time gap. So I wasn't surprised to find Uncle on the job when I phoned him.

"Come for coffee," he suggested, which meant come directly to his office.

The front of the café looks much like the other espresso shops and trattorias on Columbus Avenue: black-tiled outside walls, windows looking into a small room with tables covered with red-and-white-checkered oilcloth. There's no menu posted on the windows, and if the casual tourist or lunch seeker should decide to step inside and check the place out, surly looks from the young man behind the bar and the old-timers playing cards and polluting the air with clouds of smoke from their hand-twisted cigars would certainly encourage him or her to look for another spot.

The bartender, a slightly older version of Gino or Delio, knew me. But my past employment with the police department still marked me as someone to be suspicious of, in his mind. He walked back to the door leading to Uncle's office and got a personal okay before letting me wander back there. While I waited, elbow on the bar, the card players, the youngest of the ten pushing seventy, sat silently, hands folded in front of them away from the cards and cribbage boards.

Uncle Dominic greeted me warmly, asking about Mrs. Damonte's health. I always enjoy visiting him at his office, because it seems to change every time I go there. It's a small room with a desk and a single phone. His communications room, where the actual bets come in, moves around constantly, the phones hooked up to breakers and microwave relays to avoid law-enforcement taps.

Uncle's clients who can't come up with the money owed often pay him with furniture or works of art. The twin ink-on-paper drawings of a woman's head on the wall behind his desk were by Matisse.

The latest acquisition was a pair of long-case clocks, each standing head height. One had a shiny mahogany case and brass leg braces, the clock's face of gilt and ivory. The other was of a darker wood, the top crested with elaborate carvings resembling the towers of medieval churches.

"Early eighteenth century," Uncle said, noticing my interest. "Do you know anyone in the market for one?"

"How much?"

"I'd let them go for twenty."

Twenty meant twenty thousand dollars. The poor client and former owner of the clocks must have been on a long losing streak. "Out of my league, Uncle. But now that we're talking about money, I may have to take you up on your offer. I'm going to need some help."

"Good, good. Tell me, how goes the hunt?"

I brought Uncle up to date, including my narrow escape from the sniper setup at 77 South Park Street.

He listened patiently, interrupting only twice, once when I brought Hootsie's name into the conversation.

"That old bandit. If all my customers were as lucky as he is, I'd have to find another line of work."

The second interruption came when I told him I was sending Gino and Delio back to him.

He protested until I explained my reasons. "I want marked patrol cars, with red lights and sirens if necessary, in the street. Rent-a-cops walking around in uniform are going to discourage people a lot more than the sight of Gino or Delio."

"What are your plans now, Nicky? These people you are dealing with, they are *violenti*. What about the police?"

"They've been after Henry Lee for years, and haven't gotten close. And I don't want to get too close to Lee either. Al Davis is the real joker in the deck. He's been a military cop, worked for the Treasury Department, been a San Francisco policeman, been with the CIA, and God knows what else. He's going to be tough, and there's not much I can tell the locals to help them. If they would listen to me. The policeman investigating the arson job at my place isn't worth his weight in salt, and the inspector in charge of the hit-and-run isn't taking much of an interest in the case. And now I've got two Internal Affairs cops after me and a friend of mine. That leaves Maurence. I think he's the weak link. That's why I need some money."

"How much?"

I hesitated. "Quite a bit. Five thousand. Ten, maybe more."

Uncle gestured with a hand in the air. "Five thousand. Ten thousand, twenty. Take what you need. Money is not a problem. Henry Lee is the problem, Nicky. Spend whatever is necessary to get him off our backs." He opened a desk drawer and withdrew a lunch-pail-size metal box. "What are you going to do with the money?"

"Hire a private investigator, Uncle."

★

Have you looked in the yellow pages for a doctor lately? Or a contractor? Or a restaurant? Not as easy as it used to be. Everything is broken up into subcategories now: the docs start at Allergy and end up several pages later at Urology. There are thirteen categories listed under Contractors in the latest San Francisco phone book, which is not all that bad if you compare it to the computer categories—an even fifty separate listings.

Private investigators haven't gotten quite that bad yet, but we do seem to specialize: civil investigations, criminal investigations, locates, insurance fraud. One firm advertises virus protection in its ad. I hope it's talking about computers. If you want a surveillance expert in the Bay Area, you go to Toni Symons.

Toni's office is located in a stick-style house on Capp Street, in the city's low-rent Mission District. The building is painted schoolbus yellow, the gingerbread trim done in white. Someone apparently hadn't approved of the color scheme and had used a spray can to register his protest: wary lines, circles, and the usual naughty words crudely sprayed from the pavement up as far as an arm could reach on the clapboard siding.

A young man with spiked, beet-red hair and hoop earrings the size of a baseball sat behind a spindle-legged desk, a telephone receiver cupped under his chin. When I asked for Toni he jerked a thumb in the direction of a rubber-runnered staircase.

The second floor was crowned with an elaborately stamped tin ceiling. The walls were wainscoted in mahogany, the floors tessellated hardwood. I said a silent prayer, hoping the idiot with the spray can never gained access to the interior of the building.

Toni Symons must have heard my heels clicking on the floor. She poked her head out of a doorway and waved when she saw me.

"Hey, Nick Polo. God, you never know who"ll pop in out of the past. Come on in. Good to see you."

Toni was on the right side of thirty, with chestnut hair, a sleek figure, and dreamy blue eyes. She gave me a peck on the cheek, then walked behind her desk, flopped down comfortably in a cushioned armchair, and asked, "What's up?"

"I need your help. I need a van and a backup car. The best people you have available."

"Ummm. One-man van?"

"Better make it two. Driver and cameraman."

"My, my. I hope you have a wealthy client."

"I do," I assured her, then realized I was the client.

"The van, with driver and cameraman, goes for a hundred bucks an hour. Backup unit, one operator in a car, goes for another fifty, Nick. That's a hundred and fifty an hour. How long a job?"

"Around the clock."

"Around the clock? Are you kidding me? Twenty-four hours?" She leaned forward and started punching keys on an adding machine.

"That's thirty-six hundred bucks. Now, Nicky, because you're in the business, and because I love your tight little buns, I can give you a ten percent discount. But that's still"—she punched some more keys—"thirty-two hundred and forty dollars."

It was more than I expected. "I'm paying cash, Toni."

"Cash? Nick, whatever you're drinking, order me a double."

"I kid you not. Cash."

"Let's call it three thousand even. Who's the target?"

"Lester Maurence."

"The Lester Maurence?"

"That's the guy." I gave Toni his home address. "His shipping yard is in Oakland. The address is in the phone book. Drives a Mercedes 190E. And Toni, Maurence is connected to some bad people, including Henry Lee in Chinatown. You know about Mr. Lee?"

"Just enough to know I don't want to know him."

"And there's one particular character I'm looking for." I gave her the picture of Al Davis that Paul Paulsen had swiped from his police file. "Make a few Xerox copies of this, give them to your people. If they see him, tell them to be careful. He's dangerous. Very dangerous." I gave her a brief history of Davis's spotty career.

Toni trailed her fingers lightly across the adding machine. "Henry Lee. CIA, rogue cops. Your buns aren't that nice, Nick. I may have to pull back on my discount."

CHAPTER 23

◀▶

Bill Linwood had given up the Marlboro Man look. Today it was Ivy League professor: brown houndstooth sport coat with leather patches on the elbows over a heavily starched ecru oxford-cloth shirt with a button-down collar, whipcord slacks, the crease sharp enough to slit a throat, and a pair of scuffed desert boots.

He greeted one of us warmly. "Jane, Jane, you look lovelier every day, and today you look like tomorrow." I got a curt nod of the head. "Ah, Polo. Come on in."

Linwood led us into the living room. On the coffee table, alongside the alleged Hemingway typewriter, an open bottle of white wine was chilling in an ornate silver-plated ice bucket, surrounded by three long-stemmed glasses.

Linwood carefully poured wine into each glass, much as a chemistry teacher might demonstrate how to handle a dangerous compound. He handed Jane a glass, then passed another to me.

"We've got a lot to talk about," Linwood said. "I thought it would be easier if we just had a bite of lunch here. Sandwiches okay with you?"

"Good idea," Jane said.

Linwood excused himself for a moment and I augured the wine bottle loose from the ice and peeked at the label. Bâtard-Montrachet. A white burgundy Linwood would no doubt claim came from the cellars of the French Imperial Palace. A little farewell gift from François Mitterrand. I took a sip. Fantastic. Mitterrand, or whoever, should have held on to it.

Jane sat down on one of the green leather couches. Linwood rejoined us, carrying a tray loaded with finger sandwiches and slices of fresh fruit and cheese. He picked up his wineglass, took a small sip, and nodded his personal approval. "Jane, I've been working on this, and it could be big. Much bigger than just an article or two. I'm talking about a book. Or maybe a TV show. Documentary, you know the kind of thing. PBS maybe. Maybe the networks. I'm going to run it by my agent, see what she thinks."

I managed to plop down next to Jane without spilling any wine. "Just what 'this' are you talking about?"

Linwood was up and into his preaching-into-the-mirror routine. Maybe the sight of his own face inspired him. He must spend hours shaving. "I called in some chips. Hit some of my sources. This Al Davis of yours is an interesting individual, Polo. I found someone who knew of him, an Agency guy, who put me in touch with another CIA chap who worked Hong Kong until a few months ago. Do you know what a *say atou* is?"

"I don't have a clue. Something to dunk fortune cookies in?"

Linwood pulled himself away from his reflection and gave me a condescending look, the type a teacher bestows on an unusually thick-headed student. *"Say atou,"* he said again, repeating it slowly, even spelling it for his dumb pupil. "Snakehead. A snakehead is the bullyboy in a smuggling operation. Quite often the cargo is human beings. Mostly Chinese. From the mainland: Fuzhou, Guangzhou, Changsha, all over the damn map. They'll do anything to get over here. If you've been there, as I have, you can understand why. They scrape together all they can, then sign contracts to work off their passage. The snakehead guarantees them jobs at a couple of hundred American dollars a week. A fortune to these poor wretches. The contract usually stipulates that once they pay off the smugglers' fee, something in the range of twenty thousand dollars, they'll be free to do whatever they want."

All this pontificating was making Linwood's throat dry. He stopped long enough to swig a bit of the Montrachet, then went back to his pulpit.

I glanced at Jane. She wasn't interested in the sandwiches or fruit and cheese. A bad sign.

"Well," Linwood continued, "snakeheads aren't limited to

human cargo. Weapons, drugs, counterfeit money, credit cards. The Dragons have hired some of the artists who once made documents for the KGB. Absolutely beautiful stuff, believe me—I've seen it. And then there's rip-offs of designer clothing, perfume, watches, jewelry. The whole spectrum."

I glanced down at the phony Rolex on my wrist. "And your source told you Davis is Henry Lee's snakehead."

"Oh, yes. He's working for good old Henry 'Papa' Lee, and for Crazy Chu in Hong Kong. No doubt about it. The Dragons like to use foreigners to do their dirty work. They're really quite racist when you think about it. You have to be pure Chinese to become a member. Nothing else." He cocked his eyebrows at me. "Your Mafia let Jews like Meyer Lansky into the fold, and even a few Irishmen. But the Dragons are purists. They bring in heroin, but don't sell it on the streets. They push that off to the blacks, Jamaicans, Puerto Ricans. *Pai yans* is what they call us Caucasians, and *yuets* are Vietnamese. They make good use of the boat people."

Jane piped in. "Crazy Chu. I just love these names."

Linwood was doing a lot of talking, but not telling me much. "Your sources—what else do they say about Davis? Why'd he leave the CIA?"

"Mutual agreement," Linwood said in a forced tone. "Davis was no longer wanted, but he knew where the dogs were buried, so to speak. He got a small settlement and a letter of recommendation for his return to the San Francisco Police Department."

"What did your source tell you about Davis's present whereabouts?"

Linwood was back at the mirror. "Nothing positive. He was in Hong Kong a month ago."

Linwood flipped open the humidor on the coffee table, selected a cigar, then, with an air of superiority, said, "What I don't understand, Polo, is your interest in this. Your real interest. Don't you think it's about time you told me the whole story?"

Linwood's eight-inch cigar had an inch of ash at its tip when I'd finished. I didn't tell him everything. But enough.

Linwood said, "This O'Hara. I dropped Jane off for his funeral. How did he die?"

"The police list it as a hit-and-run. No suspects."

"What's his connection?"

"Scratchy was living in the streets. He's an ex-army tunnel rat. I figure he found what he thought was a nice warm hideout. HKI Inc., at 77 South Park. A business operated by an A. Dunhill. Dunhill is Al Davis."

"Dunhill? Davis was using the name Dunhill? You're sure of that?" Linwood asked.

"Yes. Scratchy saw or heard something at HKI Inc. He gave me three vehicle license plates to run. One car belonged to Lester Maurence, another was leased to HKI Inc. The third license plate turned out to be on Lee's Rolls-Royce." There didn't seem much point in not telling him about the watch. I slipped it off my wrist and handed it to him. "Scratchy left a pawn ticket with Father Tomasello. He pawned this."

Linwood carried the watch over to the window, parting the curtains to let the sun stream in as he closely examined the watch.

"Are you telling me this isn't legit?" he asked.

"Right. It's gold. No doubt about that. But the insides are worth about five bucks."

Linwood nodded his head knowingly. "Clever bastards. They've been smuggling gold for years, out of the mines at Kumara or Moho, up by the Soviet border. Stealing it, then smuggling it out of the country. Their cost? Probably less than a hundred dollars an ounce. They're smart enough not to dump it all on the open market, but peddle it to jewelers and industrial plants, quadrupling their investment." He bounced the watch in his hands a few times, then reluctantly handed it back to me. "This is an even better idea." He returned to the couch, tilted his head back, and blew some smoke up at the maplike ceiling. The smoke looked like clouds drifting across the Atlantic Ocean.

Linwood said, "Why do you think Davis came back to the San Francisco Police Department?"

"I know why he came back, but the speculation at the time

was he'd work for a year or so, then take a city pension to add to his federal one. He wouldn't be the first to do it."

"No doubt true," Linwood conceded, "but as it turned out, Mr. Davis wasn't thinking of a city-sponsored pension. He had other ideas."

Jane joined the conversation. "You mean the stolen floppy disks."

Linwood raised an eyebrow at the interruption. "Yes. Exactly. Do you know what kind of materials were kept in Intelligence detail files?"

Jane again. "There's always been rumors—a lot of juicy inside political stuff."

Linwood looked as if he was going to pat her on the head. It would have been a big mistake. "Well put. Some quite juicy stuff indeed, I've been told. The investigators in the Intelligence detail were often assigned as bodyguards to VIPs. I've learned—and this is strictly confidential—that a couple of the more enterprising investigators were always wired. Recorded some highly confidential conversations. It has always baffled me just how stupid some people can be. They consider servants, chauffeurs, bodyguards, to be deaf-mutes. I could tell you some stories about the Clinton campaign that would absolutely amaze you."

Jane picked through the sandwiches, selecting one that looked like tuna and olives. "So," she said in between bites, "where does all this lead us? What's in it for me, Bill? I don't write books. Or television shows."

Linwood raised a hand in a lazy salute. "Don't worry. There's more than enough for everyone. My sources say there's trouble brewing among the Dragons. Changes are coming. Crazy Chu wants to relocate. Henry Lee has to be worried about Chu moving here to San Francisco, and moving him out to some place like Portland or Vancouver. It would mean a great loss of face to Lee."

Linwood was all worked up. "I want to find Al Davis. You two have local sources, local connections. Any ideas?"

I took a sip of the wine. It was lukewarm and somehow had

developed a bitter taste. "What exactly are your plans if Davis can be found?"

"The man's a mercenary," Linwood declared. "He'll change sides on a whim. He wants money. We may not have as much as Papa Lee, but we've got something better. Information. On him. Maybe not enough to warrant an arrest, but enough to cause him some major anxiety." He leaned back, crossed one leg over the other, and smiled. "If I really go after him, either in an article or a book, he'd be dead meat. Chu would put out a contract on him."

"What's to stop Davis, or Lee, or Chu, from putting out a contract on you?" I asked Linwood.

The suggestion seemed to shock him. "On me? No. They'd never do that. Not in their interests. It would cause too much publicity. Too much heat." He tapped his cigar ashes into the ice bucket. "Besides, they don't know I'm after them yet. I haven't caused any waves, Polo. But you, you said you met with Maurence. I don't know if that was a good idea."

Linwood pulled the wine bottle from the ice and pointed it toward Jane's glass.

She waved it away. "What are you going to do now, Bill? Can you get any more information from your CIA sources?"

Linwood streamed some wine into his own glass, not offering it in my direction. "I'm working on it. Janey, I was hoping that you could do a little digging at the paper. On Maurence. Check with the people who cover the City Hall beat, see if there's any dirt on the honorable supervisor, especially anything that would show a connection between him and Henry Lee. I know it's been done before, but we have to dig deeper. Maurence is the perfect man for Lee. Not just the shipping connection, but as supervisor he can really help Lee. You know the kind of stuff—tax breaks, political appointments, pushing building contracts to Lee's friends, changing zoning rules. The possibilities are endless." He graced my presence with a warm smile. "Polo, I think you should really work on finding Davis. He must have some old contacts around here. But stay away from Maurence. I'll handle him. And Lee. Don't go near him."

"Anything else?" I asked sarcastically.

It went right over his head. Or maybe under something.

"No, no," Linwood said jovially. "But let's keep in touch on this, shall we?"

Jane stood and started toward the door. If you didn't know her, you would think that nothing was amiss. But I did, and it was. I could tell by her walk, the set of her shoulders. The lady was mad.

Linwood followed at her heels. I waited until he was out of sight, then flipped open the humidor and swiped a cigar.

CHAPTER 24

◄►

"What a pompous ass," Jane Tobin shouted once we were in the car and a half block from Bill Linwood's house. " 'This could be really big, a TV show or a movie,' " she said in a pretty fair imitation of Linwood's pompous tones. "He wants us to run around for him, doing the digging, then he'll make all the bucks. He didn't give us much information we didn't know already, did he? I'm glad you didn't pass on much either. Nothing about breaking into HKI Inc."

"It would have made me look awfully stupid."

"Aren't you used to that yet?"

Ouch. I pantomimed pulling a knife from my heart, then stopped for a red light at Twenty-fourth and Dolores streets. "What did you think about Linwood's suggestion that you dig into Maurence's background for some shady dealings with Lee?"

Jane gave me a scalding look. "I'm already doing that. And I'm not about to share—"

We were cut off by the chirping of my car phone.

"Hello? Mr. Polo?"

"Yes." I recognized the voice right away. Shy Celli. Car phones. I held out against buying one for about as long as I could, but when you use a phone as much as I do, and after you've stopped a half-dozen times at public phones only to find the receiver ripped off or the coin box pried open, or things on the floor you don't want to get within a mile of, you give in. Still, I try to limit any conversation on the damn things to an absolute minimum, because they are so damn easy to bug. I punched the speaker button and cradled the receiver.

"I hope you don't mind me calling you like this," Celli said. "I'm sorry about the other night. I don't know what gets into Les sometimes. He, he was quite upset. At you. Then after you left, at me. That's what I want to talk to you about. I need some help."

"What kind of help?"

"It's Les. He's—well, it's hard to discuss on the phone. Can we meet somewhere?"

The driver behind me beeped his horn to tell me the light had turned green. "Why don't you let me call you back in a few minutes?" I asked, turning left onto Dolores Street.

"Les will be home any minute. Can I come to your office?"

"My office is in my home, and I—"

"Wonderful. I'm an excellent cook. Let me come over and cook for you."

"No, that's not necessary, and things are a little hectic at my place now."

"What if I just stop by for a quick drink? About seven? I'd really appreciate it, Mr. Polo. I'm desperate."

I glanced at Jane. "All right. Seven o'clock."

"Wonderful. See you then."

Jane reached over, her hand encircling my wrist as I flicked the speaker button to the off position. "A lady in distress. According to Linwood, a sexy lady." She did her Linwood imitation again. " 'I couldn't take my eyes off her voice.' Jerk. How did she get your car phone number?"

"From my business card. I left one with Maurence."

"Mind if I come over and take a look?"

"Sure. Why not?"

"I promise I'll leave as soon as Ms. Celli gets there."

"Stick around. I may need protection."

"You have Mrs. Damonte for that," Jane said casually. "Drop me off at the paper, Nick. I have a couple more calls to make. I'm picking up some good stuff on Maurence. But I'm not going to share it with Linwood."

"Are you going to share it with me?"

She let go of my wrist. "Maybe. After I see what this Celli woman looks like."

Ah, the gods of love were back on my side. Jane mad at Linwood and even a little jealous of Shy Celli. I tried to get her to open up as to just what Lester Maurence information she was getting, and from whom.

"Wait'll I get the full story," she said, like a true reporter.

I went back to the flat. The two security guards had already come on duty. Both were sturdy, middle-aged Irishmen with soldierly faces. Their uniforms were very similar to those of the San Francisco Police Department: blue trousers, light blue shirt, revolver holstered at the hip. Their cars, which were double-parked around the construction workers' pickups, had a strong resemblance to the department's: black with white markings and light bars on the roofs. I explained the ground rules and advised them of the possible dangers, then headed to the office and called Toni Symons to see how the surveillance was going. So far Lester Maurence had done nothing but leave his house and drive to his shipping company in Oakland.

I called an inspector I knew in the Fraud detail to find out if he had any ideas on the counterfeit Rolex watches.

"Happens all the time, Nick. There's a flood of them on the market. Rolex, Patek Philippe, Baume & Mercier. Some of them look real good. For about the first month they're out of the box."

"Ever hear of any that were made out of real gold? The watch and the band. First-class reproductions."

"I've seen gold-plate jobs that held up real well for a while. But real gold? No, can't say I have."

I decided to give the computer a shot at Alan Davis. It was a good thing I loaded the printer with paper. The database gratefully terminated its search after 150 listings. I went through the reams of paper, discarding the obvious. I carried the remains, a total of some twenty-two full-print pages, into the kitchen.

The doorbell rang, taking me away from my useless research. It was Jane Tobin. She passed on my offer of coffee, going to the refrigerator and taking out a bottle of mineral water. She pointed the tip of the bottle at the sprawl on the kitchen table.

"What's all that?"

"The negative results of an afternoon spent running Al Davis through the computer. Most of that junk has to do with one of the most hated men in the Bay Area, the Al Davis who moved the Oakland Raiders to Los Angeles. I'd certainly like to be his attorney."

"I had better luck digging through the newspaper's old library filings," Jane said, opening a handbag big enough to have held the *New York Times* Sunday edition. "There were three stories about his leaving the Intelligence detail with confidential files."

She handed me the information. The first story was headlined "San Francisco police inspector suspected of tampering with computer files."

Davis was listed by name. The details were murky, and nothing specific was mentioned about just what it was that Davis had allegedly tampered with.

The follow-up story was just as short, taking up two lines of computer paper. "SFPD inspector suspected of tampering with computer files resigns. District attorney's office is considering filing charges."

It was three months later when the last story surfaced: "SFPD inspector involved in possible computer high jinks out of country. Former Inspector Alan C. Davis thought to be in the Philippines. The DA is looking into possibility of extradition."

Apparently he didn't look into it very hard. Davis disappeared from newsprint, never to be heard from again.

"What do you make of it?" Jane asked.

"Hard to say. Extradition costs a fortune to set up and follow through. Davis was too clever to be pinned down easily. The Philippines was probably just a stopover. If he was ever really there."

"But someone had to go after him," Jane protested.

"Who? The San Francisco cops and the DA wanted him for sure, but there's only so much money to go around, and only so many cops. Remember that video we rented last week? *The Fugitive,* with Harrison Ford."

"Sure. Good old Dr. Richard Kimball."

"And the cop who was chasing him."

"Inspector Girard."

"Right. Chased him all through the movie. And in the 1960s TV series, Girard chased David Janssen as Kimball for about three years. Good show, good movie, but, as the song says, that's entertainment. There's no way any law enforcement agency would or could spend that kind of money running down one man. The only way the cops in real life can catch a real Richard Kimball is if he runs a red light, gets stopped for speeding, or does something else to cause them to run a warrant check. Or if he tries to get a job and uses his own Social Security number, or files for unemployment insurance. It all boils down to money. If Kimball had enough money and played it smart, he would never get caught."

"In other words," Jane said, "crime pays, when you can afford to go first-class."

"Nicely put."

Jane took a pull from her mineral water bottle. "Take a look at this." She went back to digging in her purse, coming out with a manila folder. She sat down at the table.

"I've been busy," Jane said in a tone that suggested that I had not. "First, I checked with the Maritime Exchange. They keep track of all the heavy shipping coming into the bay. At least the freighters. For some reason they don't chart the tankers." Jane leaned back in her chair and burrowed her hands through her hair. "You'd think the freighters would be checked too, with all those oil spills." Her eyes fluttered, as if storing away the information in her brain for a future column. "Anyway, the top page in the folder is a list of all the ships that came into the bay and docked at Maurence's shipping yards in Oakland."

I dutifully opened the folder and looked at the list. Twelve names.

"Most of them are massive container vessels," Jane advised. "Almost eight hundred feet long, carrying fifteen hundred or more of those aluminum cargo containers. The containers are all buttoned up. The Port Authority has inspectors to meet the ships, but they can't possibly open all those containers. Still, they do perform some random samplings. So, if you are smuggling anything in, there's always a risk it will be found. Look at the name of the last ship, Nick."

I dutifully trailed a finger down the list. *"Pae Sha Yu."*

"Right. It's Chinese. For Shark, Nicky. Shark. Like Scratchy's notepaper."

"Shark. Then who, or what, is Duke?"

Jane shook her head resignedly. "I can't find out everything. The *Pae Sha Yu* is an old four-hundred-foot tramp steamer, held together by rust and barnacles."

"You've seen the ship?"

"No, no. Kenny told me about it."

I put a hand under my chin and leaned on the table. "Kenny?"

"After I left the Maritime Exchange I went to the Masters, Mates and Pilots Union. Every time a ship enters port, the captain has to relinquish control of the bridge to a pilot, who guides the ship through bay waters to dockside. Kenny piloted the *Pae Sha Yu,* taking control a few miles outside the Golden Gate and bringing it over to Maurence's docking facilities." She drained the remains of her mineral water, then continued, "Kenny said the boat was a real rust bucket. The captain was Vietnamese. Couldn't speak English. One of the hands, a rough Asian kid, about eighteen, translated. Kenny said the kid kept a watch on him, like he was afraid Kenny was going to steal something."

"Interesting," I said, "but it really doesn't tell us much."

"No, but Kenny says the *Pae Sha Yu* was light-bellied—the top of the screw was breaking water."

"Meaning she didn't have much cargo aboard." I went back to Jane's folder. The listing for the *Pae Sha Yu* showed it leaving Hong Kong on June 6, docking in Oakland on the 14th. Three days before Scratchy was killed.

Jane said, "Kenny said it's unusual for a ship to make a trip like that without a full cargo. You can't make any money like that. He called a friend of his in the Stevedores Union, who put me in touch with the crew chief who unloaded the *Pae Sha Yu.*

They unloaded machine parts and electronic equipment. The crew chief backed up Kenny. Not enough aboard to make the trip worthwhile."

I looked at Scratchy's phony Rolex on my wrist. "It's the cocktail hour. How about a drink?"

Jane looked past me and said, "Hello, how are you feeling?" as Mrs. Damonte entered the kitchen.

Mrs. D doesn't have much use for Jane. Mainly because she sees Jane as a threat. If I happened to marry Jane and we had children, Mrs. D would never get the flats. She gave a grudging hello to Jane, then switched to Italian, complaining about the two security guards. She missed Gino and Delio.

I told Mrs. Damonte that I was having a visitor. A lady visitor. That seemed to pique her interest. She looked at Jane and bobbed her head merrily. I asked Mrs. D to check and make sure the two guards were stationed in front of the flats, where they could easily be seen.

What comes about as close as possible to being a smile came to Mrs. D's lips as she left the kitchen. Another woman bumping Jane out of the picture and being able to order rent-a-cops around. What could be better?

"What was that all about?" Jane asked when she heard the front door close behind Mrs. Damonte. "She looked pleasant. Maybe she's starting to like me."

"I think you're right," I fibbed.

Minutes later Mrs. Damonte came back and said something about *polizia*. I didn't pay much attention, thinking she was talking about the security guards. I was wrong.

Someone coughed loudly, then said, "Well, well, what have we got here?"

I looked up to see the smiling faces of San Francisco police inspectors Ben Butler and Russell Flann.

CHAPTER 25

◀▶

Butler reached for Jane's manila folder. I slapped his hand away. "What the hell do you two clowns think you're doing?"

Flann waved a document in front of his face as if it was a fan. "Take a look at this, Polo. It's a search warrant."

He dropped the paper onto the table. I gave it a quick once-over. It was a warrant, all right. With my name and address. It entitled the bearers to search the premises for any documents relating to any San Francisco Police Department documents, including reports, records, and requests.

"What have we got here?" Flann repeated, bending at the waist to get a better look at the material in Jane's folder.

Jane slapped the folder closed, scooped it up along with my computer checks, and jammed all the materials into her oversize purse.

"Just leave them right there, little lady," Butler ordered.

Little lady? Jane's glowing peaches-and-cream complexion reddened. "Screw you, mister. These are my personal property."

"Leave them be," Butler bellowed. "We've got a search warrant."

"Well, put it where it'll do some good," Jane responded hotly. "My name is Jane Tobin. I'm a reporter for the *Bulletin,* and if you think you're going to mess with me, you're sadly mistaken."

Russell Flann tapped the side of his head with an index finger. "Jane Tobin. Tobin. Yeah, I've read your stuff. Funny, I always pictured you as a short, fat Bella Abzug type."

Jane smiled sweetly. "You're welcome to your little fantasies, Officer."

"Inspector," Flann corrected her, then turned to me. "Let's go see your office, Mr. Polo."

I had no choice but to lead them there. They started digging through the file cabinets and the desk. I leaned against the wall and tried to look unconcerned.

Jane was at my elbow. "Can't you do anything to stop them?"

Maybe there was something I could do. It would be a disaster if Flann or Butler came across an old criminal check or DMV printout that I'd forgotten to feed to the shredder.

I went to the kitchen and used the phone to call Father Tomasello.

"Nick. We missed you on Tuesday," the good father told me when we were connected.

"Sorry about that, but I've been concentrating on Scratchy's death, Father. Speaking of that, a friend of mine, Inspector Paul Paulsen, told me he spoke to you. Well, Paul ran a couple of police checks for me, trying to run down Scratchy's friends. Now two guys from the Internal Affairs unit have shown up at my place and are tearing my office apart."

"Is there a chance they might find something . . . that could cause you concern?"

"Yes. Paulsen could be in a lot of trouble. Me too. They've got a search warrant, so it's all legal. There's not much I can do, but I thought that a call from you to the chief, or maybe the mayor, might help."

"I'll see if there's anything I can do. Are these men there right now, Nick?"

"As we speak, Father."

"Search warrants. They're signed by a judge, aren't they?"

"Right." I dug the warrant from my pocket. "James T. McDonald. I don't know him."

Tomasello chuckled. "I do. Loyola graduate. The Jesuits. You know what those black-robed devils can do to your mind. Hold the fort, Nick. If I can get in touch with McDonald, we'll be home free."

I was on my way back to the office when the doorbell rang. Jane and I got there at the same time. I opened the door. There stood Shy Celli, holding a bottle of champagne in one hand.

"Did I come at a bad time?" she asked. "I know I'm early, I can come back later if—"

I almost tripped over myself backing up. "No, no. Come on in." I made introductions. Jane and Ms. Celli flashed insincere smiles at each other and murmured nice to meet yous.

The phone rang as Shy Celli handed me the bottle of champagne. It was still cold. The label read Dom Pérignon.

I hurried toward the ringing telephone in the office, the floor of which was now half covered with manila file folders from my cabinets.

Russell Flann was on his knees flicking through the folders. He smiled up at me. "Sorry for the mess."

I picked up the phone, feeling like smashing it over his head.

"Is this Mr. Polo?" The voice was hard and unfriendly.

"Yes."

"Judge McDonald here. Can I speak to Inspector Flann or Butler?"

"My pleasure, Judge," I said loudly, catching the attention of both men. "Judge McDonald wants to talk to you chaps." I dangled the receiver from its cord and let it fall in Flann's direction.

Ben Butler looked at his partner with concern in his eyes.

Flann took the phone, said, "Yes, Judge," several times, then started to argue. "But you signed the warrant, and—"

Back to "Yes, Judge." He got to his feet, kicked some files out of the way, and tossed the receiver in my general direction.

"Polo's been playing games, Ben," Flann said to Butler. He paused, took a deep breath, pursing his narrow lips. "Judge McDonald says the search warrant is invalid."

"But he can't do that," Butler protested. "The asshole just signed it a few hours ago."

"Don't worry about cleaning up, fellas," I advised them. "I'll take care of it. But I would appreciate it if you'd leave. Like right now, since you've got no right to be here."

Flann started toward me, Butler jumping between us like a referee at a boxing match. "Come on, Russ. Let's get out of here."

"There's always another judge," Flann called out over Butler's shoulder. "We'll be back."

"They say that about big bands, too. But I don't believe them."

Flann apparently wasn't a music lover. He tried pushing Butler out of the way to get to me.

"Come on, Russ, dammit. Not now. Not here. It's too crowded."

Flann tore his eyes from mine and looked behind him to see Jane and Shy Celli in the hallway. He blinked rapidly, said, "Fuck it," and stomped through the hallway and out the front door. One of them slammed the door behind them, the noise reverberating through the flat.

"Who were those men?" Shy Celli asked.

"Cops," Jane told her. She patted her purse. "I'll go over this material, Nick. Talk to you tomorrow." She nodded to Shy Celli and exited the front door. Another slam job, not as loud as the previous one.

Shy Celli began taking off her belted white cashmere coat. The coat was of a style called polo. No one in my family has ever gotten a nickel's worth of royalties for the coat, or those popular shirts or the shaving cologne going by the same name. Seems unfair, especially since the actual surname of Ralph Lauren, who owns the Polo Company, is Lipschitz. I mean, I understand the name change, but why pick on me?

Shy had managed to overdress and underdress at the same time. She was certainly overdressed for a casual visit to my flat. The underdressing came with the styling. She wore a long teal gown, with sleeves of a sheer material. A teal band wrapped around her neck and crisscrossed her chest, leaving the sides and lower portions of her breasts exposed. She dropped her hands to her sides and pushed her left leg out of the dress's thigh-high side slit.

"Do you like it?" she asked.

Assuming she meant the dress, I answered for my compatriots. "Every man in America likes that dress."

Mrs. Damonte came strolling down the hall dressed in her

going-out clothes. The same black dress she always wore was now covered by a black woolen coat I'd gotten her for one of her birthdays. The only way I can tell that she's dressed for a wild time on the town is her shoes. No hightop tennies—these were serious leather jobs, brightly polished and laced up to the ankles.

"Who died?" I asked, assuming she was off to a wake.

"Bingo night," she answered primly.

I made with the introductions again. Mrs. D gave Shy Celli a quick once-over, then in Italian told me she was going to meet her friends and would be back around ten o'clock.

Shy Celli told her to have a good time. In Italian.

Mrs. D liked that. A lot. I could tell by the way her lips parted. Almost a smile for Mrs. D.

She continued in rapid Italian, complimenting Mrs. Damonte on the beauty of her coat and advising her that it was windy outside.

Mrs. D's lips parted again, and I could see a portion of her teeth! Shy Celli was scoring some heavy points here.

"Grazie," Mrs. D told her. *"Sei molto bella."*

This was getting sickening. She'd told Shy she was very beautiful. The nicest compliment I can remember her ever giving Jane was that she did a good job washing the dishes.

They kept it up like that for a minute or two, ladling Roman beatitudes on each other. Mrs. D informed me that there was plenty of *bollito misto* left from lunch in the refrigerator. She had taken to feeding the construction crew and the security people. *Bollito misto* is sort of an Italian Mulligan stew: a stewing chicken, a beef roast, and some *cotechino* sausage cooked over veal shank bones, then cabbage, onions, garlic, everything but the kitchen sink thrown in. You can use the broth as a soup. Mrs. D drains the meats and makes a *salsa verde,* a green sauce with anchovies, basil leaves, parsley, white wine, and olive oil. One of her best dishes, which is saying something.

"Good luck at bingo," I said, then disappeared into the kitchen to open the champagne.

When I came back, Shy Celli was in the living room, running a hand over my CD collection.

"May I play something?" she asked in a sultry little-girl voice.

"Sure."

She selected Ella Fitzgerald, the Irving Berlin songbook album.

"I just love Ella. That's how I learned some of my English. Listening to her records."

I put the champagne glasses on the coffee table and slotted the CD into the player. "I've heard that you sing."

She began humming to Ella's "Blue Skies," then swaying to the music. "I try. Or tried. Gave it up." She laughed lightly. "Or it gave me up."

She sat down on the couch, picked up a glass of the wine, and patted the cushion beside her, inviting me to get close.

She raised the glass to her lips. Her tongue poked its head out, licked the edge of the glass, then withdrew. "To love songs," she said.

"Cheers."

"That wonderful woman. Who was she?"

"Jane Tobin? She's a reporter for the *Bulletin*."

"No, no. Mrs. Damonte. She's adorable."

I've heard a lot of descriptions of Mrs. D. That was a new one. "She's the downstairs tenant. Her flat was firebombed. She's staying here now. In my bedroom. Until her place is fixed up."

"Oh, the poor woman. It must have been very traumatic for her."

"Yes. Very. You wouldn't happen to know who was responsible, would you?"

She swung her legs off the floor, kicked her spike-heeled shoes off, and put her stockinged feet on the couch. "How would I possibly know?"

"Henry 'Papa' Lee was mentioned as a possible suspect."

"Henry Lee? Come on. He wouldn't do anything like that. Who mentioned Henry?"

"I'd better not say."

Shy Celli dipped her delicate nose toward the champagne, then said, "I really don't know Henry all that well, Nick. I did know some of his associates in Hong Kong. I'd never deny that. They were very good to me."

"Crazy Chu?"

She inhaled and sighed. I couldn't help but notice the tension that movement caused on the front of her dress.

"You've been doing some research, haven't you? Peter Chu was very helpful, Nick. My father worked for him. My father died when I was very young. Peter took me in. Educated me."

"Tell me about your father."

"He was Italian. My mother was Portuguese and Chinese. Father was an exporter. He died in a boating accident in Macao."

"Is your mother still alive?"

She shook her head, causing her hair to sway slowly back and forth in a pendulum motion. "No. Mother died shortly after I was born."

"You've led an interesting life."

She tilted her head back and raised her arms above her head. "Lord, have I ever."

What the hell was that dress made of? Much to my amazement and disappointment, everything stayed in place. "Did you meet Lester Maurence in Hong Kong?"

"Oh, yes." Her hands dropped to her lap. Reverberations, but nothing dropped out. "Les was a charmer back then."

"He's in business with Peter Chu and Henry Lee, isn't he?"

"Les is in business with everyone, including the Pentagon. It's Les I wanted to talk to you about." She picked up her glass, drained it, and asked if there was any more champagne.

I went back to the kitchen for the bottle, making a quick check of the refrigerator. Once the Dom Pérignon was gone, she'd have to get along with Château Supermarket.

Shy began telling me of her life in Hong Kong, the way Peter Chu treated her, sending her to the best schools, making sure she met the right people.

"He must have wanted something in return," I suggested.

Ella Fitzgerald started belting out "Always," and Shy closed her eyes, humming lightly, her right hand floating through the air as if she was conducting the orchestra.

"I was a virgin until I was fifteen. Then Peter gave me a thorough sexual education. He wasn't the only teacher. He had specialists attend me, some on intercourse, others on the oral aspects and massage. There were special hours in the day when this took place." She opened her eyes and looked at me. "From nine to noon it was the basics. Reading, writing, and arithmetic. He was very strict. Then, after lunch, from one to three it was the arts. Singing, ballet, painting, sculpting. Then came the sex. Not just hands-on instruction, but introducing me to literature, films, anything to do with sexual gratification." Her tongue went through that poking-out routine again, then she continued, "Bondage and sadomasochism weren't the rage they are now in America. But I was taught all the ropes." She flashed her teeth in a tired smile. "So to speak."

I topped off both our glasses. "What was graduation like?"

"Different cultures, Nick. They view sex as a part of life, an extension of life. Not just a quick romp in the hay. When I got older, twenty-one or so, I began seeing less of Peter Chu. But he set me up in a beautiful apartment and made sure that I was well taken care of. That my singing career was given a chance to succeed."

"Crazy Chu found another younger protégée, no doubt."

"No doubt at all. He was always very open about that. I was never the one and only. I—met some of the other girls."

"And eventually you met Lester Maurence."

She straightened up, arching her shoulders as if she was in sudden pain, her hands going behind her back. Still those puppies didn't fall loose. Amazing.

"Yes, Peter introduced me to Les."

"I had a friend working out of Hong Kong in those days. Al Davis. Big, tough guy with white-blond hair and unusual teeth. Ever run into him?"

Her beautiful face remained placid. "Davis? Common name. What did he do?"

"Worked for the government. The United States government. The CIA. I think Al also worked for Crazy Chu."

"Peter had so many people working for him, Nick. I only met a very few."

I picked up my glass and watched those very expensive

bubbles rise. "Someone told me that Peter Chu is in bad health. That Henry Lee is ready to step in and take his place."

"I wouldn't know anything about that."

"I thought that Maurence might have mentioned it."

"Les doesn't confide his business activities to me, Nick."

"What does he confide to you?"

She started pushing her tongue in and out ever so slowly. I wondered if that was one of the techniques Crazy Chu had taught her in Hong Kong. "I think Les wants to get rid of me, Nick. Permanently. That's why I wanted to talk to you."

CHAPTER 26

◀▶

The only comment Shy Celli made when the Dom Pérignon ran out and we switched to the bottle of supermarket champagne was that it was "a little sweet."

We moved to the kitchen. I opened a bottle of Chianti and put the budget bubbly in the refrigerator for another day.

I microwaved bowls of the *bollito misto,* cut up some French bread, and set the table while Shy told me her fears of Lester Maurence casting her out. Maybe from a high place.

"He's just been so different lately, Nick. Hot-tempered. Abusive."

She dipped the tip of the bread into a small plate of olive oil and balsamic vinegar (great stuff-no cholesterol, no fat, and tastes a hell of a lot better than that high-priced spread).

"What did he say after he kicked me out?" I asked.

She paused for a moment, as if marshaling her thoughts. "He just went ballistic. He slapped me and yelled at me for letting you into the house." A hand went to her cheek. "He's been getting rough. He—he always liked rough sex, fantasy stuff, you know, the old male-macho rape thing."

"I'm not sure I do know," I said, taking the food from the microwave.

"I shouldn't be telling you this, Nick. I don't know why I am, except I'm scared. Really scared. But Les likes to play fantasy-sex games. Sometimes I'm the lonely housewife and he's the burglar and sneaks in and rapes me. Or he'll get dressed up in a cowboy suit, and I'm the slutty town whore. Or he's a priest and I drive him crazy with a sordid confession. You know. Things like that."

"He must have a hell of a wardrobe."

She sampled a spoonful of the *bollito misto* and made appropriate yum–yum sounds. "I didn't mind. Really, sometimes it's really fun. We all have these secret fantasies we'd like to live out. But he's changing. He's bringing others into our sex games. He wants me . . . I can't . . ."

"Why don't you just leave him, Shy?"

"The usual reason. Money. I'm used to the good life, Nick. I don't want to give it up."

"How long have you been living with Maurence?"

"A couple of years now."

"See an attorney. Common-law wife, palimony. You'd walk away with a fortune."

"Walk. That's the key word, Nick. Les would have no problem coming to the conclusion that he'd save a lot of money if I just disappeared. Permanently."

She picked up her glass of Chianti and stared into it as if it was a crystal ball.

"I would think that Crazy Chu could help you. Or Henry Lee."

She placed a finger on the rim of her glass and ran it around a couple of times. "I thought of that. But it won't work. Peter doesn't owe me anything. He's in business with Les. So is Henry Lee. Besides, Les is a man. I'm just a female. Decoration. A pleasure toy. An aging pleasure toy. A whore. I'm very, very expendable. Les isn't. If I spoke to Peter, he'd think that I was getting old, ungrateful, unreliable. The first thing he'd do is call Lees. The second thing he'd do is have me killed. And send Les a bill for services rendered."

"What makes you think I can help you?"

"The way Les acted after you left the house. He was ranting and raving at what a bastard you were. How you were sticking your nose into his business. How he was going to take care of you. Kill you. That gave me the courage to contact you. We're both in the same boat, I guess."

That caught my interest. "Did he say just how he was going to accomplish that?"

"No. Just threats about killing you, getting rid of you, that kind of thing. Then he punished me for letting you into the house."

"How?"

"He called some people. One of his fantasies. A rape scene. I was the lonely housewife again, only this time it was a gang scene. A gang bang is the popular term, I believe. Les stood there and watched."

"What kind of people? White? Asian?"

"Asian. Vietnamese."

"Were they young? Old? Professional-looking?"

The questions seemed to surprise her. "There were six of them. Four were middle-aged, the other two young. Very young. I don't know what they do for a living. They had rough hands and stank like hell." She pushed her food dish away. The wineglass followed. "Do you have any brandy? Or Scotch? I need a real drink."

I went to the cabinet for a bottle of Rémy Martin cognac. I could hear Shy's chair scrape on the linoleum. When I turned around she was walking out the kitchen door, her movements slow, methodical, as if she was wading through water.

"I'm going to make use of the powder room," she said.

I gave her directions and cleared the table. I poured a couple of healthy, or maybe, if you listen to the doctors, it should be unhealthy, slugs of the cognac into balloon snifters. I found Shy Celli back in the front room, digging through the CDs. She selected an Andre Previn–David Rose album, featuring themes from old MGM movies. She accepted the glass and handed me the CD, which I dutifully put into the stereo unit. Lush strings and Previn's distinctive piano began playing *The Bad and the Beautiful*. A rather nice description of Shy Celli, I thought to myself.

She settled onto the couch again, and knocked down half the cognac in one gulp. Her shoulders shuddered as if she suddenly suffered a chill. "Are you going to help me, Nick? I'm taking a chance on you. Really taking a chance. Just coming here. If Les knew that, knew what I told you, he'd kill us both."

"Maybe you shouldn't have told me."

Her hand was pushing the glass to her mouth. It stopped halfway. "I'm sorry. I just—I didn't know who to talk to."

She started to get up. I put a hand on her shoulder. "Don't go. You've told me now. Let's figure out if there's something we can do. Did you ever hear any conversations between Maurence and Henry Lee? Did Lee ever come over to the house?"

"Oh, sure. He's been over quite a few times. And we've been out to dinner with Lee. But they don't talk business when I'm around."

"But you've never seen a man like this Al Davis I described to you? White-blond hair, funny teeth."

"He sounds interesting, but I've never seen him."

I stalled for time by sipping at my drink. How much to tell her? How much of what she'd told me was the truth? How much longer could that dress hang together?

"Does Maurence keep any records, business records, at the house?"

"Yes. He has an office at home. He does a lot of work there."

"Is everything locked up?"

"There's a safe. A wall safe. I don't have the combination. Filling cabinets. I've never checked if they're locked or not."

"Does he use a computer?"

"Oh, yes. Does he ever. Hours at a time."

"Do you know anything about computers, Shy?"

She leaned back and crossed one long leg over the other. "A little. I was toying with writing a book. Fiction. You know. If Danielle Steel can make millions, I figured with my background to draw from, I'd give it a try." Her tongue popped out for a breath of air again. "I found out it's not as easy as it looks."

"If I agreed to help you, I'd need some help from you. We need something we can use to keep Maurence off your back."

"Like what? I'm sure he keeps everything of value in the safe."

I finished my drink and put the empty glass down next to hers. "Maybe there's something on the computer. On its hard disk. Would you be willing to take a look?"

She leaned forward. "I'd be willing to do almost anything, if you agree to help me."

"Maybe we can help each other."

She may have taken my statement to mean something I hadn't intended it to mean. Or did I?

"What time was it that your friend, the adorable old lady, said she'd be back?"

"She said ten o'clock."

She reached her hands behind her neck. I could hear the seductive sound of a zipper being undone.

"Look, Shy. I don't think you should—"

Her hands came free. She pressed one against my lips. "Shhhh. Don't talk. Let me do everything."

Shy slipped off the couch, onto her knees. The two crisscrossing dress straps fell down, but not quite off. She grabbed each by its end and pulled. There was a sticky sound, like a Velcro strap being pulled free. The dress came away. There were two fingernail-size red marks on her breasts, alongside her hardened nipples. She saw my interest.

"Body glue. It's the only way to keep that damn dress on."

Body glue. What chemical genius came up with that one? What will they think of next? The sound of another zipper being undone snapped me away from further technical questions. The zipper was mine. I reached down and gently grabbed her shoulders. "No, Shy. We can't. Not now."

She looked up at me with wounded eyes. "You don't want me, do you?"

"Listen, Mrs. Damonte's liable to come in, the security people are outside, and that lady you met, Jane Tobin, she and I—"

"No," she said harshly. "That's not it." She got to her feet, turned her back to me, and put her dress back together. "It's those men, isn't it? The way I've been living. The way Les has forced me to live. You're afraid. Afraid you might catch something from me." She swiveled on her heels to face me, hands on her hips, lips drawn back in a sneer. "I went to a doctor right away. Tests. Lots of tests. All negative. But we never know nowadays, do we? Some little microscopic bugs could be hibernating, just waiting to do their damage." She dropped her chin to her chest, ran her fingers through her hair, and let out a sob. "God. He's even robbed me of this."

I stood up awkwardly and patted one of those bare, beautiful shoulders. "Listen, Shy, that's not it, it's just that—"

She slapped me across the face, hard enough that I staggered backward.

"Bastard," she yelled. "You're like all the rest. Where's my coat?"

I walked to the closet and got the coat, holding it out to her. "Shy, I—"

"No, no, don't. It's my fault. I apologize. I went over the line there." She blotted her eyes with the back of one hand. "I'm losing it, I guess."

I held the coat out and she slipped into it, then started for the door. "Nick, I'll do what I can for you on the computer. Call me tomorrow, okay?"

"Sure."

She opened the door, then turned back. "Use my private number—555-0639. In the afternoon. Okay?"

"Yes. Listen, I want to—"

She held up a hand to cut off any further words. "Call me tomorrow."

I closed the door after her, then wandered into the kitchen and poured myself some cognac. My sport coat was draped over the back of the chair Shy Celli had been sitting on. I dug out the cigar I'd pilfered from Bill Linwood and lit up. Something about Shy Celli didn't ring true. The seduction scene at the end was too pat. The slap across the face certainly wasn't a pat, though.

I picked up the kitchen phone to call Jane Tobin. No answer at her place, and no one at the *Bulletin* knew where she was. Or at least they wouldn't tell me if they knew. Bill Linwood seemed to have blown himself out of the water as far as Jane was concerned. But you never know. You never know. I poured myself more cognac. I was still sitting there when Mrs. Damonte came home. She looked as gloomy as I did. It must have been a tough night with the bingo cards.

CHAPTER 27

◄►

Do you remember the old TV series *Banacek?* George Peppard played the hero—a suave, handsome insurance investigator who lived in a mansion in Boston and drove a classic Packard convertible when he wasn't being driven around in a stretch limo by his trusty chauffeur-butler. Banacek only worked on exotic cases: missing armored cars, stolen priceless statues or jewels. He always received ten percent of the insured value of the stolen goods, so he was raking in fees in the hundred-thousand-dollar neighborhood all the time.

Despite all this, Banacek could be thrifty. He smoked long Cuban cigars, and, if not finished with an expensive stogie, would snuff it out, put it away, and finish it up later.

In the morning, I headed for the kitchen, only to find Mrs. Damonte at the sink, the tail end of the cigar I'd left in the ashtray revolving madly as it was sucked into the garbage disposal.

A tired-looking security guard was at the table, polishing off breakfast. From the remains on his plate, it looked like an herb omelet and homemade *panettone* bread.

"Puzza tremendante," Mrs. D said, waving a spatula at the vanishing cigar.

Translation: It stinks to high heaven. I grunted a reply and went to my former bedroom to take a shower.

Mrs. Damonte was gone when I got back to the kitchen, so I had a quick cup of coffee, then carried a refill and a slice of *panettone* into my office and called Jane at her apartment.

"How was the dragon lady?" she asked in a sleepy voice.

"She gave me a long sad story, but I think she was just here for a look at the place and to feel me out."

Jane let out a loud yawn, and I could picture her sprawled out lazily on her bed. "So who put sweet Shy up to it? Maurence? Lee? Davis?"

"Probably all of the above. It shows they're still worried about me."

"You didn't get to look at all the stuff I dug up on the *Pae Sha Yu*. I got the skipper's name. Captain Tak Pui Tsang."

"Spell it, please."

She did so, and I scribbled the name on a notepad.

"There's no way we're going to be able to find Tsang. The ship sailed back to the Far East, Nick, but I've got an idea."

"Let's have it."

"We call Maurence. At his office. Tell him we know all about the cargo on the *Pae Sha Yu*. Drop Captain Tsang's name. Maybe mention those counterfeit Rolex watches."

"So far the surveillance has been a dud. It might get Maurence moving."

"You've already called over there, with your phony cop story about Scratchy. What if I call? If I don't get through to Maurence, I'll leave a message with his secretary. I think it's worth a shot."

I did too. "Okay, but just to be safe, let's use a pay phone, so there's no way they can trace the call back to you."

Jane yawned again. "This is my day off. How about breakfast? There are pay phones at Butler's. Come on over."

Jane was all business and half dressed when I got to her apartment. Skirted, bra'd, she was wiggling into a lapis-blue blouse. Why is it that even the most basic bra is sexier than a skimpy bikini top? Why is it that a basic black bra, which is the type Jane was wearing, is sexier than a basic white bra? Why is it—?

Jane brought me out of my whys, spinning on her heels and asking me to button her blouse up the back.

Why is it that fingers that could be as dexterous as a safecracker's in unbuttoning a blouse become clumsy, bananalike appendages when buttoning the same garment?

"Tell me more about your meeting with Shy Celli last night, Nick."

I gave Jane Shy's version of her life.

"I wonder how much, if any of it, is true. She's beautiful, I'll give her that, and that coat she was wearing was cashmere, the perfume Jean Patou Sublime."

I was glad Jane hadn't asked for a description of what was under that coat.

"Did you really send her packing last night?"

"Scout's honor."

"You were never a scout, Nick. But I'll trust you anyway. What are your plans, after I make this call to Maurence's office?

"Wait and see if anything happens, I guess."

"Any reason you can't do your waiting here? At my place?"

"None that I can think of."

Jane made the call to Maurence's office from a pay phone right on Union Street. She was good, demanding to speak to Maurence's personal secretary when she was told Maurence wasn't in the office yet.

"Tell Les," Jane said, giving me a sly wink, "that we've talked to Captain Tsang about his cargo on the *Pae Sha Yu,* about the full cargo that left Hong Kong and the cargo that was off-loaded here, and before we talk to the authorities, or Mr. Chu in Hong Kong, we'd like to meet with him."

"And just who is 'we'?" the secretary asked in a salty voice.

"Ms. Rolex. Tell Les I'll be in touch."

Jane hung up, smiling as I applauded her performance.

"Are you really hungry?" she asked.

"Not particularly."

"Let's just pick up something at a bakery and get back to my place."

Jane's bed was a mixture of croissant crumbs, our discarded clothes, and the morning paper when the phone rang shortly after noon.

I'd given Toni Symons Jane's number to call in case anything interesting came up.

"Nick. We've got something," Symons said. "Your boy went to work this morning. Left his home about nine. Got to the shipyard about nine forty-five. Came right back out, a little after ten, and headed back to San Francisco. Fisherman's Wharf. It looks like he had a meeting set up. He went inside the Wax Museum. The operative in the van got some film of him entering and exiting the museum. We weren't able to film him inside, but the backup hung around and filmed the exit for about fifteen minutes. I think you'll recognize somebody."

Jane and I donned our togs and hurried over to Toni's office. She had the surveillance tape set up in a video machine.

I introduced Jane as Toni started the tape.

"This is Maurence backing out of the house on Buena Vista this morning, and some footage of him driving across the Bay Bridge." She pushed the fast-forward button and the images blurred. "Nothing much there for you." She slowed the tape down as Maurence parked his Mercedes in the company parking lot and entered the building, reappearing on the tape seconds later as he exited. Toni fast-forwarded again. "Back across the bridge to San Francisco and out to Fisherman's Wharf."

The van's camera zoomed in on Maurence as he parked in the lot behind the Boudin Bakery and looked around nervously as he sprinted across Jefferson Street and into the entrance of the Wax Museum.

The time recorder on the bottom left-hand corner of the film showed 10:58. When Maurence reappeared, hurrying down the building's staircase, it showed 11:14.

"Not a very long meeting," Toni said, extracting the tape and slotting another into the machine. She punched the go button and the tape started. The camera's position was much lower than that of the van's periscope-style video recorder.

"Great spot for us," Toni said. "Fisherman's Wharf, I mean. Every other person out there has a camera of some kind draped around his neck, so my girl had no problem blending in. Maurence drove back to his house, by the way. The van's sitting down the block from there right now."

There was a small stream of people, lots of adults with children in tow, exiting the museum. Jane spotted our man first. At 11:19, according to the indicator on the screen.

Toni Symons froze the tape. "This guy looks like the one you told us to be on the lookout for, Nick."

It did indeed. It was Al Davis himself. "That's the man, all right."

Symons punched the play button, and we all watched as Davis exited the museum and stood there, eyes squinted, panning the street. He stopped and stared right into Toni's investigator's lens for a second, then started straight toward the camera, all elbows and kneecaps as his image slowly enlarged on the screen. The camera lens panned quickly to the right, then the screen dissolved.

Toni Symons said, "Jackie, my camera gal, has been in the business a long time. When it looked like your friend spotted her, she scooted. Said the guy kept following her, but she lost him by ducking into Sabella's Restaurant."

Toni extracted the tape and used a scribe to put the date and initials on the tape's plastic casing. "I guess you'll want this, Nick."

My mind was still whirling. "Yes. Can you make a copy for me?"

"Sure. No problem, Nick."

"You had the Buena Vista house under surveillance yesterday, right?"

"We had Maurence under surveillance. He didn't leave the shipyard until almost seven last night. Drove straight home. Didn't make a move until this morning." She thumbed through the files on her desk, picked up a folder, and read from it. "That's all there was, Nick. I can show you the film of him coming and going if you want."

"No. But while your crew was there, after Maurence came home last night, they'd have noticed and filmed anyone else coming into the house, right?"

"Damn right." She tapped a fingernail against the folder. "There's no notation of anyone coming or going. I've got a good crew on this. If someone made an appearance, they'd have picked him up."

I looked across at Jane. "Seems like Shy Celli never got home last night. Toni, get hold of your team. Tell them to drop the surveillance on Maurence now and get the hell away from him.

Your backup car, too." I walked over and shook her hand. "You did a great job. Send me a final bill."

"Sure," she agreed. "What are you going to do now?"

"Good question," I said softly.

CHAPTER 28

◀▶

"Any suggestions?" I asked Jane when we were back at my car.

"Let's eat."

She's always so practical. We headed back to my place and raided the refrigerator. The Spanish call them *tapas,* appetizers served in between meals. *Merende* are the Italian version, and Mrs. Damonte had made a platterful of *piadines,* sort of like small tortillas, stuffed with prosciutto and goat cheese.

"What are you going to do about Shy Celli?" Jane asked, licking some of the goat cheese off her fingers.

"I don't know what to make of her."

"What about pressuring Lester Maurence? Showing him the videotape?"

"Maurence might laugh it off. There's nothing on the tape to positively put him in Davis's pocket. But if your phone call panicked him into a meeting, maybe the videotape would really send him over the edge." I went to the kitchen wall phone and dialed Maurence's office. He was out. I left the name Mr. Rolex and said I'd be in touch.

"We've got to find out where Davis is, and what happened to whatever it was he had in storage at 77 South Park," I said.

"That building could hold an awful lot of phony Rolex watches."

"Watches or whatever, they had to get them off the ship before it came into the bay."

"The guy at the Maritime Exchange said it could have unloaded anywhere outside the Gate, then been brought in to San Francisco, Berkeley, Oakland, Alameda. Anywhere."

"The captain of the *Pae Sha Yu* was Vietnamese."

"Right," Jane said. "There's been a lot of press about fights between local fishermen and Vietnamese immigrants. The immigrants don't understand our laws, the restrictions on fishing rights and net fishing. They're in a bind. They have to flee their homeland, then they come over here and can't use the skills they've used all their lives because of our regulations. A lot of them turn to smuggling."

"I've got an old friend who might be able to help us out on that."

Jane stood and carried the now empty platter to the sink. "Good. Drop me off at the *Bulletin* and I'll see what I can come up with in the library on local smugglers."

"Friend" might not be the right description for Dante. "Old" was, though. Picture Sylvester Stallone continuing to work out until he was in his mid-seventies and you have an idea what Dante LaCosse looked like. Only Dante did it without benefit of weight trainers, steroids, or liposuction. He did it the old-fashioned way. Hard work. Unfortunately, my father had exposed me to both—Dante and hard work—when I was still in high school, sending me down to the Wharf to work for LaCosse during summer vacation. Dante operated one of the tiny "one-lungers," single-cylinder fishing boats moored near Fisherman's Wharf.

You can sit in one of the wharfside restaurants and watch the fishermen repair their craft, mend their nets. They look distinctly European, Italians mostly, a sprinkling of Greeks and Slavs. They act European, too, using their native tongues and bastardized code words on the marine radio, always careful not to give away their positions for fear that other boats will come over and poach on their catch. About the only English I heard over the radio that summer was "Mayaday, Mayaday, Coasta Guard, sava my boat."

When the Coast Guard radio operator responded to the emergency call and asked for the boat's position, all he got was another "Mayaday" and some rapid Italian. Translating the messages and relaying them to the Coast Guard was one of the few things I'd done during those long three months that Dante approved of.

"Colorful" was the way tour guides described the fishing boats and those who worked them. I didn't feel at all colorful that summer. I felt sick, scared, and exhausted, but never colorful.

Dante and I had never become close. The sight of me hanging on for dear life while throwing up on his crab pots had not endeared me to Mr. LaCosse, but he hadn't thrown me overboard out of respect for my father.

Dante greeted me cordially. His skin was tree-bark brown, the muscles tightly corded. Even his face looked muscled, all angles and planes, with wrinkles that looked as if they'd been carved in with a knife. He extended a clawlike hand, the fingers and palm calloused into granite.

There's not much room for socializing on those boats. There's a cabin big enough to hold two people, if they're standing up. All available space is taken up with wells to hold the day's catch of crabs or rockfish.

I spoke Italian. "A quick question, if you have the time, Mr. LaCosse."

He grinned, showing a missing front tooth. "Use English. I think you can call me Dante now. How is your uncle?"

"Fine."

"You still police?"

"No. Private. I investigate things for insurance companies. Dante, if a ship was coming into port, a big ship, but there was cargo that the owners wanted off-loaded before it got into harbor, how would they do it? Where would they do it?"

"Big ship?"

"A freighter. An old freighter, a rust bucket."

Dante squatted down and leaned his back against the wheelhouse, turning his face to the setting sun. "What they unload? People?"

"Maybe. Maybe not. I'm not sure."

"What kind of people? On the boat?"

"The boat came from Hong Kong. The captain was Vietnamese."

The tide was rolling the boat back and forth. I could feel a lump forming in my throat. I grabbed the railing to steady myself.

"Viets. They tough bastards. Don't give a shit for nothing. The whole family works the boat. Wife, kids. I admire how they work. But no license, they don't give a shit. They use gill nets, they don't give a shit."

He dug a toothpick from his shirt pocket and stuck it in his mouth, dangling it from his lips as if it was a cigarette. "We have problems here. Some of them want to take over. The bad ones. I work here over fifty years, they come over and want to take my spot. Lots of problems. A few are real bad. Pirates. They don't fish. They steal the others' fish." He rolled a hand as if it would help him come up with the right words. *"Portano di contrabbando.* What you call them?"

"Smugglers?"

"Sì, smugglers. We have a lot of trouble with them, but they finally move. Down the coast. They keep their boats down in Mission Bay. If I had a ship, and wanted to lighten it, I'd do it south, out of the shipping lanes. Then have the boats come in to French Beach. That's what I'd do."

I thanked Dante and headed back to my car. French Beach was about twenty-five miles south of San Francisco, a small seaside community nestled right in the middle of Pillar Point Harbor, a few miles north of Half Moon Bay. Half Moon Bay had become more famous for its yearly pumpkin festival than for anything else. Thanks to heavy fog and poor roads, the area had remained relatively free of the urban explosion that had taken over most of the Bay Area.

I dug the Thomas Guide map book from the car's trunk and looked at the outline of French Beach. Not much there—small clusters of streets along the waterfront. The builder, or the city planner, had apparently been a fan of higher education. Street names like Harvard, Princeton, Yale, Vassar, Clemson, and Stanford showed on the map. One street right on the waterfront, with a line sticking out into the harbor, caught my eye. It was named Duke.

Jane's inquiries at the *Bulletin* had brought forth a slew of stories about Vietnamese fishermen's encounters with the state Fish and Game Department and local fishermen. A bloody fight over docking rights in Berkeley had left two men dead. There was nothing in the paper's library involving the fishermen and French Beach.

The roads were as bad as I remembered, but the fog was nowhere to be seen. A full moon brightened the cloudless sky. I pulled off Highway 1 and throttled down to cruising speed over the rutty, undulating road leading into French Beach.

"This is—quaint," Jane said. "Very New Englandish."

The road took us past small, ramshackle homes. More like cabins really, and though they were several blocks from the water, many had boats of varying sizes and pedigrees sitting on blocks in their driveways. A colony of Noahs waiting for a flood.

A neon sign for the French Beach Inn was the first indication of any activity. The inn's parking lot was filled with pickup trucks and several 4×4 off-road vehicles. I pulled over, got out of the car, and walked over to check the 4×4s. Not a green Toyota among them.

Country-and-western music spilled out into the lot from the inn's bar. A tall guy in a crushed Stetson and faded jeans came out to the lot and gave me a mean-eyed squint.

"You lose somethin', mister?" he asked.

"No. Just thought I recognized the car of a friend of mine. Al. Guy about my age with blond-white hair."

I apparently gave Mr. Stetson the wrong impression. He hunched his shoulders and ground his right fist into his left palm. "We ain't got them kind of bars down here, buddy. Why don't you go on back to Sandy Frannycisco."

Jane came to my rescue, her shoes making crunching sounds on the gravel. "Anything wrong, Nick?"

Stetson gave her a long look, then his eyes came back to me. He smiled and winked. "Sorry about that, buddy," he said, then dipped his hat to Jane and sauntered over to a battered blue pickup truck.

"What was that all about?" Jane asked.

"He thought I was going to ask him to dance. Let's check out the bar."

Business was good. Thirty or so. More Stetson hats. Waylon or Willie or one of their clones was blaring out something about empty farmland and a broken heart on the jukebox. The female members of the cast scrutinized Jane closely, not liking the competition. I was the only guy in the place with a sport coat and loafers. There was that drop in volume that happens when strangers come into a place. It lasted a few moments, then things cranked back up to normal.

We went to the end of the bar and ordered two Buds.

"Not an Asian in sight," Jane said, scanning the crowd. She got a howdy and a wave from a huge bearded man wearing a straw hat and leaning on the jukebox.

"And no Al Davis. I'll hit the bartender, you take Hoss Cartwright over there at the jukebox."

The bartender had dark, curly hair and a face that tapered to a narrow chin. I pushed the change from a ten-dollar bill in his direction and asked about Davis.

"Yeah, I seen your buddy. Thought he bleached that hair at first, but you can tell he ain't the kind to do that. Someone gave him a ration of shit one day and he was real sorry he did. Got the shit kicked out of him. Hasn't been in for a couple days, though."

"That's Al, all right. Know where he's working? Someone told me on Duke Street."

"Only thing on Duke Street is a pier and a warehouse. Don't think your friend would have much to do with them."

"Them?"

He leaned across the bar and lowered his voice. "Slants. You know. Gooks. First they fucked us in that war, now they're trying to fuck us out of our jobs."

Somebody started clapping, and I turned to see Jane dancing with the big cowboy. The song was up-tempo. Something about a broken heart and a runaway dog.

Lots of twirls and spins, the big guy throwing Jane around with his huge paws as if she was a feather. More clapping when the music ended. Heart still broken, dog still lost.

Jane came to the bar with her partner. He doffed his hat and dusted his hair back with the flat of his hand. "That's a fine woman you got there, buddy."

I was beginning to wonder if someone had pinned a "Buddy" sign on my shirt. He wanted another dance, but Jane begged off. "Be back later, Arnold."

Arnold held his hat across his heart. "I take that as a promise."

I grabbed Jane by the elbow and steered her outside. The jukebox kicked in again. Something about a broken heart and transmission problems.

"Arnold?" I said, once we were safely out of doors. "A cowboy named Arnold?"

"He's a broker with Merrill Lynch. Lives in Half Moon Bay. He says there's been trouble between the locals and the Vietnamese. The local fishermen aren't taking kindly to the Asian competition."

"Anything on Al Davis?"

"I only had a few minutes and one dance," Jane protested.

"The bartender recognized my description of Davis. Said he got in a fight with one of the regulars and cleaned his clock."

"You can relate to that," Jane said, as I unlocked the car door.

CHAPTER 29

◄►

The rutted road we'd followed to the French Beach Inn looked like a German autobahn compared to the ones leading to Duke Street. More run-down houses, small warehouses, marine repair shops, and beached boats everywhere. Hand-painted signs, painted with shaky hands, advertising Fresh Fish, Real Fresh Fish, and the ultimate, Best Fresh Fish.

I consulted the map, found Clemson Street and then Duke Street. It wasn't much of a street. A worn-down, narrow macadamized strip with knee-high weeds sprouting along the side, leading to a gravel parking lot. The lot fronted a dark brown warehouse, some fifty by a hundred feet with a metal saltbox roof. Streaks of rust showed red in the roof's channels. A slit of light shone through a crack in the sliding doors that hung from the roof to the ground. A wooden pier stuck out into the water from the back of the building. A round-stern seagoing tugboat was tied to the end of the pier. There were lights on the ship, and I could see a couple of dark figures outlined by the moon, moving aboard in no particular hurry. The water was a dark, gunmetal gray.

"I don't like the looks of the place, Nick."

"I agree." I maneuvered the car a half block away and into the driveway of a marine repair shop, nudging it alongside a sad-looking sailboat on a trailer. The boat's mast was broken off at the center, looking like a pencil snapped in half by an angry student.

Jane began tapping out a nervous tune on the dashboard with her fingernails. "Are we just going to sit here?"

"I don't particularly feel like walking in there. Especially without a couple of basketballs. Let's hang on for a bit. See what turns up."

What turned up forty minutes later was a cream-colored van that parked in the gravel lot. Four young Asians in dark clothes and knit caps exited the van. One of them used a key to unlock the building, rolling both doors back a few feet. They disappeared inside and appeared moments later on the pier, walking down to the big tugboat. I tried counting their strides when they came back into sight. A hundred and twenty-eight is what I came up with when they all had boarded the ship.

"Four in, four out," Jane said softly.

"And no bombs or machine guns went off. I'm going to take a peek. Man the horn. If you see them coming back, or someone coming in, give a beep. And kick over the engine."

"You expect me to sit here and play Miss Moneypenny to your James Bond?"

"Would you rather be a basketball? Three quick beeps on the horn if you hear anything." I leaned over, took a mini-flashlight from the glove compartment, and put it in my breast pocket. Then I bent an arm behind Jane's head and wrested a .38 snub-nosed revolver from the passenger-seat headrest. I placed the gun in Jane's hand. "Just in case Goldfinger shows up, Miss Moneypenny. Fire it in the air and hope the good guys hear you."

I tried remembering my military training. Serpentine running pattern, hugging the shadows, eyes on the door. They'd left it open a crack. I stopped and looked back toward Jane. Just the front of my car showed, no indication of Jane at all. I took my .32 out of its hip holster and stuck it in my front pants pocket, hand on the grip, finger on the trigger. I kept to the bare patches on the ground, avoiding as much of the gravel as I could, stopping to peer into the van's window, seeing nothing, moving on toward the building door. I stopped to listen, eyes closed, concentrating on my ears, just as the drill sergeant had so strongly advised. "Concentrate. Concentrate. Make yourself listen. Make yourself hear. The snap of a twig, the click of a rifle's safety slipping off. It can save your life!"

I concentrated. I listened. I heard old wood creaking. Distant traffic. The wind. I could hear my Adam's apple move when I swallowed. But nothing else. Nothing that would give me an excuse for running back to the car.

I looked through that crack in the door. A greasy cement floor leading straight back to wide-open doors onto the pier. I nudged the door open slowly, making room for my head to fit through. There was debris everywhere—discarded cardboard cartons, wooden crates, empty pallets. Two forklifts were parked near the pallets. Two stacks of cardboard boxes, stretching out some twenty feet in length and reaching some ten feet in the air, formed a corridor leading to a series of doors toward the back of the building. I took a deep breath and edged my way through the crack in the door, hugging the wall, heading for the relative safety of the pallets and forklifts, making my way to the stack of boxes. There was printing on the boxes, in Chinese or some other Asian language.

The boxes were held together by steel bands. I pushed against the cardboard. There was a give, as if the contents were soft. Or at least not hard.

The place stank of old fish. A steel door with a pull-down handle caught my attention. A refrigerator room, or an icehouse. I was creeping toward it when the car's horn went off. Three quick beeps. I ducked back in between the row of cardboard boxes. I could hear footsteps, laughter. Coming from the pier. I edged around the boxes so I could see them come into the building. Three young Asians with navy watch caps. Probably three from the van who had come in earlier.

They headed toward a door bracketed by a wall of pebbled-glass window panels. One of them opened the door, entered the room, then moments later ran back out, screaming. His two companions pushed him aside and went into the room, only to exit almost immediately. The three of them got into a hot discussion. One started running my way, only to be pulled back by the others. More arguing, screaming. Then one of them headed for the pier, running at full steam toward the boat.

The other two started my way again. I backpedaled and

ducked around the boxes, crouching behind a stack of pallets. They stopped for another round of arguments at the steel refrigerator door. One of them opened it, only to be pulled back by the other. More arguing, then they hurried to the front entrance. I could hear a vehicle's door open, slam shut, the start of a motor, then wheels screeching through the gravel.

I waited a moment, then ran to the front of the building, just in time to see the cream-colored van's taillights wobble out of control for a moment, straighten out, then fade into the darkness.

Jane was out of the car, gun in hand. "What the hell happened in there?" she demanded.

"Damned if I know. You beeped the horn, they came in, took a quick look in a back office, and went berserk."

"I saw them coming down the dock. Look." She stuck her hand holding the gun out to the pier. The tugboat was pulling away.

"Something got them excited." I gently touched Jane's arm and freed the .38 revolver. "Let's find out what it was."

The office door was still ajar. I kicked it all the way open. The moonlight slicked pencil-gray lines through the venetian blinds onto the pale green linoleum floor.

The flies. The damn flies are always the first to get there. I wrapped a handkerchief around my hand, found the light switch, and flipped it on, making sure there was nothing on the floor that would take a print, or that there weren't someone's prints visible that I might mess up. I saw nothing but grimy linoleum.

He was sprawled across a metal desk, sitting in a high-back office chair with cracked vinyl armrests. An educated guess would be that he was sitting right there when he was shot.

I approached the body slowly, on the lookout for anything that the crime lab might consider a clue. I didn't want to disturb any such thing, and I certainly didn't want to leave anything that could be traced back to me.

The body had blond-white hair. Al Davis. Al Davis was not the kind of man to get shot in the back of the head, unless he was bound and gagged first. Who could have gotten up behind him like that?

An educated guess on the time of death? And that's about all it ever is, unless it just so happens that, as in an Agatha Christie plot, the bullet passes through the victim and hits a clock, or his wristwatch. Then you've got an absolute time of death. And every once in a while, it does happen in real life.

There was too much blood on the desk blotter for one of Lady Agatha's victims. Real life, or death, is so damn messy. The bullet had entered Davis's head just behind his left ear. The gun had been somewhere between four and twelve inches from Davis at time of firing.

Am I starting to sound like Agatha's famous sleuth, Hercule? No, you don't need all those "little gray cells" to figure out the basics.

A contact shot, where the gun is held against a flesh-and-blood target, leaves a ragged entry hole, the results of the gases created by the bullet expanding the skin and bone.

A shot fired from a few inches to a foot away leaves dispersed powder burns concentrated right around the entry hole, which is a neat contusion ring, actually smaller than the diameter of the bullet, as the skin is broken and stretched inward at impact, then contracts. Which is exactly what the back of Davis's head looked like. I didn't check the exit wound, which often resembles a Salvador Dalí painting.

Davis's head was lying on its right side. His left eye was open, the cornea dull and filmy.

He'd been wearing a blue-and-white-striped dress shirt. One arm was splayed across the desk. I lifted it gently. There didn't appear to be any rigor mortis. Rigidity usually shows up somewhere between two and four hours after death. Which leaves a lot of leeway, doesn't it?

The flies, *Mosca domestica,* just plain old miserable houseflies, seemed to be multiplying—working their way into Davis's eyes, nose, and mouth and the entrance hole in the back of his head, laying their eggs. As disgusting as it sounds, this often helps a pathologist determine the time of death.

So, back to our educated guess on the time of death. A couple of hours. Maybe. Maybe more. It was pretty cool in the building. Room temperature is another consideration that comes into play.

I looked around the room. The usual office stuff: another desk, filing cabinets, computer, copy machine. I backed away as if walking on eggshells.

"Is that—"

"Al Davis himself," I told Jane.

"We'd better call the police," she said, her eyes still on Davis.

"Right. We'll use my car phone. Let's see what's in the refrigerator first."

A blast of cold air enveloped us as soon as I opened the door. There were boxes of fish. Little boxes, big boxes, some the size of coffins. Little fish, big fish, salmon, rock cod, petrale. And Shy Celli. Naked. Lying on the icy wood-plank flooring, her arms behind her back, her feet tied at the ankles with thin wire that appeared to be a coat hanger. Her eyebrows were frosty, her mouth open, her skin a blue-white. Lying alongside Celli was Lester Maurence, eyes wide open, an amoeba-shaped blotch of blood showing through his white-on-white dress shirt.

"Oh my God," Jane said, choking back a sob, her breath hitting the air like smoke signals.

I crouched down and touched Shy's leg. Cold as a popsicle. There were bruises around her breasts, her neck. The wire binding her feet had cut into her flesh. No visible bullet wounds, knife wounds. Her neck was at a slight angle. Maybe they broke it. Maybe she broke it banging her head on the floor while struggling to get free. Lots of maybes.

Maurence was wearing his shoes, pants, the shirt, and tie. The wound on his chest could have been caused by a bullet or a knife. There was too much congealed blood to tell without probing.

We backed out of the icebox, the reefer door closing with a solid thunk. Jane was rubbing her hands up and down her arms. "Let's call the cops, Nick."

Right. I stared at the row of cardboard boxes. "I wonder what's in those damn things?"

"How long will it take the police to respond to a call?"

I shrugged my shoulders. "Maybe five minutes. Maybe twenty. Depends on where the nearest radio car is."

Jane nodded her head. "Let's open a box first, then."

Cops just love to respond to a homicide call and find a private investigator there ahead of them. I'd put my gun in the car's trunk, and the one Jane was carrying back in its hiding place in the headrest. I was waiting with Jane at the entrance to the building when the first radio car pulled up.

A one-man car, the one man a tall, lanky guy with a soup-strainer mustache. He didn't like what I had to tell him. He liked the sight of Davis, Lester Maurence, and Shy Celli even less. He called for help, and kept his hand on the grips of the revolver in his holster until they arrived. They came in waves. By the time the full team arrived, six marked cars, two unmarked cars, an ambulance, and the medical examiner, I had gone through my story a half-dozen times.

Jane had the same experience. Soup Strainer had questioned us together; the others had separated us.

In addition to all the police vehicles, a dozen or more civilians drawn by the red lights arrived, then the news boys and girls. I recognized Jane's straw-hatted dancing partner and the bartender from the French Beach Inn.

Jane knew most of the press people. A photographer from the *Bulletin* was among them. As soon as I'd called the police from my car phone, Jane had dialed her paper. Bill Linwood was not part of the group.

I didn't know any of the cops. A lieutenant was as high as the brass from the sheriff's office got. Lieutenant Meekan. He was a thin, patient-faced guy who looked like he never got enough sleep. We were sitting on metal folding chairs positioned a dozen steps from the office where Davis's body was. Lab technicians passed by us at frequent intervals. A uniformed officer sat alongside Meekan with a tape recorder in his lap.

"Once more, please, Mr. Polo."

I went through it again. This time they had asked my permission to record the statement. They like to do that.

Question you a few times, fill their notebooks with your quotes, then for the final-final, record it, asking questions from those notebooks.

"What made you think that Mr. Davis might be here?" Meekan asked, after I was through with my narrative.

"Just lucky. I thought that Davis was involved in a smuggling operation."

"And who told you this?"

"Bill Linwood."

"Fill me in on that."

I filled him in. For about the fifth time. The Linwood-to-Davis-to-Maurence-to-Lee connection.

"And you're telling me you had Mr. Maurence followed? By another private investigator?"

"Correct."

"And who was your client, Mr. Polo? Who was paying for this investigation?"

"I was."

Meekan moaned, leaned back, and dry-washed his face with his hands. "You do this a lot? Take on crime all by yourself? Kind of like Batman?"

"Mr. O'Hara was a friend of a friend. I got started, and just couldn't stop."

Another uniformed cop tapped Meekan on the shoulder and handed him a piece of paper. Meekan gave it a quick glance, looked over at me, then went back to the paper. He didn't like what he was reading. I had a feeling the document in his hand was my rap sheet. I was right.

Meekan heaved himself up from the low chair. "Maybe you'd better come to the office."

CHAPTER 30

Meekan's office was in Redwood City, a good thirty-minute drive. But on this trip I wasn't allowed to drive. I gave Jane the keys to my car. She said she'd drop over to the sheriff's office and pick me up as soon as she phoned the story in to the paper. First things first.

More questions, more recorded statements, more brass. A roomful of captains now, as well as representatives from the Immigration Department and the FBI, and some people in gray suits who didn't identify themselves. The names Henry Lee and Lester Maurence had brought in the heavy hitters. And I was the punching bag. The usual threats: loss of license and jail time. The usual responses: I was only doing my duty. I could have left the scene and not called the police. The usual response to responses: What are you covering up?

Not much, really. I left out the parts about breaking into 77 South Park, Jane's telephone call to Lester Maurence, and my conversations with my uncle, but I gave them most of it.

Jane saved me. Her story backed mine up. If she hadn't been there I'd have at least spent the night behind bars. They finally released me, letting me keep all my possessions, except the phony Rolex watch.

"Do you have any idea what is in those cartons in the warehouse?" was Meekan's final question.

"More Rolex watches?"

"A couple of the cartons were ripped open."

I didn't say anything.

One of the gray suits leaned over and whispered something in Meekan's ear.

Meekan nodded, went through the dry-washing routine again. "Miss Tobin is waiting out in the hall. You can go, Polo. Thanks for your cooperation."

Ah, I like a man with a sarcastic sense of humor.

Jane was there as promised, a soft-drink can in hand, talking to a uniformed sergeant. She smiled when she saw me. The sergeant didn't. Jane offered me the Coke. "You must be starved."

For a big city with a lusty reputation, San Francisco rolls up its streets early. Most restaurants shut the doors by ten or eleven. After-hours joints are pretty much a thing of the past, so we ended up at the Sugar Plum, a twenty-four-hour coffee shop on California Street. The waitress looked as tired as I felt, but the ham and eggs helped to get my mind back into gear.

"At least they didn't use a rubber hose," Jane said softly. She was feeling pretty good. Not only had she gotten her story into the *Bulletin*, but she was all over the TV news. "Bill Linwood is going to be furious."

"Especially after the cops jump on him. I had to tell them about Linwood's tipping us off to Davis's being a snakehead for Henry Lee."

"Mr. Lee isn't going to like that," Jane said.

I paused, a forkful of scrambled eggs inches from my mouth. "You're right about that."

Jane tore off the top of one of those fifty-cent-piece-size packages of jam, took a sniff, then spread the jam on her muffin with a knife. "Do you think Davis killed them both, Maurence and Celli?"

"I don't know. I doubt if Davis was dead for more than a couple of hours before we got there."

"That poor woman. I wonder what they did to her before she died."

I thought of Celli's blue-white body. "It probably wasn't pretty. She preceded Davis. So did Maurence. They'd been in that icebox for a long time."

"So who killed Davis?"

"My guess is the betting favorite will be Henry Lee. He'll be the cops' favorite too."

"Mr. Lee isn't going to be very happy with you, Nick."

"He's going to have to get in line. Linwood, the sheriff, the FBI, the CIA, Toni Symons."

"Why Toni?"

"They'll question her about the surveillance job on Maurence. Try and find things that aren't there."

"Did they ask you about the Levi's?"

The Levi's. Two corridors of cardboard boxes filled with denim jeans. Model 510 button-front Levi's. Thousands of them in those boxes. "They asked me about the boxes. I played dumb."

She reached a long arm across the table and patted my cheek. "You're so good at that, darling."

Darling. That took away some of the sting.

"I was talking to a customs agent, and he—"

"Where?"

"At the warehouse, after you left with the police. They tore into those cartons. We could have saved ourselves the trouble of sneaking a peek. Rip-off Levi's all over the place. Apparently it's big business. They make them in China and they smuggle in millions every year. Not only here, but to Europe, Russia, Africa. Pay about five bucks for them, peddle them for three or four times that here in America. Double and triple that in Europe and Russia."

Somehow smuggling imitation jeans just didn't have the same pizzazz that diamonds or emeralds did. Or Rolex watches.

I crashed at Jane's apartment. And crashed is the word. I was asleep before my pink, shell-like ears were within striking distance of the pillow. That was somewhere after two in the morning. Jane had the TV on at six, channel-surfing to catch sight of herself.

I buried my head under the covers, but it was no use. She kept kicking me whenever her moment of glory came on the screen. No pictures of me, but my name was mentioned prominently.

By Jane Tobin. "Mr. Polo and I had reason to believe," and "Mr. Polo and I called the police as soon," etc., etc.

"What do you think?" she asked, when the clock struck seven and the national morning shows came on.

"I think I'm going to need a nap today. What do you think?"

Her hand went to her forehead. "I think I'll cut my bangs. They look a little long."

The phone rang. Jane picked it up, a mischievous grin coming over her face in a matter of seconds. "Gee, Bill. I'm sorry. But I didn't have much choice." She nodded her head and winked at me. "No, no. The bodies were there. What else could we do?"

More nods, more winks. Then she said, "Nick? No, I don't know where he is. Back at police headquarters, probably."

I couldn't handle any more winks. I headed for the shower. Jane brought in a cup of coffee while I was toweling off.

"Mr. Linwood does not think very highly of you this morning. The police are en route to talk to him as we speak."

"Poor baby." I sampled the coffee. Instant. "I think all of us will be talking to the police for a long time."

I can't speak for Linwood, but I made three trips to Redwood City in the following three days, along with getting visits at my place from U.S. Customs Service investigators, the Justice Department, and an assistant U.S. attorney with a high opinion of himself. And a low opinion of me. The feds seemed a lot more interested in the Levi's then they did in finding out who killed Al Davis, Maurence, or Shy Celli.

It went on like that for a week, then died a natural death, the story slipping gradually from the newspaper's front page to the second page, to a playing-card-size item buried among the obituaries and weather reports.

I felt strangely depressed. I dug out my police academy class photograph. A total of fifty-one mint-fresh cops getting ready to graduate and hit the streets, all smiles and bright eyes. Davis was in the back row, his fanglike teeth just barely visible. I was up front, grinning from ear to ear, partly because I'd just been fitted with the front bridge that replaced the teeth Davis had knocked out of my mouth.

Al Davis. I certainly wasn't going to shed a tear because he was no longer among the living, but I felt cheated. Davis was the focus of my investigation, my fears, my hatred. I wanted to find him, catch him myself, be personally responsible for his going to jail. Have a final confrontation with the bastard.

But in a way, maybe I was responsible. Jane's call to Maurence, Davis's spotting Toni Symons's camera operator—those were all my doings. Which also meant that I was responsible for both Shy Celli's and Lester Maurence's death. Poor Shy. She never really had much of a chance in life. Crazy Chu taking her under his wing and training her as if she were a pet, a hunting dog. Once too old to go into the water and retrieve the birds, she was dumped off to Maurence, who himself was getting bored with her, ready to push her down another step on the degradation ladder.

Jane had had her share of hassle time with the cops, but she was none the worse for wear, turning her experience into several articles on the ramifications of international smuggling.

The cops had no real leads on the murders of Davis, Maurence, and Celli. Davis had been shot with a single semijacketed soft-nose 9mm bullet.

Shy Celli's official demise was listed as "Death by Freezing." The autopsy revealed that she had been subjected to a "multi-partner sexual assault" prior to being thrown into the icebox. Semen from "five separate donor sources" was found in her body.

Maurence's death had come much more quickly, from a knife to the chest.

The seagoing tugboat had yet to be found, and the feeling was that it had been scuttled at sea. Perhaps with some of the crew still aboard. "These bastards don't leave anything around," a customs agent advised me. "Pick up a boatload from the Chinese mainland, keep the young ones, the pretty ones, and throw the others overboard. After picking their pockets clean, of course."

Bill Linwood was not talking to either me or Jane. Oh, he did call me once. A short, graphic call, telling me what he thought of me and what I could do with myself. I expected something more eloquent from a famous foreign correspondent.

Paul Paulsen was back from his fishing trip, sunburned, windblown, and with an ice chest full of fish, which his wife refused to cook. The Internal Affairs investigation seemed to have died a natural death.

The really good news was that Mrs. D's apartment was finished. Jane stopped by while Mrs. D had her full corps of codger commandos over to see her "new" place, while I packed her belongings for the journey back to where they belonged.

I was making another trip, this time for her kitchen appliances, when I stopped in at the office and checked the answering machine. Just one call, but it was a good one.

"Mr. Polo. My name is Henry Lee. Please call me. I think it would be to our mutual benefit if we got together."

He left a number. I called. The phone was answered with a simple "Yes?"

"Nick Polo calling for Henry Lee."

"Ah, Mr. Polo. Thanks for being so prompt. I was hoping we could get together. I'll send a car for you, if that's convenient."

"Convenient for who? I've heard some of your passengers end up with one-way trips."

"Do not believe everything you read in the papers, Mr. Polo. No matter who writes it. If you feel threatened, inform one of your police friends. Or your uncle. Our meeting shouldn't take more than half an hour. If you're not out and free by then, you can have your friends break in and rescue you. I give you my word that you will come to no harm. And my word is respected, Mr. Polo. Thirty minutes. I assure you, it will be a profitable half hour."

CHAPTER 31

◀▶

I was a little disappointed. The back of the Rolls wasn't as roomy as I'd thought it would be. Before I got into the car, I introduced the young Asian driver to Jane Tobin.

"She's a newspaper reporter," I advised him. "If she doesn't hear from me in half an hour, she'll call the cops."

Jane pulled a small camera from her purse and got a picture of the driver and one of me climbing into the backseat.

The driver sat there stone-faced, waiting for me to close the door. Once I was seated, the Rolls purred away from the curb. It was only a half-dozen blocks to Pagoda Alley, but it was an interesting trip, sitting behind those dark windows, watching the rubberneckers gawk at the car. I wondered if they stared because it was a Rolls, or because many of them knew it belonged to Henry Lee.

Stoneface parked in front of Lee's brick building on Pagoda. The door was opened by another Asian. Willie "Pork Chop" Marr himself.

He gestured with a finger for me to follow him into the building. There were four doors and a small elevator in the lobby. We got into the elevator, where there was barely enough room for the two of us. There were no numbers indicating which floor we were heading to, and the elevator moved at such a fast pace I wasn't sure how far up we'd traveled. We lurched to a stop, and the doors hissed open to show a barrel-vaulted hallway, the center split by track lighting.

Marr gave another gesture with his index finger, and I followed him down a polished parquet floor to a courtyard garden terrace. A waterfall plunged over a mossy stone wall and into a dark pool filled with lily pads. Wisteria dripped down from a redwood arbor's pillars. A path of herringbone-patterned bricks led to a slate-roofed gazebo.

"Ah, Mr. Polo. I'm glad you decided to come."

He was just a couple inches over five feet and had the thick neck and heavily muscled shoulders of a wrestler. His hair was coal-black and combed straight back from his forehead. He was wearing a well-tailored charcoal-gray suit, white shirt, and heavy silk black tie. His eyes were gray-black, the color of licked stones, and slightly magnified behind thick-lensed steel-rimmed glasses. There was a wet-looking shine on his expensive black shoes. He had the talcum-powder smell of someone who has just left the barber shop.

"Come," Henry Lee said. "Let's have some refreshments."

Milk-white wicker chairs circled an ebony table inside the gazebo. An unopened bottle of Seagram's VO whiskey, an emerald-colored ice bucket, and two matching glasses sat in the middle of the table. A bright yellow bird swung back and forth in a small bamboo cage hanging from the center of the gazebo's roof.

There was a sharp cracking sound as Henry Lee broke the sealed cap of the whiskey bottle. He scooped ice into both glasses, then dribbled in the VO.

"Your health, sir," he said, raising his glass.

"Which I hope to keep," I said, taking a tentative sip.

Lee settled himself into one of the wicker chairs. "Please, sit down. We have much to talk about."

"Such as?"

Lee snapped his fingers, and Willie Marr hurried over carrying a small saddle-brown leather box. He handed it to Lee, who then passed it to me.

"Your time is valuable, Mr. Polo. I realize that. Please accept this as compensation for my imposing on you."

The gold inscription on the box said ROLEX. I opened it. A gold watch, a match for the one Scratchy had pawned.

Lee seemed to read my thoughts. "I assure you, this is the

genuine article. I understand that you were forced to leave the imitation with the police."

I freed the watch from its setting and bounced it in my palm. "Real gold? Just like the one I left with the sheriff?"

Lee leaned back in his chair, the wicker making creaking, arthritic sounds. "Exactly."

"And what am I supposed to do to earn this little trinket?"

"You were at the warehouse in French Beach before the police arrived?"

"Yes."

"And after they arrived, did you happen to see them examine the materials in the cartons?"

"The Levi's?"

Lee stuck an index finger in his glass and circled the ice cubes. "The Levi's, yes. We know about them, Mr. Polo. But was there anything else there? Other items?" He pointed to the Rolex. "Similar to that?"

"Not that I saw. Maybe they were on the boat."

"No," Lee said firmly. "They were not. Tell me, if you don't mind. Exactly how did you come into possession of the watch now in the police department's custody?"

"And if I choose not to tell you?"

Lee made a steeple with his hands and surveyed his fingertips. "You're free to go at any time, Mr. Polo. But I'd prefer that you stay and help me."

"Why should I help you? You firebombed my house, damn near killed a dear friend in doing so."

"Incorrect," Lee said softly. "I had nothing to do with the problems at your property."

"No? How about a man called O'Hara? He was run down a block away from Davis's place on South Park."

"The man you called Lester Maurence about? Again, I had nothing to do with his death. I know nothing of the man."

"He was interested enough in you to write down your Rolls's license plate."

Lee arched an eyebrow. "Really?"

"Yes. He wrote down Lester Maurence's plate too. And the plate of the vehicle that Al Davis had rented."

"Again, I assure you, I had nothing to do with this Mr. O'Hara's death."

Lee was full of nothings. "And I suppose you had nothing to do with Davis's, or Lester Maurence's, or Shy Celli's death."

"Absolutely nothing." He dropped his hands to his lap and leaned forward. "I am very anxious to find out who is responsible. Very anxious. I am willing to pay a reward to the person who tells me who did it."

"The police think you did." I nodded my head toward the pond. "Or your employee, Pork Chop."

"The police are incorrect. Mr. Davis was a businessman. We had done business together for some time. I had no reason to kill him. He was useful. Very useful."

"How useful? I know he was a *say atou,* a snakehead. A *pai yan,* a white man, who did some dirty work for you. He worked for Crazy Chu in Hong Kong. But he came back to San Francisco. To the police department. That was for you, wasn't it? He broke into the computer and turned the records over to you, right?"

Lee didn't acknowledge anything, but at least he didn't throw an "incorrect" at me.

"And Maurence was useful. And so was Shy Celli. Was it your idea to have her come to my home and pour out her heart to me with that sob story?"

Lee took a dainty swallow of the VO, then smacked his lips. "Miss Celli came to your home? When was this?"

"The day before I found her body down in Mission Bay."

He inhaled deeply, then blew the air from his lips as if it were cigarette smoke. "No. I did not know about that. Miss Celli had many gifts, many talents, but intrigue was not one of them. This sob story she told you. Just what was it?"

It was my turn to lean back in the chair, sip the booze, and blow out air. What the hell was Lee's game? If he had killed Davis, Maurence, and Shy Celli, why bother with little old me? Why all the smoke and mirrors? I hefted the Rolex again. The second hand was pecking away at time. "Have you got a phone handy?" I asked.

Lee snapped his fingers again, and Willie Marr came trotting over with a palm-size cellular phone. I dialed my place. Jane answered. "All is well," I told her. "Give me another half hour."

Lee was a good listener. I gave him a brief outline of the story Shy Celli had told me. His face remained impassive.

"A gang bang. A group of Asians. Vietnamese, she said. And all Maurence did was watch. The autopsy on Shy showed she'd been subjected to more of the same. Before she was dumped in the freezer alongside Lester Maurence."

"I was not aware of this. She should have come to me."

"She said that if she did, you, or Crazy Chu, would have her killed."

A bit of a hard edge came into Lee's voice for the first time. "Mr. Chu does not enjoy being addressed by his nickname. But I assure you, his reaction to Shy's story would have been quite different from what she feared."

"How many watches are missing?"

Lee lifted his eyes to the bird cage. "You are an interesting man, Mr. Polo. An enigma. An ex-policeman, an ex-prisoner. You are friendly with a newspaperwoman. There are times when I find newspaper articles about myself and my associates to be very beneficial. There are also times when I find them very distasteful." His eyes drifted down and focused on mine. "I am quite willing to pay you for your time, for the information you may develop. However, I would not accept your passing this information on to anyone. Anyone at all."

"Sorry. If I happen to stumble across anything that points to you as being responsible for Shy's death, or Davis's, or Lester Maurence's, or anyone else's, I'm going right to the cops."

"That doesn't concern me. You will find no such information. Ms. Celli was of no interest to me. Mr. Davis can be replaced easily enough. Lester Maurence not so easily. I would like to find the reason and cause of his death. But what I'm looking for now is property that belongs to me."

"The phony Rolex watches."

"Possibly."

"They were at the South Park warehouse, weren't they?

Then Davis moved them. Down to French Beach? Is that where they originally came to shore? I had the watch examined by an expert. He said it was the best counterfeit Rolex he'd ever seen. Six ounces of gold. Real eighteen-karat gold. Each watch is worth over a thousand dollars just for the gold alone. But the watches could be peddled for five or ten times that amount, if merchandised properly. How many are missing?"

"Let's use a round number to make things easy. Say a thousand. I want you to find them, Mr. Polo. You have been involved in this from the beginning. I'm not quite sure what your role was. Perhaps you were working for Davis. A silent partner. I always knew he had someone here on his payroll. It didn't matter to me when he was alive. It doesn't matter to me now. I think you were Davis's partner. And I think you are the one man who can retrieve those watches. I will be very grateful to you for doing so. I will also be grateful to your reporter friend, Miss Tobin. And your uncle, Pee Wee. If you do not find the watches, however, I will be most ungrateful. Most ungrateful indeed."

How nice. The Dragons' version of "I've got an offer you can't refuse."

"Can I ask a few questions?"

"Certainly."

"Shy Celli. What happened to her after she left my place?"

"I have no idea."

"She didn't go back to Maurence's house. I'm sure of that. Did she come here?"

Lee shook his head slowly. "No. She did not."

I turned to look at the ominous figure of Willie Marr. He was standing as motionless as a window mannequin. "Would he know where she went?"

"No. Now I have a question. How did you come into possession of the watch you gave the police?"

"It came from the South Park warehouse. You've been there."

"Have I?" Lee queried, the voice turning hard again.

"Yes. Or maybe it was Marr or one of your other men. But

the Rolls was there. That's where O'Hara saw it. O'Hara found a way into the building. He saw you, or Marr, along with Davis and Maurence. Heard you talking. He dug out one of the watches and hocked it at a pawnshop. I found the pawn ticket and got the watch."

Lee's forehead wrinkled in a disapproving smile. "A pawnshop. How did you come into possession of the ticket?"

"Mr. O'Hara left most of his worldly possessions in the care of a priest. The priest gave it to me."

"And you told the police all of this?"

"Yes. They must have questioned you by now."

Lee's nostrils flared. "They are discussing matters with my attorney," Lee said harshly. He stood up, brushing the arms of his suit coat. "Mr. Polo, I have the feeling you are spinning fairy tales. All this effort on your part for a man like Mr. O'Hara. No. It doesn't ring true. I want you to return the missing merchandise to me. Within a week. A week. Do you understand?"

CHAPTER 32

◄►

Willie Marr led me back to the elevator. When the doors closed behind us, he jabbed an index finger into my stomach. "You're the one who was screwing with the Rolls in the alley, aren't you? You and the woman. You find the boss's watches or I'm going to hurt you. Both of you."

Up close and personal, Pork Chop was uglier than I'd thought. There were balloons of scars over each eye. He unsheathed a smile like a knife when the elevator bumped to a stop. "You remember what I say. Tell your girlfriend what happened to Shy Celli could happen to her."

He walked me to the street, slamming the door after me. There was no Rolls in wait this time. I hiked it back to my place.

You're probably way ahead of me, but I didn't figure it out until I got back to the flats just in time to see Mrs. D's slightly tipsy girlfriends descending the stairs in a happy mood. Some of them even smiled at me. Mrs. D had probably told them I was for hire in case they were contemplating moving.

Jane Tobin was waiting anxiously for me at the front door. We went inside and I got a pot of coffee going.

"Come on," Jane complained. "Quit stalling. What happened?"

I handed her the Rolex box. "A gift from Mr. Lee. He says it's the real McCoy."

"What the hell are you going to do with it? I hope you're not going to keep it. Guys like Lee don't give away expensive presents unless they want something even more expensive in return."

Jane opened the box and held the Rolex by its band.

"It looks just like the one Scratchy left in the pawnshop."

"Yes. The one the San Mateo Sheriff's Department took from me. I have a feeling Susan McCord may never get that little treasure back."

Jane slipped the watch on her wrist and snapped the clasp shut. She rode it all the way up to mid-forearm before it snugged to a stop.

"Lee claims he had nothing to do with the deaths of Shy Celli, Lester Maurence, and Al Davis."

"Sure," Jane scoffed. "Just another innocent bystander."

"He just might be telling the truth," I said, reaching for the coffeepot.

Jane screwed up her face and handed me back the Rolex. "You bribe easier than I thought, Nick."

I dropped the watch on the table, then opened my cupboard. I was delighted to see it back in its natural state of chipped and mismatched cups, now that Mrs. D's fine china was safely stored in her own cabinets. I poured each of us a cup of coffee, then sat down at the table, suddenly feeling drained of energy.

"He might be telling the truth," I repeated. "He denies knowing anything about Scratchy's death."

"And I'm sure you believed that, too," Jane chirped skeptically.

"Yes. I'm sure if there was a reason, if it was profitable for him to do so, he'd have done them all in without a second's hesitation. Davis was someone he used, someone who was pretty useful. Maurence was invaluable. I can't figure out any reason for him to whack Maurence."

Jane picked two sugar cubes from the bowl and rattled them in her hands as if they were dice. "So Henry Lee is as pure as the driven snow. What did he want to talk to you about?"

"He's worried about some missing merchandise."

"The Levi's," Jane suggested.

"No. He doesn't seem too worried about those."

"The watch. Or should I say watches? How many are there?"

"A thousand. Our friend Pork Chop was there. He recognized me from the night we were peeking at the Rolls in the alley. He remembered you, too. He strongly suggested I find those watches for his boss. Lee made the same suggestion. Said he'd be grateful to me and you and my uncle if I find the watches. Very ungrateful to all of us if I don't. He expects results in a week."

"And if the results aren't good?"

I tried to keep my voice light and cheerful. "He will be disappointed. Henry Lee is not a man who likes to be disappointed."

"Why does Lee think you know where they are?"

"He said that he thinks I've been Davis's partner from the start. 'Silent partner.' He was trying to feel me out, then throw a scare into me."

"Well, I don't know about you," Jane said, "but I'm scared. I don't like someone like that threatening me."

Neither did I. "We'll just have to find the watches."

"You know where they are?"

"No. But I think I know where to start looking."

"Well," Jane snapped, "are you going to let me in on this little secret or are you going to sell the information to Linwood for another goddam book? Who's got the watches?"

"I'm not sure, Jane. But I've got a hunch. Russell Flann or Ben Butler. Or both."

From the look in her eyes, my statement startled her. "How the hell did you come up with Flann or Butler? Was it Lee's idea?"

"No. Their names never came up. But Shy disappeared after leaving my place. She never went back to Maurence's house on Buena Vista. Toni Symons's surveillance van would have spotted her."

"She could have gone right over to see Henry Lee."

"She could have, but Lee says she didn't." I held up a hand to hold off her protests. "Yes, he could be lying, but why? That's the whole thing with Lee. Why bother to lie? To even talk to me? If he was positive that I was Davis's partner, he'd have kept quiet, pulled me in off the street one night and let Willie Boy have a go at me.

"Shy Celli leaves my place and no one sees her until we find her body in that icebox. She said she was going to help me look into Maurence's computers. She was afraid of Maurence. Afraid he'd kill her. She was afraid of Lee, said he'd have her killed if she went to him or Peter Chu with her sob story. When I mentioned Al Davis's name, she said she'd never heard of him."

Jane ran a fingernail around the rim of the coffee cup, her eyes squinted shut in concentration. "I still don't see the connection with Butler or Flann."

"They were here when Shy Celli arrived. They both saw her. Henry Lee is sure Davis had a silent partner. What if Davis did have someone working for him? Who better than a cop, who could keep him informed of what was going on? If one of them was Davis's man, the first thing he'd do when he saw Shy at my place was call Davis. And I asked Flann about Davis. Flann was working Internal Affairs when Davis was under investigation for dipping into the computer banks. Flann told me Davis was dead. Said he was positive about it. Something about him dying in the Philippines."

"Butler. Flann." Jane propped her chin on the palm of her hand and stared into her coffee cup. "One of them, or both of them? If your little theory is right, then there's a good chance they killed Celli. And Maurence. And Davis. But why? None of it makes any sense."

I picked up the Rolex and exchanged it for the Seiko on my wrist. "If you add in a thousand watches, it might."

Back to the old standby. Legwork. Or fingerwork, really. The computer got a workout as I ran Russell Flann and Ben Butler through the computer. I didn't want to call Paul Paulsen for help. Yet. And there was no sense running Butler and Flann through DMV files. For obvious reasons, police officers leave their home addresses off DMV records, listing police headquarters on all of their personal ID.

Jane had some luck on the phone, conning a clerk at the personnel detail into releasing some minimal information on both officers by saying she was doing a story on Internal Affairs for the *Bulletin*. She picked up a middle initial on Butler, which would help sort out the data checks, and dates of hiring on both, as well as the fact that Flann had gone on a week's vacation. Starting two days ago.

"Butler didn't join the department until four years ago," Jane said, showing me the scribbles on her notepad. "But Flann's a veteran. Twenty-eight years."

"Someone might have tipped Davis that they were on to him for copying those files. Giving him time to flee the country. Who better than Russell Flann?"

Jane scrunched up her nose to show her estimation of my idea. "That's pretty thin."

Butler was negative in the database records, outside of one piece of property listed to him in Walnut Creek. He'd purchased it two years back and still had a sizable mortgage.

I concentrated on Flann, finally picking up a divorce action out of Marin County. Three years ago.

"There's not going to be much in a three-year-old civil case," Jane protested.

Bright and early the next morning, we headed for Marin County. Russell Flann. Somehow it fit. Like one finger in a glove. I had to find a way to get the rest of the hand in there. Flann was the one who first threatened me with a subpoena for my office, told me Davis was dead, and was so upset when the subpoena was withdrawn.

Checking public records is a boring, tedious job. Marin County makes it almost pleasant, because the court clerk's office, along with most of the county offices, are housed in Frank Lloyd Wright's masterful Civic Center. "Big Pink" was one of Wright's last commissions, a beautiful low-lying complex, all curves and arches. The building is truly pink, the roof sky-blue, topped off with a needlelike gold spire. Long, narrow skylights run the length of the building, accommodating the well-kept internal gardens.

I filled out the proper form, and within minutes the proper-looking clerk handed me the Flann file. Marriage resolution. Kim Flann, petitioner; Russell Flann, respondent.

I skimmed through the papers, looking for financial declarations. The Flanns had two children, both boys, ages seven and eleven when the action was filed. Mrs. Flann listed her occupation as housewife, Flann listed his as policeman. There was a rundown on their holdings—a house in San Rafael, a couple of cars, a boat, miscellaneous furnishings, an assortment of mutual funds and blue-chip stocks.

The agreement they both signed gave Kim Flann the house, both cars, the furnishings, the investments, and child support. Flann kept his pension and boat.

The items of interest to me were the Flanns' Social Security numbers and an item typed on the back of a subpoena. It showed he had been served with legal papers aboard the *True Blue*, Marina Yacht Harbor, Gate 6, Sausalito. The process server had been a diligent devil, even listing the berth: Y17.

Someone once told me that if you took away the freeways, the congested auto traffic, the congested pedestrian traffic, and everything built after 1920, you'd swear you were in the south of France, rather than Sausalito. Sausalito was originally built as a rural vacation spot for San Franciscans, who lived all of eight miles away. Of course, there was no Golden Gate Bridge in those days. Now the surrounding cliffs are fence to fence with houses and apartment buildings, the waterfront road clogged like all waterfront roads nowadays.

The Marina Yacht Harbor is at the north end of town, a cluster of weathered piers sticking out like long, arthritic fingers into the murky bay waters. The reason the waters are a bit murky is that many of the vessels tied to the piers never move. Houseboats in the true sense of the word. Like houses, the boats are equipped with living quarters, kitchens, and bathrooms. The inclusion of bathrooms made it advisable not to visit at low tide.

The boat tied up at berth Y17 was a lopsided sloop, its masts holding no canvas, the fiberglass decking bleached and peeling. Old rubber tires lashed to its sides served as bumpers. No numbers or name on the bow. If Flann was living on this derelict, he was either an honest cop or a stupid one. I didn't think he was either.

We heeled and toed it down the shaky planking, avoiding danger spots. Jane wondered out loud why people who live on boats insist on having dogs.

A Brillo-haired man with flaky, sunburned skin and wearing old gray flannels cut off at the knees was watering potted geraniums from a sprinkler can on the deck of his gable-roofed houseboat two slots down from Y17.

"Hi," I called out to him. "I was looking for the *True Blue*," I said, pointing back toward Y17.

He twisted the sprinkler can my way as if it was a weapon designed to protect him. "That's it, mister."

"Does Russ Flann still own it?"

"Nah. Sold it to some kids. They come down on weekends, party, leave a mess."

"When did Flann take off?"

He put the can down and shoved his hands in the back of his jeans. "What's your interest?"

You never know for sure how to play these things. If he knew Flann and liked him, he wasn't going to tell me anything. If he didn't like Flann, he'd open up. "Financial," I said.

"He's a cop, you know."

"Cops have financial problems, too."

That drew a deep chuckle. "Some do, some don't. Flann's a jerk. Always was. *True Blue*," he sneered. "Sold it to those damn kids, after painting the name off the bow. Bought himself a new boat. Big fancy thing." He looked down the dock. "Too fancy for this place, I guess."

I gave him a friendly wave, then stopped and called back to him, "You don't happen to know the name of his new boat, do you?"

"The *True Blue II*. What else?"

CHAPTER 33

◄►

It took me a day to find Flann, another day to be sure, and two more days to get ready for him. None of the local marinas knew of the *True Blue II*. Attempts to develop a home address for Flann through conventional channels were unsuccessful. It was the Social Security number in the divorce action that turned the trick, with a little help from my money guru. A credit check showed a wide variety of charge cards, the usual Visa, MasterCard, Discovery, as well as some upscale stores: Neiman-Marcus, Nordstrom, Eddie Bauer. The listed address on most of the cards was good old 850 Bryant Street, San Francisco. The Hall of Justice.

But Flann made a boo-boo. His bank account listed a postal box. A real, good old United States postal box. Getting the address shown on the application form from Uncle Sam is an easy matter. All you need is a subpoena made out to the party renting the box. So, I made out a phony subpoena.

The post office in San Rafael looked like it was stamped out of the government's cookie mold. A counter with six windows, four of which were permanently welded shut and one of which was always vacant.

I showed the subpoena to the blue-shirted clerk. He didn't know what to do about it, so he called his supervisor, a pudgy-faced guy with a toothbrush mustache. He didn't know what to do with it, either.

"Listen," I explained. "This is a civil subpoena duces tecum requiring the personal presence of Mr. Russell Flann to appear in superior court in San Francisco. The only address we have for Mr. Flann is this postal box. If you do not relinquish his address to me, I will serve the subpoena on you, and you can come to court and explain your position to the judge. That's the way the law works."

He made a clicking noise with his teeth and scratched his jaw, then took the subpoena into his office and closed the door behind him. He had me sweating for a few minutes. If pudgy-face checked with his supervisor, he'd find out what I told him was correct. However, if he checked with the court, he'd find there was no such case or trial as shown on the subpoena form I'd typed up.

He came back in about two minutes, handing me back the subpoena and a palm-size piece of pink notepaper with the name Russell Flann and an address: 1224 Marina Drive, San Rafael.

1224 Marina Drive was a nice ranch-style home off San Rafael Creek. You could sail your boat from your backyard and within minutes be in San Rafael Bay. A ten-minute cruise would take you south to the Richmond–San Rafael Bridge. Another minute or two and you'd be alongside San Quentin Prison.

The cars parked in the driveways of the nearby homes were mostly small BMWs, a Lexus or two, Volvo station wagons, and Buicks and Oldsmobiles. No Rolls-Royces or Ferraris. This wasn't the land of the filthy rich, just the nicely smudged rich.

The house was owned by a Marin County Realtor, who told the man from the Equity Credit Corporation that his tenant was never behind in his four-thousand-dollar-a-month payments. He also told me that Flann had moved in over two years ago.

A jaunty tomato-red Alfa Romeo two-seater convertible was parked in front of Flann's house, the top down, the seats pushed forward to prevent sun damage. I pulled into Flann's aggregate cement driveway alongside a Ford Taurus that was almost an exact duplicate of my own car. My jalopy looked like a slightly battered unmarked police car, with whip antenna and a red emergency light. The cord for the light plugs into the car's cigarette lighter, and the light itself is on display on the passenger seat so meter maids will think it's the real thing. Flann's was the real thing.

I turned off the engine, rolled down the window, and waited a minute. The only sounds came from the swishing of a neighbor's lawn sprinkler. I took a deep breath and decided it was show time.

Flann's front lawn was neatly trimmed and emblazoned at intervals with tricolor beds of salvia, alyssum, and mums. No one responded to the front doorbell. I walked around the side of the house. A woven-wire gate with a flip latch was all that kept me from entering the property. I called out Flann's name and flipped the latch open.

I could hear a radio, someone's voice proclaiming the benefits of an insurance policy. Most of the backyard was taken up by a small kidney-shaped swimming pool. Three black inner tubes and three black balls that looked as if they'd been punched out of the center of the tubes floated aimlessly on the sky-hued water. Solid walls of twelve-foot-tall bamboo plants provided privacy from the neighbors on both sides of the property.

The dock where Flann kept his boat was no more than ten yards from the pool. It was empty. The radio spilling out the commercials was sitting on the dock. The commercial was over and a booming voice came on. The speaker identified himself as G. Gordon Liddy.

I crouched down and switched the channel to KCSM on the FM dial and found the soothing, rich tones of Coleman Hawkins's tenor sax playing "Body and Soul."

I found a shady spot near the pool, settled gingerly onto a nylon-webbed lounge chair, undid my tie, and waited. I was half dozing when the sound of the boat pulling into the dock woke me. I checked my Rolex and found I'd been in the chair for almost an hour.

The man in charge expertly guided a gleaming white two-masted schooner to the dock. The boat looked like it stretched out over twenty-five feet.

A woman with white shorts and a yellow spandex tank top jumped off the boat and ran to the bow. A man with a mop of curly gray hair and sunglasses tossed her a mooring line. She fastened it to a dock cleat, then ran toward the stern of the boat and repeated the procedure. She had a long-legged, long-waisted dancer's body, a honey-colored tan, and shoulder-length blond hair as bright as brass. She looked like a girl you'd expect to see behind the wheel of an Italian convertible. She looked like a girl you'd buy an Italian convertible for, if you could afford it.

She swiveled, gave me a curious glance, then bounced back onto the boat. She and the man had a short, animated conversation. It ended with her looking back my way, her lovely face crumpling into a frown.

Poor girl. It looked like I was spoiling her afternoon. She disappeared down below decks for a moment, reappeared, then jumped ship and scooted past me without so much as a nod.

The man was wearing baggy sand-colored pants and a chambray shirt, the sleeves rolled up to his elbows. It took me until then to recognize him as Russell Flann. The moplike toupee over that smooth pate had fooled me. He disappeared down the same hatch the girl had taken. When he popped back up there was a gun stuck in his waistband. He put one bare foot on the dock, hesitated, then finally planted the other, as if he was reluctant to make full contact with dry land.

"You'd better have a damn good reason for breaking into my property, Polo, because I'm going to call the local police in about two minutes."

"Careful you don't get splinters," I said, pointing at his feet. "You can get an infection. Even die from it."

He padded toward me, one hand resting on the butt of the gun. It looked to be a revolver. "What the hell do you want?"

"Just to talk. Maybe buy a watch." I held my hands out slowly, peeling back my jacket sleeve, flashing the Rolex at him. "Like this one."

Flann just stood there, staring at me, biting down on his lower lip.

"Nice place you have here, Russ. If I'd known how well a cop can live on his salary, I'd never have quit the department."

More glaring. More lip chewing.

"Of course, you could have inherited some money. But you

didn't. I talked to Kim. Your ex-wife. She told me quite a bit about you. About meeting you in Vietnam. Falling in love. Having a child. Then moving to America. Another child. Nice kids. Kim showed me their pictures. They're going to good schools. Private schools, thanks to the money you're providing. Kim appreciates it. I think she still loves you. Be a shame if that money was cut off because you went to jail. That where you first met Al Davis? Over in Nam?"

Flann looked like he was ready to explode. I pointed toward his boat. "Looks like your girlfriend didn't do much of a job tying down. It's started to drift."

When Flann swiveled to look back at the sailboat, I pulled my .32 from its holster. It was pointed at his stomach when he turned back to face me. "Your gun, Russ. Just use your fingers. Take it out and lay it gently on the ground."

"Don't act stupider than you already have, Polo. You're not going to do anything with that gun."

I aimed at the swimming pool and pulled the trigger. One of the inner tubes bucked and started hissing air, spinning in a mad circle until it deflated and started sinking to the bottom.

"People don't worry about hearing gunshots anymore. A backfire, a TV on too loud. It's all right with me if your neighbors call the cops. Now, Russ. The gun. You know the drill."

Flann's hand moved slowly to his waistband, freeing the revolver with his thumb and forefinger, holding it away from him as if it was a dead mouse. He bent down at the knees, placing the gun on the tiling around the swimming pool.

I moved toward him, and he shuffled backward to the pool. "Jump in, Russ. The water's fine."

"Listen, if you think—"

I pulled the trigger again, casually aiming at one of the round balls, casually missing it by a good three feet. "Jump!"

Flann screwed up his face, looking like he was about to protest. Then he edged toward the pool, jumping in awkwardly, his head going underwater momentarily, the sunglasses falling from his face. When he came up the toupee looked slightly askew. He treaded water for a bit, then reached out and hung on to the side of the pool.

"I'm not wearing a Fargo," I told him, using the police terminology for a listening device or wire, "so everything we say is just between us boys. I want the watches."

"I don't know what the hell you're talking about."

"I think you do. And if I tell Henry Lee about you and Davis, he'll think so too. You wouldn't want that."

Flann wiped the back of his hand across his mouth. "I still don't know what you're talking about, Polo. I'm going to have your ass for this."

I dragged a chair over to the pool and sat down. "Russ, give up. The ball game is over. If you don't tell me, Henry Lee will send his top dog over to talk to you. Willie 'Pork Chop' Marr. He'll chop your arm off, then beat you over the head with it until you tell him what he wants to know. I cut a deal with Lee. I deliver the watches, he pays me, and everyone lives happily ever after."

"You made a deal with Henry Lee? That wasn't very bright of you."

"Oh, I think it was."

"I'm glad you think so, Polo, but I don't. First, I don't know what the hell you're talking about. Second, if I did any of the things you suspect me of, I sure as hell wouldn't cop out to it."

I slapped the barrel of the revolver against my palm in a slow steady rhythm. "Kim is looking real good. She told me to be sure to say hello to you, Russ."

"You really met with her?"

"Yes. Down at her house in Los Angeles. She seems happy down there. Your kids like it too. I get the feeling she's thinking of getting married again."

"You're still full of shit, Polo. You can't prove anything."

"You're not listening. I don't have to. I just dump everything into Henry Lee's lap. I'd rather not do that, Russ. Not because of you, but because of your wife and kids. You know how the Dragons are. If you tried skipping, they'd find them in Los Angeles. Butcher them, you know that. That's their style. Kill everyone, so there's no witnesses, and no friends or family members who might try and come back in a few years and settle the score."

There was enough truth in the statement to get to Flann. He leaned his head against the pool tiles and groaned.

"What I don't understand is why you killed Davis. Now, Shy Celli and Lester Maurence, I'd bet my money on Davis being responsible for them."

No response, but I could almost see the wheels spinning under that soggy toupee.

"Someone played rough with Celli before she died. Who was that? Davis and his Vietnamese smuggling crew? Or were you there, too? Henry Lee isn't going to lose much sleep over the loss of Shy Celli, or Al Davis for that matter. Hell, you can come in from the cold and take over for Davis directly. But Maurence, that was bad news. Lee is very upset about Maurence. He's going to be hard to replace."

Flann wiped a strand of toupee hair from his forehead and looked up at me with sorry eyes. "You talk like you and Henry Lee are big buddies."

"We have a business arrangement."

"The watches."

"Right. He gets the watches back and he's a happy man again. And you and I can split the reward."

"Reward?"

"A quarter of a million dollars."

"Humph. Do you know what those watches are worth?" he asked testily.

"A quarter of a million each, Russ," I told him. "No questions asked. That's a lot of money. That and what you've salted away over the years should keep you happy. People who get too greedy end up like Al Davis. You know that. We give Lee the watches and walk away. Think about it."

"And you think I'm going to trust you, Polo?"

"I'm the only chance you've got."

Flann dipped his face into the water, snorted, then dog-paddled a few feet until he could stand on the pool's bottom. I let him get to a point where his head and shoulders were above water. "That's far enough, Russ. Talk to me. Who killed Shy Celli and Lester Maurence?"

"I thought you just wanted the watches."

"I do. But I'm curious. Humor me."

His toupee seemed to be sagging more by the moment, inching slowly forward. "Davis killed them."

"Where'd you hook up with Davis?"

"Nam. Where else? In Saigon. I was in MI. He was CIA. We scratched each other's back a few times."

MI. Military Intelligence. "Yes, I bet you did. Then you hooked up with him again when he came back to the police department."

Flann finally got around to straightening his toupee. He used both hands, moving it slowly, as if it weighed a ton. "No. We'd done some business in Nam. Both made a few dollars. I'd had enough of it."

"But Davis didn't. He came after you, didn't he?"

Flann started walking toward the shallow end again. "It's getting cold in here."

"Tough. Tell me about Davis."

"This isn't going to get you the watches, Polo. What the hell do you want?"

"I want us both to live a long, happy, prosperous life. But I want the story, Russ. All of it. After all, if we're going to be partners, we shouldn't have any secrets."

Flann digested this with a seasick look. "I knew Davis had come back, but I didn't go near him. At first. I had married over in Nam. Dumb thing to do, but I did it. Then the captain came in with a case. They were worried about Davis. About him copying computer data from the Intelligence detail."

"So you went and told your old comrade-in-arms about it."

"Yeah," Flann admitted. "I talked to Davis. He was grateful."

"How grateful?"

"Plenty grateful. If it wasn't for me, he'd have been arrested. He got out of the country just in time. I didn't hear from him for a while. Then he called me, said he needed a partner."

"A silent partner," I said, quoting Henry Lee.

Flann began moving again, the water down to his waist.

"I guess you could say that."

"What about Scratchy O'Hara?"

"The bum? What about him? Dumb bastard got into Davis's warehouse. Took a watch. Just the one. Al thought it was me at first. He found the bricks where the old bastard had tunneled in. Just waited for him one night. Made the dummy talk." Flann smiled for the first time. "The bum mentioned your name, Polo. That really got to Al. He flipped. Beat the shit out of the bum."

"Then the two of you dragged Scratchy around the corner and ran him over, right?"

"Yeah. But I think he was already gone. Davis really worked him over."

"Then Davis firebombed my place."

"I don't know anything about that."

"But Shy Celli? You do know about her, don't you? Seeing her at my place. That must have been a shock. How'd you recognize her?"

"I'd seen pictures of her. Davis had pictures of all the players in the game: Lee, his henchmen, Maurence, everyone. Even you, Polo. He showed me your academy graduating class picture. He was really looking forward to getting rid of you."

"Were you there when Shy Celli was killed? Before she was killed?"

Flann shook his head. I thought the toupee would start sliding again, but it held firm. "No. I had nothing to do with her. Or Maurence. That was all Al's work. And his buddies, the fishermen."

I cocked the revolver. Flann heard the noise and stopped moving. "It just doesn't ring true, Russ. Why shoot Davis?"

"You should be grateful I did, Polo. You were next. You and that bitch reporter. Davis was going to get you both. He really hated your guts."

"You didn't kill him to save my life, Flann."

"No," he admitted wearily. "Mine. Al was wrapping things up. Getting ready to disappear completely. I'd seen him do it in

Nam. He had a network of six agents over there. All Viets. They were bringing in some really good intelligence, troop movement, ammo dumps, all kinds of stuff. Of course, Al was peddling info to the other side and pulling in literally tons of heroin from the Triangle. He got wind that one of the agents was going to dump on him to headquarters. He didn't know which one, so he killed them all. Then, their families, anyone they were close to. I always figured he was sorry he missed me, but I got out of Saigon just in time."

"You seem to be a real lucky guy, Russ. So you just walked in and popped Al in the back of the head."

"Yep. He was drunk. Davis was a mean, tough, miserable bastard, but he couldn't drink worth shit."

"Which left you with the watches."

Flann strode awkwardly to the end of the pool, climbing the shallow-end steps. He stopped to shake himself like a dog, sending rivulets of water in all directions. "Leaving us with the watches, Polo."

CHAPTER 34

◄►

Flann's confidence seemed to have returned. He stripped off his shirt. His chest was covered with gray hair that matched his toupee.

"How about your partner, Ben Butler? Did he help you out?"

"Butler," he snorted. "He's a dickhead. He hasn't got a clue. Just wants to put in his eight hours, then run home to his wife and kids."

"When did you pick up Shy Celli?"

"Soon as she left your place. I dropped Butler off at the Hall of Justice, then called Davis and doubled back. We were waiting for her when she left your flat. I pulled her over with a red light. Davis did the rest."

Flann was toweling himself off with his wet shirt, all the time moving in the direction of the revolver I'd made him take from his waistband. I stepped over and kicked the gun into the swimming pool.

"Aw," he complained. "You don't trust me. And I thought we were going to be partners."

"I'm not greedy. I can get by with a quarter of a million bucks. Where are the watches?"

He twisted the shirt in his hand, wringing it out like a wet towel. "What's to keep you from shooting me after I tell you? Keeping all the money yourself? Or keeping the watches?"

"Henry Lee. You may feel like messing with him, but I don't."

"But Lee doesn't know about me yet. Just you do."

"Right. And I'm a blabbermouth. Where are they, Flann?"

"Where do you think?" His head did a quarter revolution, out to the water. "On the boat."

He really didn't have a chance, but I guess he had to try. Al Davis might have gotten away with it, but not Russell Flann. I started to swivel toward the boat, and he lashed out with the rolled-up shirt. It wrapped around my arm like a snake. Flann followed with a bull-like charge at my chest, his hands clawing my face. I drove my left elbow into his stomach, following with an open-handed palm to the bridge of his nose. He made a startled, grunting sound, and I brought the elbow back into play, aiming at his nose. It burst like a ripe tomato, spraying polka dots of blood in all directions. He sank slowly to his knees, stunned, arms at his sides, helpless. I knew I'd regret it later, but at the time it seemed like a hell of an idea. I brought my arm back, straightened my knuckles, and used my hips to drive my hand into that bloody face. Flann tottered, then fell backward, his head making a cracked-ice sound when he hit the ground.

I bent over and checked his pulse. It was strong. I used the wet shirt to stop the flow of blood, then walked over and climbed aboard the *True Blue II*.

Russell Flann was a murderer, a smuggler, a crooked cop, quite possibly a rapist, and, to top it off, a damn liar. No watches on the boat. But they weren't hard to find. Flann was still out like a light. I dug his wallet from his soggy pants. There were pictures of his ex-wife, Kim, standing alongside their two children, grouped under a swaying palm tree. She wore a sarong garment, the kids had on swimming trunks. Another picture of someone in a swimming outfit, the brassy blonde who'd jumped ship just a little while ago showing herself off in a tangerine-colored string bikini. Then there was Flann's personal ID, over a thousand dollars in cash, and a receipt for a storage locker in San Rafael. I extracted the cash, then went back to his pants pocket for his key ring. There were six keys: two car keys, three that were probably to his house, and one small bright and shiny new one.

★

The new key fit the lock on the door at the storage locker. It was more of a garage than a locker, big enough to store a good-size truck. There was no truck. Just cardboard boxes stacked to the ceiling. I broke one open. It was filled with smaller boxes, each saddle-leather-colored with the name ROLEX in gold relief. I put one of the boxes under my arm and carried it back to my car, then decided what the hell, and went back for another one.

It was almost noon the next day when I made my way back to Pagoda Alley. Henry Lee didn't look at all surprised to see me. After all, I was a *pai yan,* there to do his bidding. A fresh bottle of VO whiskey sat on the table in the gazebo.

"Ah, Polo," Lee greeted me. "You are prompt. I like that." He undid the whiskey bottle's cap and went through the niceties of pouring us both a drink.

He raised his glass and toasted me. "Your health. Your continued good health, sir. You have something for me?"

I handed him the key to the storage locker's lock and the receipt I'd taken from Russell Flann's wallet.

He studied the receipt. "You are sure that the merchandise is there?"

"It was an hour ago. I'm not sure if that's the only key, though."

"And who else might have a key?" he asked sharply.

"The man who took them from Al Davis."

"And the name of that man?"

"That wasn't part of our deal, Lee. You just wanted the watches. You've got them now." I took a long sip of the VO. For such a smooth Canadian blend, it felt like kerosene going down my throat.

"I would like to know the name of this man." He cocked his head to one side. "If there is such a man."

"There is. Davis's silent partner. He's not too bright. The cops will probably get to him pretty soon, so if I were you, I'd reclaim those watches pretty damn fast."

Lee snapped his fingers, and Willie Marr dutifully appeared. Lee shot off some rapid Chinese, then handed Marr the key and the receipt. Marr gave me a squinty-eyed sneer before he took off.

Lee reached for the VO bottle and waved it at me. "Another drink?"

I drained what was left in my glass and set it on the polished ebony table. "No thanks. Time for me to toddle off."

"I'd prefer it if you waited until I hear from Mr. Marr."

"I'd prefer to go home and get drunk. By myself. If you want me, you can always find me."

Lee bobbed his head in agreement. "Yes. Indeed I can. But a deal is a deal. I told you there'd be a reward for finding my merchandise."

"I'll keep the real Rolex you gave me and we can call it square."

"Square," Lee said softly, as if it was a strange, foreign word. "I will find out who this silent partner of Mr. Davis's was. You know that. You might as well tell me now."

"A deal's a deal, Lee. I kept my end of the bargain. You keep yours. Just stay away from me, my friends, and my relatives. Davis's silent partner, he's dog meat. The cops will have him before you can get your hands on him. He has a family, but he's divorced. They knew nothing of what was going on. I want them left alone, too."

Lee pursed his lips together and studied me for a moment. "You may go," he finally said.

I went.

All in all, it turned out about as good as I could have hoped. Willie Marr picked up all the watches and transported them to a warehouse in Oakland, near the airport. Lieutenant Meekan of the San Mateo County Sheriff's Department had followed through with his promise to me. He coordinated efforts with the FBI and the customs people, who followed Marr by helicopter, then put a surveillance on the warehouse. The watches were moved three days later, onto a cargo plane headed to New York. Thanks to the FBI, the plane mysteriously blew a couple of tires after landing at Kennedy Airport. The blown tires caused a delay, and the cargo had to be off-loaded on a run-up pad. One of the lifts broke and a box fell. When it broke open, there were all those damn watches. Lee's New York Dragon friends were rounded up as they claimed the cargo.

Henry Lee might be suspicious, but there was no real way he could trace the bust to me. Just one of those things. Bad luck, or *joss,* as the Chinese say.

Russell Flann had panicked and tried sailing away from all his troubles on the *True Blue II.* He'd gotten as far as the Santa Barbara Channel before the Coast Guard caught up with him. He had his moment of glory on TV, shown being herded off the Coast Guard cutter, the wind blowing strongly. Flann's face was bandaged, and one hand stayed nervously clamped on his toupee.

Everyone who counted seemed to be reasonably happy. Except me. I still had an empty, hollow feeling in my stomach. You get that feeling when people die and your actions play a major part in the way things turn out.

Scratchy. If I hadn't run those plates for him, if I had talked to him, found out just what the hell he was really up to, maybe I could have changed things. Maybe.

Shy Celli. She'd come to me for help. I hadn't believed her. Had politely kicked her out of my home, and right into the hands of Al Davis and his thugs.

Lester Maurence. No tears lost there, and Al Davis was the kind of person who makes a failed Catholic hope that there really is a hell, commanded by a devil with a sharp pitchfork. "Vengeance is mine," saith the Lord. I think Mickey Spillane said the same thing.

Russell Flann was going to spend the rest of his life in prison. But that probably wouldn't be so very long. Prison wouldn't stop Henry Lee from seeking his revenge. Vengeance. Revenge. Both are highly overrated.

But, as they say, life goes on. Things turned back to what passes for normal in my life: work, Tuesdays at St. Matthew's Kitchen, dates with Jane. Bill Linwood was making a minor comeback in Jane's life, wooing her with a side job helping with a script for a TV documentary on the homeless. Linwood even came to work at the kitchen a couple of times to "get the real feel of things." Would you think it catty of me to say he's a lousy dishwasher?

Mrs. Damonte was happy as hell with her remodeled flat, and planned a dinner, inviting Dallera, the contractor; a few of his workers; poor old Hines, the adjuster; Uncle Dominic; and even Gino and Delio. I finessed an invitation for Jane.

It was a Tuesday, the day things started to turn around, the blues fading away to an icy whiteness. Maybe it was the passage of time, maybe it was the therapy of a long day scooping out spuds and turkey wings. Jane and I were having a drink at my place before descending to Mrs. D's.

The afternoon mail contained the best piece of news I'd seen in some time, a letter and photograph from St. Louis. Susan McCord cradled the latest addition to the family, a six-pound-seven-ounce wonder named Terry McCord, Jr. There was a nice note attached to Susan's picture, thanking me for sending her father's watch. She wasn't sure just what she was going to do with it. Her husband seemed to think it was worth holding on to until the price of gold went up.

I'd sold the real Rolex Lee had given to me. I got ten thousand dollars cash from one of Hootsie's contacts. It was enough to pay off Uncle Dominic's loan. The thousand dollars from Russell Flann's wallet would just about cover all my other expenses.

According to Lieutenant Meekan, there was still a chance the sheriff's department might return the phony Rolex Scratchy had pawned. "But don't hold your breath," Meekan advised. I wasn't worried.

Of the two counterfeit Rolexes I'd confiscated at the storage locker, one went to Susan McCord, and the other was snuggled on my wrist.

Jane suggested having one more glass of Chablis, because Mrs. D could be a little slow in passing out her vino.

"I'm starved," she said, taking the last sip from the glass. "I wonder what she's cooking?"

"Whatever it is, it'll be great."

We trooped down the stairs, arms entwined, leaning against each other. Mrs. D was there to greet us. When she opened the door an unmistakable odor drifted from the kitchen. Turkey.

"Oh, shit," Jane said softly, but not soft enough.

"Non capisco cos'è che non va?" Mrs. D demanded to know what was wrong.

"Nothing," I soothed her in Italian. "It must be something she had for lunch."